A Second Helping of Murder and Recipes

A Hot Dish Heaven Mystery

Also by Jeanne Cooney:

Hot Dish Heaven: A Murder Mystery with Recipes

A Potluck of Murder and Recipes

It's Murder, Dontcha Know

A Second Helping of Murder and Recipes

A Hot Dish Heaven Mystery

Jeanne Cooney

North Star Press of St. Cloud, Inc.
St. Cloud, Minnesota

This book is dedicated to my children, Elizabeth, Pete, and Jim.
While I hope you always work hard and do your best,
I pray you never take yourselves too seriously.

ISBN: 978-0-87839-718-1

This is a work of fiction. Names, characters, places, and incidents are the products of the author's imagination or are used fictitiously. Any resemblance to actual events or persons, living or dead, is entirely coincidental. In other words, the sheriff and deputies in Kittson County are talented and dedicated and, collectively, have a great sense of humor. Right?

Printed in the United States of America

Published by
North Star Press of St. Cloud, Inc.
St. Cloud, Minnesota

Part One

Make Sure Everyone Has Gone through the Buffet Line

A Second Helping of Murder and Recipes
Cast of Characters

Emerald Malloy—Minneapolis newspaper reporter
Margie Johnson—Owner of the Hot Dish Heaven café
Barbie Jenson—Editor of the local newspaper
Deputy Randy Ryden—Local sheriff's deputy
Buddy and Buford Johnson—Local farmers and Margie's nephews
Vivian and Vern Olson—Margie's sister and her husband
Little Val and Wally—Vivian and Vern's daughter and her husband
Father Daley—Local Catholic priest
John Deere—Local farmer
Dinky and Biggie Donaldson—Local farmers
John Hanson (the President)—Local businessman
Raleigh Cummings—Beet truck driver from out of town
Janice Ferguson—Kennedy city clerk
Hunter Carlson—Local farm worker
Sheriff Halverson and Deputies Gus, Jarod, and Ed—Other local law enforcement

Chapter One

I swerved to miss the sugar beets that littered the road. It was the end of October, and I was back in the northern Red River Valley, only thirty miles south of the Canadian border. Once again, it was all because of hot dish.

The air was cold, and the wind was strong, howling at me through my car windows. I was driving east along Highway 11, just outside of Drayton, North Dakota, on the Minnesota side of the river. I was headed for Kennedy, the sun riding low on my shoulders. The beets I was attempting to avoid must have fallen off the trucks used to haul them from the fields to the pilers.

Don't let me fool you with words like "pilers" or even "sugar beets" for that matter. I really don't know much about either. I'm not a farmer. My name is Emerald Malloy, Emme to my friends. I'm a twenty-six-year-old reporter at the Minneapolis paper. I write for the Food section, although the word "write" may likewise give you the wrong impression. Mostly I compose lead-ins for articles that highlight recipes. But a few months ago, during my first trip to Kennedy, Minnesota, I not only gathered hot dish, Jell-O, and bar recipes for a feature on "church cuisine," I solved a murder.

It made the front page. I got a piece of the by-line and everything, which should have thrilled me because I thought I wanted to be an investigative reporter, a far more prestigious position than glorified errand girl, my current job. But in the end, I actually ached for the people involved in that terrible crime and felt more than a little guilty for my part in exposing it. Consequently, when my editor explained that the article had earned me a full-time position on the crime beat if I wanted, I told him I'd have to think about it.

So that's what I'd been doing the last few months. Thinking. And since I can multi-task, I'd also volunteered to return to Kennedy for more recipes from Margie Johnson, the owner of the local café, Hot Dish Heaven. It turned out our readers loved seeing their favorite old-time recipes in print, so we were planning another full-page spread.

When I called Margie to ask if I could visit again, she said, "Ya betcha. Just be careful once ya get off I-29 there. The state highways and county roads are slick with mud and scattered with beets. See, harvest isn't quite done yet."

The beets were much larger than I'd expected, although, in truth, I wasn't sure what to expect. I knew sugar beets were used to create an alternative to cane sugar. I also knew they were big business up here, making unassuming millionaires out of many of the Norwegian and Swedish farmers who lived in the area. I just didn't think they'd look like potatoes on steroids—the beets, not the farmers. Yet they did. Giant potatoes with thick brown skins.

I turned onto County Road 1 as Willie Nelson sang from my CD player, "On the road again. I can't wait to get on the road again." I bounced over a few more beets and the large clumps of dirt accompanying them, certain Willie would have changed his tune if actually in the car with me.

Up ahead I spotted what I presumed was a "beet piler." It was nothing more than massive mounds of sugar beets in an open field, each mound surrounded by heavy equipment. Several trucks piled high with more beets idled in single file nearby, while people rushed around outside a small guard-like shack.

Aside from that activity, all was quiet. The roads were empty, and the flat, treeless fields that stretched to the horizon were barren and windblown. It made for a bleak picture, one that reminded me of something Margie had once said: "This may not be the end of the world, but we sure as heck can see it from here."

By the time I entered Kennedy, the sky had fallen gray. Outside the Maria Lutheran Church, red and gold leaves blanketed the ground, preparing for the cold winter ahead. A few even scuttled across the road in an apparent but futile attempt to flee the area before the first Arctic blast.

A dirty white pickup truck moved past me in the opposite direction, the driver acknowledging me by briefly raising his index finger from the steering wheel. I nodded in return, bumped across the railroad tracks, and hung a right onto Highway 75, pulling in across from Hot Dish Heaven.

Only two pickups were parked along the highway that also served as Main Street. But the makeshift parking lot next to the grain elevator was crowded with vehicles and men, about five or six of each, constituting quite a gathering in a community of 193 people. I didn't recognize anyone, but that didn't surprise me. While after just one visit, I knew more people here than I did in Minneapolis, where I lived a solitary life, I couldn't expect to be familiar with everyone. Not yet anyway.

I exited the car and leaned forward to touch my toes. Following a six-hour drive, stretching was necessary. I'd stopped only once for the bathroom and refills of gasoline, Diet Coke, and M&Ms. Righting myself, I adjusted my sweater and, with a shiver, wrapped my short corduroy jacket tightly around me, all the while wishing I'd worn a heavier coat.

I hurried across the road. The wind, smelling of dirt and damp leaves, pushed me the entire way. There were few trees around to stop its efforts.

A small white-haired dog sat near the café. As I approached, he edged away. "Don't be afraid," I said to the cute little guy in my friendliest voice. He nonetheless scampered down the sidewalk. "Your loss," I shouted. "I would have offered you treats." He hesitated, as if he'd heard and understood. He even glimpsed over his little doggy shoulder. But when all was said and done, he continued on.

I opened the heavy metal door to Hot Dish Heaven and peered inside. It looked deserted. I didn't see anyone. Not even Margie. Although I did hear her singing to the juke box. It was playing Maura O'Connell's version of "Livin' in These Troubled Times."

I knew the song because my parents had been big music fans, particularly folk and country-rock, and I'd continued the tradition. "Brings you down to buy a paper if you read between the lines that no one seems to have the answer to livin' in these troubled times." I smiled at the thought of a sad Irish folk song playing in a café owned and primarily frequented by stoic Scandinavians.

Nothing had changed in the place. It was small and dark, the walls covered in plaster and wainscoting and topped with faded advertisements, both professional and handmade. The booths were upholstered in black vinyl, marked by intermittent pieces of duct tape, while the tables in the middle of the floor and the counter up front were framed in chrome and topped with stained Formica.

"Anybody home?" The aroma of hot dish invited recollections of my previous visit and prompted all kinds of emotions. A veritable casserole of feelings, you might say.

"Oh, my goodness!" Margie scurried from the kitchen, drying her hands on a towel that ended up flung across her shoulder. "If you aren't a sight for sore eyes."

She enveloped me in an embrace so tight I could only manage to mumble, "'ood t' see 'ou."

"Now, let me getta look at ya." She stepped back and scanned me up and down. "Uff-da, you're still so skinny I bet ya hafta run around in the shower just to get wet." She grinned. "Otherwise, ya look wonderful. I love your hair, ya know." She yanked one of my long, orange curls. "As ya might recall, we have very few redheads up here."

That may have been an exaggeration. I'd never spotted any redheads in the area.

Most of the Scandinavians who called the northern Red River Valley home were tall, with blond hair, blue eyes, and solid builds, much like Margie herself, even if Margie, admittedly in her early sixties, was now more gray than blond. I, on the other hand, was a rarity in these parts. Being Irish and just five-foot-five, with long, curly, carrot-colored hair and emerald-green eyes, I stood out in Kennedy like "a bagpiper at a lutefisk dinner," as Margie often said.

I thought the world of Margie Johnson. During my previous visit, I'd ended up incapacitated for a few days, and she took care of me. In spite of repeatedly telling her it wasn't necessary, I loved every minute of it. Having lost my mom at a young age, I guess I craved motherly attention. And since Margie had never married or had children of her own, she must have enjoyed providing it. Throughout those four days, we spent hours visiting and became fast friends, in spite of our age difference. And while I'd often spoken with her on the phone between then and now, it wasn't the same as seeing her in person.

"You look great," I told the solid-framed woman in front of me.

She patted the sides of her head, taming the strands of hair that had escaped her ponytail. After that, she tugged on her tee-shirt, which, along with her jeans and sneakers, comprised her work uniform. "Your eyes must be goin'," she said with a moderate Scandinavian accent. "Kind of strange for someone so young."

Somehow my smile grew wider, no doubt nearly splitting my face. "Tell me, do you have time to sit and catch up, or are you too busy preparing for the big feast?"

Margie was cooking for the beet banquet her nephews, Buddy and Buford, were hosting that evening in the "middle room," as the space that bridged the café and the adjacent VFW was known. The meal was to show their appreciation to the people who'd worked for them during the recent harvest. Margie said it was something most of the local farmers did every year.

"Well, I gotta keep cookin', so why don't ya come on back to the kitchen, and we'll talk some there, while ya relax."

"Okay," I replied, my nerves oddly contradicting the notion that the rest of my day would be relaxing.

What did they know that I didn't?

Chapter Two

Margie put her arm around my shoulders and led me to the kitchen after first pulling the plug on the juke box.

"You still haven't gotten that thing fixed?" The switch on the juke box had fizzled prior to my last visit, leaving the cord alone to do the job.

"Yah, well," she stated hesitantly, "I'm not askin' that outfit in Grand Forks to take care of it. They're too spendy. So I'll hafta wait for the guy down there by Stephen. But he's busy too. First, he was fishin' in Canada. Then, there was harvest. Soon, he'll be deer huntin'. And after that, the holidays . . ." She didn't seem all that concerned. "At least it's not as bad as last fall when the phone went out. With field work, huntin', and ice fishin', the phone guy in Karlstad didn't make it over till darn near spring. If it hadn't been for my cell phone, I'd been forced to use two cans and a string."

We stepped into the kitchen, where the warmth from the oven swaddled me like a cozy blanket. The faint smell of baking bread wasn't half bad either. "Yum."

Margie gave me another one-armed squeeze. "I still can't get over ya bein' a food reporter, given what a terrible cook ya are."

I squinted, feigning ire. "But I'm a good eater. And I can copy down recipes with the best of them, right?"

She nodded. "Oh, for sure, kiddo. Business has been boomin' ever since that newspaper of yours published the piece about me and my food. I've had folks in from as far away as Crookston and Thief River. And like I told ya over the phone, I even got a nice review from that famous food critic at the *Grand Forks Herald* there." She paused. "As I might of mentioned, though, messin' up that Carrot Bar recipe has caused more than a few problems. Poor Amy Burdeau, over by Alexandria, wrote me about her bars. They turned out to be nothin' but mush."

I sighed, something I never did before coming to Kennedy. "Margie, I've told you about a hundred times how sorry I am about that."

For some unknown reason, Margie's recipe for Carrot Bars appeared in print minus two cups of flour and three quarters of a cup of vegetable oil. And while the paper was quick to publish a correction, Margie reminded me of the error every time we spoke.

I pulled the strap from my shoulder, set my purse on the metal work table, and sat down on a nearby stool. Margie wiped her hands along the front of her tee-shirt, across the words, "Let Me Spend Eternity in Hot Dish Heaven." She always wore a tee-shirt or apron that highlighted that same plea, just in different colors. Today's shirt was royal-blue with white lettering.

"If ya care to, Emme, ya can stack dinner plates on the counter while we gab." She made the passive request—the only type normally uttered by Scandinavians—as she checked the stovetop. It was teemed with various hot dishes. "We'll be feedin' about seventy, countin' the workers and their families. The counter will serve as our buffet table, just like the last time ya were here."

I nodded and headed for the large painted cupboard at the back of the kitchen. I knew my way around since I'd helped out when the café and adjoining VFW had co-sponsored a benefit dinner-dance during my previous visit.

"I'm glad ya got here when ya did," my friend went on to say. "The temperature's droppin'. The weather's supposed to get real ugly." She lingered before explaining, "There's a storm front in Canada, and it's headed our way. We might get a fair amount of snow tonight. And the way the wind blows 'round here, snow always means a possible blizzard." She grimaced. "Another Halloween blizzard. Good thing everyone makes their kids' costumes big enough to fit over snowsuits."

A guilty expression seized her face. "I suppose I should of called and told ya." She raked her bottom lip with her top teeth. "I just didn't want ya to cancel your trip. Besides, those weather folks never know what they're talkin' about. The storm could very well miss us altogether."

She stirred the contents of a large frying pan. "But to be on the safe side, plan on pluggin' in your car." She peeked in my direction, her eyes twinkling. "Ya do have a head-bolt heater, don't ya?"

I shook my head while placing a stack of mismatched dinner plates on the counter. "No need. My townhouse came with a garage."

She chuckled, waving her spoon. "I was just pullin' your leg anyways." She drew in a deep breath. "And if ya do have trouble gettin' it started in the mornin', I have jumper cables ya can use." She chuckled some more as she inspected another dish.

"That reminds me of a funny story." Margie loved to tell tales. I suspected that back in time, the blood of an Irish storyteller had found its way into her family. "Some big shot from California was here recently to check out the canola plant down the highway there." She bobbed her head to the north. "And when he saw the cords hangin' from the grills on all the cars, he decided they must be electric. He told everyone back home he'd never seen such a 'green' community."

After allowing a snicker over the idea that some people didn't know that in extreme northern climates, cars had to be "plugged in" to keep the engines from freezing up, Margie got serious again. "But like I said, I should of given ya a 'heads up.'"

I dismissed her apology with a wag of my hand. "It's not your job to keep tabs on the weather for me. I could have checked on it myself. Instead, I listened to music the whole way up here. And because I had no intention of delaying my trip, I didn't pay any attention to the weather reports earlier in the week."

As I spoke, I imagined being snowbound in Kennedy for a few days. In my mind's eye, I saw a crackling fire, a bottle of wine, a couple of long-stemmed crystal glasses, and a wooly blanket tossed across a braided rug. It actually made me giddy, a condition I apparently failed to mask, as evidenced by the smile that lit Margie's eyes.

"You're thinkin' about bein' stranded with Deputy Ryden, aren't ya?"

At the mere mention of the man's name, my cheeks grew warm, and I was positive they were flushing as red as my hair.

Randy Ryden was a Kittson County deputy sheriff. I'd met him the last time I was in town. We hit it off. Well, not at first, but before the night was over. And since then, we'd talked on the phone twice and had exchanged four or five e-mails. We also went out to dinner when he was in the Twin Cities two weeks ago, visiting his folks. For that date, I shaved my legs and the whole works, hoping we'd end up back at my place, taking our relationship to the next level—the horizontal one.

I realize that makes me sound sleazy, but believe me, I'm not. It's simply been a while since I've experienced any "intimacy." The closest I've come lately was a month ago, when I spent an evening with "Ben and Jerry," and a mouthful of Chunky Monkey slipped off my spoon and down the front of my pajamas, making my taa-taas tingle.

As for my night with Randy Ryden, he got called away before anything happened, though not before inviting me to stay with him when I was in town this go-round. And I planned to do just that. As soon as he returned from western North Dakota.

He was helping in the oil fields. Not working with oil but doing law enforcement stuff. The oil boom had caught the police out there off guard, so cops from around the region were lending a hand. Until he got back, which he expected would be the following afternoon, I'd bunk in one of two rooms above the café. Margie rented them out to short-term guests. It was Kennedy's answer to the Holiday Inn.

"Margie, I'll admit I like the guy, but that's all I'm going to say on the subject." In truth that's all I could say without getting tongue-tied and overheated. I couldn't help it. Randy Ryden was tall, dark, and handsome, with a large portion of strong thrown in for good measure. He had a build that reminded me of rugged mountains—the kind I wanted to climb all over. And more importantly—or at least as importantly—he was genuinely nice, not something I was used to. "As I've told you countless times, my track record with guys isn't great. So I'd rather not jinx myself by talking about what's *not* going on between Randy and me."

Margie's smile remained in place as she poured two cups of coffee and handed me one. "Well, if ya don't wanna share your secrets with me, that's your business, I suppose. But it seems kind of cruel since I nursed ya back from the brink of death."

I rolled my eyes. "Don't be so dramatic. I had a concussion, nothing more. I was hardly at death's door."

I did my best to sound nonchalant, but my chest tightened as I spoke. I guess I still was "working through the psychological aftermath" of nearly being killed the last time I was here. At least that's how my therapist had explained my on-going battle with anxiety.

That's right. I see a therapist and have for some time. Even so, I remain pretty messed up. Makes me wonder about people who've never sought counseling. Kind of scary, huh?

"Well, if ya won't spill your guts," Margie playfully whined as she retrieved a Tupperware container from the fridge, "how about fillin' 'em with a little somethin'?" She tugged at the plastic lid. "I know ya hate sweets." Believe me, she was being facetious. I was—and happily remain—addicted to sugar. "But you'll like these. The recipe's from Michelle Pierre, a friend of a friend down in St. Paul. It's for the best banana bars ever."

I grabbed a bar and bit into it, savoring every moist yellow morsel and ignoring the likelihood that Margie was using these sweet treats to weasel information out of me—information of the romantic variety. It was a risk I was willing to take considering my love for baked goods. Especially Margie's baked goods.

See, Margie was not only a hot dish wizard, she was an award-winning baker. She'd won lots of county-fair ribbons over the years and, at my insistence, had finally entered a dozen different desserts in this year's Minnesota State Fair. She walked away with three firsts, five seconds, and four thirds. That's right. Twelve for twelve her first time out.

Despite that, she'd cast off her success by saying, "Well, I sure as heck didn't deserve this many ribbons."

I, in turn, had argued that she was the best baker around, and with my penchant for sweets, I counted myself an expert on the subject. I also begged her to quit being so modest.

To that she'd thoughtfully replied, "Well, maybe you're right. I'm gettin' arthritis, and I don't deserve that either, so maybe—just maybe—it all evens out." I had to bite my tongue to keep from laughing.

"Margie," I said, my mind returning to the here and now, "how did . . ." My voice trailed off. I'd planned to ask her how these incredible bars had "fared" in the state ribbon competition but got distracted by another anxious feeling.

And despite being in Margie's warm kitchen, I shivered.

Chapter Three

BIRDS HAVE TINY BRAINS. Still, they know when to fly away, whether it's to avoid danger or inclement weather. People aren't that smart.

At least not my old boyfriend, Boo-Boo. He'd been calling me again. He didn't seem to understand that he should fly away—far, far away—even though I'd urged him to do so repeatedly.

I guess I shouldn't be too critical though. While able to sense doom and gloom easily enough, I, too, have failed to respond appropriately at times. Case in point, my disastrous relationship with the aforementioned small-brained professional baseball player, whose idea of a great double-header was having bleached-blonde twins do him simultaneously.

Even before I learned of that particular peccadillo, the warning signs flashed and screeched like red lights and whistles at a train stop. Yet I refused to take heed. So a little more than a year ago the heartbreak express ran right over me when I opened the door to Boo-Boo's Chicago hotel room. I'd planned to surprise him midway through his road trip. And "surprise" him I did. I also surprised the two women in bed with him—the previously noted and surgically enhanced twins.

I wasn't sure why I recalled that horrid day now, while standing in Margie's kitchen. It might have been that the anxiety snaking through me was similar to what I felt back then. Or maybe any thought of snakes automatically triggered recollections of Boo-Boo.

Back in Hot Dish Heaven the door opened to Barbie Jenson, the editor of *The Enterprise*, the local weekly newspaper. She was also Margie's best friend, though a decade or so younger. During my last visit, I'd gotten to know her and was quite fond of her. She was different from Margie. Not as motherly. More outrageous. More worldly. Unlike Margie, who'd never strayed far from home, Barbie had lived in St. Paul for years, where she was a newspaper reporter. She only moved back to the valley to raise her children and care for her aging parents. Her kids were now grown and gone and her parents, deceased.

"Oh, good, you made it." Barbie spoke on a harried breath while strutting to the kitchen, her tight jeans swishing as her chubby denim-clad legs brushed against each other. "I've got something to tell you both." She pulled me to her bountiful bosom for a cursory hug complete with air kisses. If I was not mistaken, Barbie was a bit bigger these days. "You won't believe what just happened." Her voice was a combination of shock and awe, matching her appearance perfectly. With full lips, arched brows, and spiked maroon hair, Barbie always came across as shocked or in awe.

Margie filled a cup with coffee and handed it to her. "Calm down and take a seat. You're as excited as a sugared-up ten-year-old. A very well-endowed ten-year-old."

Barbie ignored the comment, but Margie was right. Barbie filled her Minnesota Gophers' football jersey with absolutely no room to spare. She was a defensive line coach's dream.

"I can't sit," Barbie said. "I'm too keyed up." She sipped her coffee and frowned. "Then again, this may help." She raised the cup. "It's so weak it might actually lull me to sleep."

It was Margie's turn to frown. "Ya don't hafta drink it, ya know."

Barbie set the cup on the prep table. "Well . . ." she said, shifting her weight from one foot to the other. Despite the chill in the air, her feet were bare in backless UGG slippers. "You know how I have to listen to the police scanner for my job and all?"

I didn't say anything, but in truth, Barbie would have found a way to listen to the police scanner if unemployed and living under a bridge. Barbie, you see, was nosy. Extremely nosy.

In the interest of full disclosure, I must say that I, too, had been called "nosy." Many times by many people, including the deputy I was presently lusting after, as well as by Barbie herself. Not that she had ever said anything to my face. Oh, no. She had, however, made a notation to that effect in her reporter's notebook—the one she so carelessly left in her open purse.

"Anyhow," Barbie said, "a little while ago I heard the radio dispatcher call Sheriff Halverson, telling him to get out to the Kennedy piler."

I pointed at her. "I think I passed that on my way into town."

"Did you see anything out of the ordinary?"

I considered the question. "Since I'd never seen a piler before, everything seemed out of the ordinary."

"Oh, too bad." She eased her expression and circled toward Margie, her voice rising excitedly. "I drove out there right away and arrived just after the sheriff. A few deputies followed me in. Some state troopers too." She flailed her arms in typical fashion. Barbie employed numerous body parts whenever she spoke. "Things were so chaotic. People were running every which way."

"And?" Margie posed the word as a question.

"You won't believe it." With palms up, Barbie paced. "You simply won't believe it."

"Spill it," Margie groused. "Then I'll tell ya if I believe it or not."

Barbie clamped her mouth shut. She wasn't about to "spill" it. She possessed information that neither of us had. And while undoubtedly eager to share it, she'd do it slowly, in drips, like a coffee maker in the morning, when you're dying for that first cup. It's what made Barbie a different type of storyteller from Margie, who pretty much blurted out everything all at once, her mouth overflowing most of the time.

"Well, first of all," Barbie said, her words measured, "as you know, the shacks at the pilers aren't guard shacks, but scale houses, with a scale along the ground on each side of them. One scale weighs the trucks on their way in. The other weighs them on their way out."

"Okay, so the pilers have scales." Margie was growing impatient. "And chickens have wings, but they still can't fly. So what?"

"So . . ." Barbie examined her short, black-polished fingernails. She wasn't about to let anyone, not even her dear friend, rush her. She wanted to toy with us. Hold us in suspense. She couldn't help herself. It was the reporter in her. I probably would have done the same. "Beneath each scale—underground—there's an area where the mechanical workings are located. You know, the sensors that make sure the trucks are getting weighed accurately." She moved on to scrutinize her thumbnails.

Meanwhile, Margie checked the schoolhouse clock that hung high above the sink. "I swear if ya were any slower at tellin' stories, Barbie, ya'd be talkin' backwards."

Barbie raised her eyes. "To access that underground area, called the scale pit," she said to me alone, apparently punishing Margie for her petulance, "you have to climb down what looks like a square manhole." She formed "Ls" with the fingers on both her hands.

Margie blew a wayward wisp of hair from her face while trudging to the stainless-steel refrigerator. She dug around inside until she found the decorative tin she obviously wanted. Grabbing it, she kicked the door closed with her heel and made her return.

Apparently sensing that Barbie was nowhere near the end of her tale, Margie was providing us with sustenance. She pulled off the canister cover, dropped it on the prep table with a clang, and tilted the container our way. The two of us snatched what smelled like chocolate-covered peanut butter cups. "Barbie doesn't like Banana Bars," Margie informed me, "but she loves these Peanut Butter Bars."

Barbie lifted her chin. "I wouldn't say I *dislike* Banana Bars. I just don't understand why anyone would make something out of rotten fruit."

Margie set a fist to her hip. "That recipe calls for regular bananas, not overripe ones."

It didn't matter. Barbie was on a roll. "And another thing. What's the deal with *lutefisk*? Yeah, I'm Norwegian, but still . . . eating dried fish that was soaked in lye? Really?"

She went on, but I zoned out. Not intentionally. It's just that the sweet smell of milk chocolate and sugar-laced peanut butter had filled my head and overtaken my senses. While the Banana Bars were great, these were incredible. After only a couple bites, the fret residing in my stomach had been evicted, and my insides were inhabited by the warmth of homemade goodness and memories of childhood.

In my mind, I saw my mom in the kitchen of our old Victorian house in southern Minnesota. She was baking peanut butter cookies that she partially dipped in chocolate shortly after they came out of the oven. While only allowing me to dip a few, she would let me lick the dipping pan clean.

"I've gotta get back to cookin'." Margie punctuated the sentence by slapping the metal prep table, bringing my reverie to a noisy conclusion. "So, Barbie, either get to the point about what happened at the piler or point yourself on out of here."

"Okay, okay," Barbie mumbled, her mouth full of the sweet and sticky peanut butter mixture. "You're kind of grouchy, aren't you?"

"No, just busy. I don't have time for all this lollygaggin'."

Truth be told, Margie did sound grumpy, or at least exasperated, but I figured it wasn't my place to say anything. I was just a visitor. What's more, she was preparing to feed close to a hundred people, a daunting task. So I kept my mouth shut other than for the occasional bite of my dessert bar.

As for Barbie, she finished her bar and brushed her empty hands together. "Okay, Margie, I'm sorry." Plainly, she wasn't. There wasn't an ounce of remorse in her tone. "I just thought you'd want to hear the whole story. But if you don't care about facts . . ."

Margie raised her eyes to the ceiling, as if she might discover some much-needed restraint there. Or absent that, a club good for clobbering her friend. She also tapped her foot in a steady rhythm that played out her annoyance. Yes, Margie could express a lot without saying a word.

"Geez," Barbie hissed. "Don't get your panties in a bind. I'll tell you." She tossed in an eye roll. "They found a guy in there. In that underground area. He was dead." She licked her fingertips. "There. I'm done. Happy?"

"Dead?" Margie repeated. She met Barbie's gaze with her own blank stare. "As in from a heart attack or somthin'?"

Barbie twisted the tips of her spiked hair, a smug look tripping across her face. She was unmistakably pleased that in spite of her complaints, Margie was captivated by the story.

And me? Well, the anxiety temporarily ousted by peanut butter and warm childhood memories had returned, nestling in my stomach.

"No," Barbie said in answer to Margie's question, "it wasn't a heart attack."

She then went mute, and in the silence that followed, two competing notions argued their respective positions in my brain. One suggested I refrain from asking about the piler guy's demise since I was still recovering from my own recent brush with death. The other reasoned that, as a reporter, I had, at minimum, an obligation to make a few inquiries. "So, Barbie," I said, the curiosity-driven view winning out, as usual, "if it wasn't a heart attack, what was it?"

Barbie slipped her eyes between Margie and me, her mouth closed up as tightly as a drawstring bag.

While appreciating her ability to create suspense, I, like Margie, was becoming irritated, not to mention uneasy, because of her delays. "Come on," I grumbled when I couldn't stand it any longer, "what was it?"

Barbie's head swiveled, as if on a stick. "Murder," she said. "It looks like murder."

Margie blinked rapidly, and I stuck the remainder of my Peanut Butter Cup Bar in my mouth, chewing fiercely. Another murder here in the Red River Valley, a place where nothing newsworthy ever occurred other than the occasional tornado or flood? How could that be?

Chapter Four

THE DEAD GUY'S RALEIGH CUMMINGS," Barbie said. "He drove beet truck for Buford and Buddy." She sent Margie a quizzical look.

Margie responded, "I don't believe I knew him."

"He was Harvey's cousin from Fargo. His only surviving relative. He stepped in at the last minute, after Harvey's heart attack."

Margie clicked her tongue against the roof of her mouth. "I'm still shook up over Harvey." She was referring to her nephews' long-time beet hauler. She'd told me about his death during one of our recent phone conversations. "I always thought he drove his snowmobile way too fast to hafta worry about cholesterol. I guess I was wrong."

Barbie plucked a spoon from the silverware bin. "Yeah, everyone really misses him. And from what I understand, Raleigh wasn't much of a replacement. He was a pain in the ass from the get-go. Always telling Buddy and Buford how to do their business." She jabbed the air with the spoon. "As we all know, farmers don't like being second-guessed. They get enough of that from Mother Nature." She ambled toward the stove. "By Raleigh's third day on the job, the twins were ready to fire him but couldn't. They were already shorthanded because of that flu bug that's going around."

"Oh, now I think I remember the guy." Margie nodded like a bobblehead doll. "Tall drink of water in his mid-thirties? Broad shoulders? A wicked smile and eyes to match?"

"Well, when I saw him, his eyes were closed, and he didn't have much to smile about, being dead and all."

I broke in. "You actually saw the body?" I'd never seen a corpse, and the thought of it made me squirm. Even so, I couldn't help but ask for details. Pathetic, huh?

Well, Emme, as we've often said, your curiosity may very well be the death of you.

It was one of the voices in my head. That's right. I occasionally hear voices. And there was a time in my life when I suspected it was a sign of mental instability. But my therapist said it was far more likely the result of being alone so much.

I was an only child, and following the death of my parents, when I was just thirteen, I moved in with my only relatives, an aunt and uncle who were neither demonstrative nor talkative. To fill the void, I supposedly developed an active imagination, complete with voices. Either that or my therapist was wrong, and I was just plain crazy.

"Yeah, I saw the body." Barbie reached for a hot pad and lifted the cover from the large skillet that sat on the left rear burner. "But only for a minute. Then the sheriff pushed me away, yapping about how I was contaminating his crime scene." She stirred the hot dish before scooping up a spoonful and replacing the cover. "He wouldn't know a crime scene if he fell into it face first."

I raised my eyebrows.

She waved the hot pad dismissively. "I'll explain some other time." She blew on her food.

"So how was the body discovered?" I couldn't help myself. Asking questions was as natural to me as breathing.

Barbie touched the tip of her tongue to the food on her spoon. "Well, at two o'clock this morning the piler was shut down because of the cold, and it didn't reopen until a little while ago. It then got really busy with everyone hauling the last of their beets. There were extra-long lines of trucks and lots of waiting. I guess one driver got bored, started texting his girlfriend, and ended up rear-ending the truck in front of him, which was on the outgoing scale. It messed up the scale, so some guys had to go down into the pit to check things out. That's when they found Raleigh Cummings."

"Well," Margie said, her eyes trained on Barbie, "if he's the same guy I have in mind, he not only thought he was God's gift to agriculture, he also fancied himself quite a ladies' man."

"How do you know that?" I asked.

"I saw him in the 'V' a couple times." She bobbed her head toward the hallway that connected the café to the VFW. "And Buddy mentioned a few things about him."

"And Buddy should know," Barbie muttered.

Margie shot her a glint of disapproval, and the newspaper lady immediately got defensive. "Oh, Margie, you know I like Buddy. And he's definitely hot. Hell, if I were twenty years younger and single, I'd offer to rock him like a porch swing in a wind storm. But you've got to admit, he's a hound. He's used to getting whatever he wants when it comes to women." She again blew on her spoonful of hot dish. "And if the stories are true, he's even contracted a few things he didn't want."

After a wink in my direction, she tipped the hot dish into her mouth. "Nummy." She drew out the "e" sound. "This is really good." She once more pivoted in the direction of the stove.

"Don't you dare double dip," Margie growled.

Barbie lifted her hands in the air like a criminal caught in the act. "I'm not. See?" She backed away, easing over to the sink and dropping her spoon into the deep basin. It landed with a ping. "Now I've got to go and see what else I can learn at the piler. Hopefully the sheriff's gone." She glanced at me. "And hopefully you'll come with me."

I had no desire to get embroiled in another murder. Asking Barbie a question or two was one thing. Actively pursuing an investigation was something else entirely. Been there. Done that. It hadn't ended well. In fact, I still was having nightmares. "Thanks, but I think I'll stay here and help Margie."

"Wait a minute. You'd rather work in a kitchen than investigate a crime?" Barbie knitted her brow. "Emme, you're a terrible cook. But you've proven yourself a damn good investigator. And I could use the help."

As nice as her words sounded, I didn't allow myself to be flattered. Barbie had an ulterior motive. She wanted me to move up here and work for her at the paper. That's why she complemented me every chance she got. Her plan was that I'd take over once she retired. But I wasn't sure about being a small-town journalist. Nor was I sure about living in a county where the largest town had fewer than a thousand residents. It would mean a sixty-mile commute for gourmet coffee or shopping. Not that I'm a snob. But sixty miles? Really?

And when it came right down to it, I only stumbled along as a reporter, in spite of how it may have appeared. Sure, I'd solved a homicide, but my efforts had little to do with investigative prowess and lots to do with an insatiable appetite for snooping, not to mention plain old dumb luck. As my dad used to say, even a blind squirrel occasionally finds a nut or, in my case, a killer.

On top of that, I still felt awful about my part in *outing* the people entangled in that earlier crime. True, Barbie knew those same folks. But her role hadn't been as prominent as mine. And apparently she could separate her personal feelings from her professional work, and her professional work didn't cause her sleepless nights. I wasn't that lucky.

"I may be a bad cook, but that doesn't mean I can't lend a hand." Yep, I wanted to avoid any more homicides. And that wasn't such an outlandish goal. I imagined it was near the top of most people's wish lists. Yet, most people hadn't dreamed of being a reporter who'd unearth the cold hard truth no matter the danger. On the flip side, most hadn't come face to face with a murderer.

"What's more," I said to Barbie as my internal debate waged, "I don't want to miss supper. I'm famished." It wasn't a total fib. I really was hungry. Then again, I was always hungry.

"Emme," Margie replied, "if you wanna go with Barbie, grab a plastic bowl and spoon from the cupboard, scoop up some hot dish, and take it with ya."

Regardless of what she may have assumed, the café owner wasn't helping me, so I hedged. "We shouldn't even be considering going out, should we? Isn't it supposed to storm?"

"Oh, it won't get bad for a while," Margie assured me.

"And it's not like we're headed into the boonies." Barbie immediately amended that remark. "Well, not any farther than we are already." She giggled.

I didn't. I was busy picking my brain for a better excuse for keeping clear of the murder scene. Since I was a bit worn out from my long drive, I wasn't doing my best thinking and settled for, "I'm sure Margie could use an extra pair of hands to get ready for this big shindig of hers."

"Goodness gracious, it's not my shindig." Margie glimpsed at the clock. "It's Buford and Buddy's. And they should be along any minute to set up."

She caught my eye and evidently confused my sudden panic with some form of anxiety-laden exhaustion because she added, "Of course, if you're too wound up from your trip to go with Barbie, ya can certainly stay here and rest."

I swallowed hard. It was a conundrum. I certainly didn't want to visit a murder scene. At the same time, I had no desire to remain in the café, where I'd meet up with Buddy Johnson and his brother.

If only there was another option—like a pap smear or root canal.

Chapter Five

As I said, I was aware the twins were hosting the beet banquet, but I'd assumed they'd waltz in at the last moment, deliver a couple remarks, eat, and leave, never noticing me hiding out in the kitchen. I certainly didn't expect them to do any prep work. They didn't seem the type.

Not that I really knew their type. In truth I knew just two things about the Johnson brothers. One, Buford was a goofball. When it came to farming, he was smart enough, but beyond that, not so much. And, two, Buddy was extremely good looking and could sing, dance, and charm the pants off of almost any woman he met. Naturally that scared me. I didn't want to tempt fate—or my pants.

During my last trip to Kennedy, I'd spent a little time with Buddy Johnson, dancing at the VFW. I love to dance. My parents taught me, and I'm pretty good at it. Buddy's no slouch either. As a matter of fact, we tore up the floor doing the country swing. But before and after, I was totally flustered by the guy. And it wasn't just because of his bedroom eyes and sexy ways. No, there was something else. A sense of danger or risk I found compelling, notwithstanding—or perhaps because of—the stories I'd heard regarding his occasional run-ins with the law.

Yes, that's right. While always a law-and-order kind of gal, I regularly fell for "bad boys"—the guys who appeared mysterious and a bit naughty. Needless to say, those relationships left me feeling lower than a chocolate-induced hangover and routinely led to costly therapy sessions focused on my lack of self-esteem.

I was tired of it. But since I'd proven less than resolute in rejecting gorgeous bad guys, I had to steer clear of temptation from the start. And in this instance, temptation went by the name of Buddy Johnson. He was nothing but misery in an attractive package. And I didn't need any more misery, no matter how appealing the package might look—wrapped or unwrapped.

What's more, there remained the matter of murder. Not that of the piler guy but the earlier one. Because some of Buddy and Buford's relatives had been involved, I didn't expect them to be quick to forgive the people who'd cracked the case—me included. Margie insisted they understood. She assured me, "Time heals all wounds." But I knew from personal experience that some wounds simply festered.

"Margie?" I said as I considered yet another idea—one that might actually save me from an awkward encounter with Buddy Johnson and his brother. "Since Raleigh Cummings, the dead guy, worked for the twins, you guys aren't going ahead with the banquet tonight, are you?" My hope was she'd call her nephews and insist that decency dictated the dinner be postponed until some future date. That way I'd get to spend the evening with her without worrying about her nephews making an appearance. I considered it a great plan.

Margie thought otherwise. "Oh, it would be a cryin' shame to put it off. I've made food enough to feed a hundred. What in the world would I do with it all? With a storm brewin', business could be slow for the next couple days. The electricity could go out. Everythin' could spoil. Uff-da, that wouldn't be good. Not good at all." She hesitated for only a second before deciding to call the boys to make sure they were "plannin' on movin' forward with the meal."

I exhaled in defeat as Margie wiped her hands on the towel that draped over her shoulder. "No, I don't see why we oughtta put off the dinner," she repeated. "No one really knew Cummin's all that well anyways. And who knows? By gettin' together and talkin', someone might think of somethin' that could help the investigation." She picked up her cell phone and began pushing buttons.

"Yeah," Barbie added in a tone that confirmed her support for Margie's plan, "if you listen closely tonight, you might learn something important. For instance, did Cummings get into altercations in the beet field? At the bar? Or maybe he got caught doing something terrible. If he thought he was a ladies' man, he might have crossed a line. Whatever the case, it led someone to get angry enough to bonk him over the head."

"Is that how he died?" I asked the question out of idle curiosity, nothing more. I certainly wasn't genuinely interested in the case. "Was it blunt-force trauma to the head?"

"Yeah," Barbie said, "it was repeated blunt-force trauma to the back of the head. The lack of blood at the scene suggests he was killed elsewhere and moved to the scale pit."

Margie set her phone on the counter. "The boys aren't answering."

Barbie put her fists to her ample hips. "What's it going to be, Emme? You staying here or coming with me?"

Before I could answer, the café door swung open, and Buddy and Buford entered on a blast of freezing air.

My breathing stalled. But I couldn't blame it on the wind or the cold. I'd expected them. And I should have expected the twins too. Perhaps intellectually I had. But emotionally I wasn't at all prepared. Consequently, I stood there like a potted plant. A cold potted plant.

"Woah!" Buford hollered to no one in particular. "It's windier out there than a sack full of farts. And it's getting damn nippy too."

"Buford!" Margie scolded. "Do ya actually eat with that mouth?" She shook her head. "You're always so gall-darn vulgar."

"Why?" he wanted to know, a confounded expression on his face. "What did I say?"

The last time I'd seen Buford, he was recovering from burns sustained in an alcohol-related grilling accident. He was bald, pink, and scaly. And upon my return to Minneapolis, my editor had described him perfectly without ever having met him. "Emme," he'd said, "while most people learn by observation, some can only learn through experimentation. And among them there are a few, unfortunately, who have to stick their faces right into the fire before they understand they're going to get burned. Your Buford, it seems, is one of those guys."

He wasn't "my" Buford. Nor was he any longer pink and scaly. His dark hair and eyebrows were growing in nicely, and his face was tan and healthy looking. Another couple months and he'd be a handsome man, undoubtedly biding his time until the next fire, real or figurative. After all, as my editor had surmised, Buford Johnson was just that way.

Buddy, conversely, was drop-dead gorgeous—then and now—despite the pale purple and green smudges presently marking the underside of his left eye.

The twins' late father was Scandinavian, while their mother was Hispanic. And when it came to looks, the boys and their sister took after their mom.

Buddy's hair was dark and wavy and a couple weeks past a needed trim. His skin resembled caramel—the kind you could barely resist tasting. And his brown eyes sparked with mischief, an expression also captured by the half smile usually at home on his lips. He was tall and lean but toned, and he looked fine standing there in a white tee-shirt covered by a blue flannel shirt that hung open over fitted jeans.

"You called as we were pulling up," he said to his aunt just prior to catching sight of me.

At that he stopped and stared, causing me a sudden attack of hysterical paralysis. That's right. I couldn't move. I couldn't speak either. So the only thing left to do was try and read the guy.

I got the sense that Margie was wrong. I was the last person on earth Buddy Johnson wanted to see. And Buford reinforced that notion by shuffling in behind his brother, clearly ready to follow his lead, whatever that might be.

A few possible scenarios played through my mind. Buddy may merely holler at me for what happened to his family and my role in it. Or he could strike out across the floor and actually punch me in the nose. Then, too, there was the outside chance he'd throw his arms around me and kiss me tenderly.

Okay, there was absolutely no chance of that kissing thing. I didn't even like the idea. I was involved with Deputy Randy Ryden, or at least I was attempting to get involved with him. So I don't know why the thought of kissing Buddy Johnson had even popped into my head. And I dismissed it as nothing more than a natural reaction to the appearance of an incredibly good-looking man and the agony I was suffering due to my aforementioned romantic dry spell.

I ordered myself to get a grip. And to that end, I drew in a slow deep breath. On the exhale, I directed myself to speak. After several false starts, I managed to push a sound from my throat. I was going for, "Hi," but it came out part greeting, part frog croaking.

Nice, Emme, real nice. That is if you lived on a lilypad and ate flies for lunch.

I silently told the voices in my head to muzzle it.

"Hello," Buddy replied. The word rumbled from deep within him like a growl.

It scared me or, at a minimum, caused me dread. And soon that dread was weighing heavily on me, seeping deep into my bones, where it mingled with desire. But not the kind of desire you probably assume. No, this was the desire to "skedaddle," as Margie would say.

Trusting my instincts, I cleared my throat and took a crack at an excuse to leave. "Sorry to rush off." My voice sounded strange, even to my ears. "I . . . umm . . . Barbie and I are . . . We have to . . . I mean . . . umm . . ." Talking was pointless, so I gave up and yanked on Barbie's arm.

I pulled her toward the door as Margie hollered, "Eh, Emme, I thought ya were hungry. If ya wait a minute, I'll serve ya up some Vegetable Hot Dish. Ya can take it with ya."

"No, that's okay." I shouldered the door. "I wouldn't want you to go to any trouble."

"Oh, it's no trouble. It's already done. It's an 'express' hot dish. I got the recipe from Deb Kapinos. Didn't ya meet her last time ya were here?"

"No, Margie, I don't think so." I shoved Barbie outside. She stumbled, barely catching herself before falling to the sidewalk. "And I'm not that hungry after all."

The door slammed as Margie called out, "Okeydokey then. See ya later."

To which my stomach responded with a growl of its own.

Chapter Six

THE WIND PROPELLED US across the highway to Barbie's SUV. At the same time, a gaggle of geese passed overhead in a "V" formation. Their honking was frantic, much like my nerves.

We jumped in the car and buckled up. Barbie turned the engine over, and the radio blasted "Hell on Heels," a song by the Pistol Annies. "I'm hell on heels, say what you will, I done made the devil a deal." I stared at my red high-top tennis shoes while reviewing my pitiful behavior back in the cafe. Not exactly "hell on heels." More like "tenuous in tennies."

Barbie cranked up the heater and spun the car around in front of the community garden. Only a few months back the garden had been abundant with colorful and fragrant flowers. Now all the blooms were spent, and the stems were shriveled and brown, bending in the wind like crippled up gardeners.

Barbie switched off the music and, oddly enough, the heater. "What was that all about?" she asked.

"What do you mean?" I tried on a tone of innocence.

"Oh, puleeze." I guess it didn't fit. "The air between you and Buddy was practically crackling with electricity. On top of that, you all but ran up my back on your way out of the cafe." She leaned into a sharp left, bounced over the railroad tracks, and headed down County Road 7.

"Barbie," I yelped, "you didn't even use your turn signal!"

She shrugged. "Don't have to. In a town this small, everyone already knows where you're going." She winked and added. "Now quit trying to change the subject."

"I'm not." I tugged my seatbelt tighter. "It wasn't electricity. It was friction." I'd never before ridden with Barbie. It was reminiscent of a carnival ride—a scary carnival ride. "He hasn't gotten beyond what happened last time I was here."

Barbie dismissed my remark with a wave of her hand—a hand I would have preferred she had kept on the steering wheel. "I think you're imagining that. As I've told you before, he's Scandinavian, like me. And we don't like discussing personal matters, especially with people outside of family. But that doesn't mean we're holding a grudge."

"Barbie, you talk about personal stuff all the time." *Often to a fault,* I added to myself.

"Well, I'm unique." She displayed a toothy grin before jerking her attention back to the road and slamming on the brakes. I lurched forward, only my seatbelt saving me from smacking my head into the windshield.

The little white pup from earlier trudged across the road, its own head bowed against the wind. "Damn dog," Barbie muttered. "I almost ran him over."

With that she was off again. And a few minutes later—though it should have been much, much longer—we hung a two-wheeled left onto County Road 1 and way too soon another into the beet piler. Barbie's car skidded to a stop, gravel spraying from under the tires. "Good, the sheriff's gone." She cut the engine and opened the door.

"Barbie," I said, snatching the sleeve of her football jersey, "I only came along for the ride." I couldn't help but add, "Such as it was." I dropped my hand. "I'm not getting drawn into a murder investigation. So I'll just wait here."

"You can't do that. You'll look ridiculous sitting alone in the car. Like a kid waiting for her mother." She rested for a beat. "But if that's what you want, I guess it's your prerogative. Just don't expect me to bring you a sucker, honey. I don't care how good you are." Fluttering her eyelashes, she eased from the vehicle, the wind gripping her door and slamming it shut behind her.

Despite Barbie's mockery, I wasn't about to leave the vehicle. She strutted toward the scale shack, where two deputies leaned against a nearby squad car. She could ask them questions all night long as far as I was concerned. I was just going to sit here. And I wouldn't look "ridiculous." I was certain of that.

I made a visual sweep of the area. The vast fields around me were upholstered in a tweed of black dirt and brown stubble against the overcast sky. The landscape wasn't pretty in the traditional sense—not like a mountain scene or a lake view. Still, there was something intriguing about it. Maybe because it had a purpose. It actually had an important job to do. And that made it fascinating.

At the piler itself, sugar-beet mountains, each at least twenty feet high and two hundred feet long, waited to be moved by a convoy of trucks to the processing plant in Drayton. Unlike earlier, though, no trucks now stood in line. And the only people in sight were the two deputies, Barbie, and me. Yep, even to someone who had never before been to a beet piler, the inactivity generated a tension that was almost palpable.

The wind howled at the car, and I pulled on the bottom of my short jacket, once more regretting I hadn't brought a warmer coat. I glanced at Barbie and muttered under my breath. She'd taken the car keys, so I couldn't even switch on the heater.

She was talking to the deputies. And even though I couldn't hear them, I knew exactly what the men were saying. Their movements spoke volumes. With curious expressions and less than subtle gestures, they were asking about me.

I made an effort to ignore them. Twisting my hair around my finger, I pointed my eyes elsewhere. But they trailed right back. And no matter how hard I fought the sensation, I did indeed feel "ridiculous." As Barbie had warned, I was akin to a kid confined to the car. And I didn't like it. No more than I had as a child.

"Shit!" I muttered as I opened the door.

I instantly chided myself for swearing. My editor had received complaints. The way he'd explained it, I came across as too innocent to swear. It threw people. It left them unsure what to think of me and, by extension, the newspaper's Food section, which was "G" rated. What's more, he said swearing was a sign of a limited vocabulary. Particularly bad for a journalist. So I was working to curb the habit. Even so, during the previous week, he'd been forced to remind me twice to refrain from swearing, "Damn it!"

I wrangled from my seat, this time mumbling, "Shoot!" No, it just didn't project the same oomph.

I trudged toward Barbie, the wind hollering at me as I went. *I'm not some kid restricted to the car,* I assured myself. *I'm an intelligent adult and a professional newspaper reporter who'll participate in any conversation of her choosing.* Even so, I wasn't about to let my guard down and get dragged into another murder investigation. And to make certain of that, I silently pledged to keep mum. I wouldn't speak. I wouldn't utter a word. I'd simply stand next to Barbie and let her take care of business. *Ugh!*

"What can you tell me?" Barbie asked the question of the deputies as I approached.

The men, in response, simultaneously tilted their heads at me, leaving Barbie to answer their unspoken question. "Like I already said, that's Emme Malloy." She pointed at me, somewhat ambiguous about continuing. After a moment, she did anyhow. "She's a reporter for the Minneapolis paper. You probably remember her from a few months back."

The deputies smiled, just barely, as if sharing an inside joke. And I went from feeling ridiculous to uncomfortable—extremely uncomfortable. "Yeah, we know who she is," the bigger of the two men said before his smile transformed into what appeared to be a smirk. "We've heard all about her."

Barbie didn't wait for them to elaborate, and for that, I was grateful. I had no idea what Randy had told them, but it must have been bad. At least that's the sense I got from their smirks. Or were they sneers? *Hmm.* Another glimpse and I decided, yes, they were sneers. Lecherous sneers.

I crossed my arms over my chest. *And here I thought Randy liked me.* My shoulders slumped. *I sure got that wrong. He played me for a fool. Then he made fun of me to his friends.* My chest heaved. *When will I get it through my thick skull that guys don't really like me? When will I realize they only want to use me?*

Emme, you're overreacting. It was yet another voice from inside my head. *You're allowing your insecurities to take control. Don't do that. And don't get all bent out of shape before you learn the facts. Ask Randy what he said. Give him a chance to explain.*

I should have been pleased that this particular voice was showing kindness, rather than hurling insults, as was usually the case. But I wasn't. I hated that the voices in my head could be so damn—I mean darn—reasonable. It was far easier for me—and way more familiar—to make assumptions and jump to conclusions based on my perceived deficiencies.

"Come on, guys," Barbie pleaded, "give me a little something here."

One of the men—the bigger one with the receding hairline—took a drag from his cigarette. "Barbie, I recall sayin' that very thing to you back in high school. It was in the band room one night after practice. Remember? It didn't get me anywhere either." He and his buddy chuckled and bumped fists.

"These two are former classmates of mine," Barbie said to me. "Guy Gunnerson." She pointed at the sandy-blonde lug with the hair-loss problem. "And his cousin, Jarod Martinson." She formed a gun with her thumb and index finger and aimed it at the skinny man with the hang-dog face and absent chin.

I raised my index finger. "Excuse me. I didn't catch that. Was that Jarot with a 'T' or Jarod with a 'D'?"

The thin man wrinkled his forehead. "It's Jarod," he stated slowly, as if I were an idiot, "with a 'J.'"

Out of the corners of my eyes, I caught Barbie's attention. "All righty then," I muttered to her in disbelief.

"Yeah, it's a wonder they're allowed to carry guns." She spoke loud enough for all to hear. "Well, it's no wonder really. It just bugs the hell out of me."

Guy snapped his cigarette onto the ground. "Oh, Barbie, you love us. You just talk mean because you're afraid if you don't, you'll paw us all over, like a cat in heat."

"In your dreams," Barbie countered.

To which Guy replied, "That's what I'm countin' on, Barbie. That's what I'm countin' on."

Jarod laughed and slapped his thigh, while Barbie shook her head.

"Hey, now," she proceeded to say after allowing the men another moment to enjoy themselves, "let's get down to business. Tell me who you've got for suspects so far."

Guy rubbed the back of his neck. "Barbie, the sheriff will have our jobs if we say anythin' to ya."

It was Barbie's turn to laugh. "No, he won't. He's your uncle. He wouldn't dare fire you." She squinted at them. "So tell me what's going on." More squinting. "You know you want to."

The men eyed each other. Barbie was right. They were nearly bursting at the seams. They definitely wanted to talk.

Guy re-adjusted his laid-back position against the squad car. "Well, I guess it won't be a secret for long," he said after fighting the desire to speak for a whopping two or three seconds. "The sheriff called the BCA. They should be here before mornin', weather permittin'."

He was referring to the Minnesota Bureau of Criminal Apprehension, a state law enforcement agency that assisted rural sheriffs and police chiefs investigate crimes beyond what they normally encountered. I knew of them because until recently I'd kept notes on anything I heard at the paper that pertained to "real" news. Like I said, I thought I wanted to be a "real" reporter.

"Yeah," he continued, his head inclined in my direction, "after she showed him up by solvin' that last murder, he wasn't about to take any chances this time around. No, sir-ree, Bob. He's makin' sure this case gets wrapped up under his watch. Don't forget, he's up for re-election in another year."

Jarod adjusted himself—in the crotch. Then he shook out his leg and did it again, as if he had to wind himself up to speak and that's how he got the job done. "And while he's waitin' for the BCA," he finally said, "he's goin' after the usual suspects, startin' with Buddy Johnson."

Guy backhanded him, causing the skinny man to gasp.

Chapter Seven

"What'd you hit me for?" Jarod asked between coughs and just prior to taking a swing at Guy. Since he was folded over at the waist, it was a feeble attempt at best.

Guy scowled. "I did it because you talk too much."

"No, I don't. I talk way less than you." Jarod worked at standing erect.

"Then maybe it's that you're an idiot when ya do talk."

Jarod coughed. "I'm not an idiot. You are."

"No, I'm not."

"Yes, you are."

I recalled Randy telling me about two of his fellow deputies. He'd referred to them as Tweedledum and Tweedledumber. I presumed I'd just made their acquaintance.

"Now, boys!" Barbie scolded. "Stop arguing! You're both idiots." The pair actually seemed pleased—for a moment. "But neither of you is as idiotic as your boss. Why on earth is he after Buddy this time?"

"Well, because, for starters, Buddy's a hothead." Guy scuffed the ground with the toe of his boot. I got the impression his feelings were hurt by Barbie's "idiot" comment. But his need to sulk was obviously trumped by his longing to flaunt his knowledge about the case, as evidenced by his continued chatter. "Word has it that him and Cummin's were in pissin' matches on a regular basis. Cummin's was drivin' beet truck for the twins, you know. And this past Tuesday night, the two of them went at it outside the Caribou." He glanced at me. A gust of wind had come up, and I was wiping dirt from my eyes. "That's the bar and grill in Hallock. The town just up the road there." He tossed his thumb across his shoulder before redirecting his attention to Barbie. "Buddy fired him on the spot. Told him not to show up for his shift that night. And that's the last time anyone saw Cummin's alive."

"So what did they fight about?" Barbie asked.

Guy puffed out his chest. He clearly enjoyed being the source of information. "Oh, you know. The usual. This and that. Everythin' and anythin'."

I was about to respond with a snort but held back, deciding that with these guys around, I might need a good snort later on.

"Cummings knew how to get under Buddy's skin." Guy was doing his best to sound authoritative. "Not that it takes a whole lot of figurin'." He offered me a knowing look. "See, he liked to say that Buddy and Buford got the farm 'handed to them.' Of course Buford just laughed it off. But not Buddy. He said they'd worked too damn hard to have some jackass shoot his mouth off about somethin' he knew nothin' about."

I wasn't privy to all the details, but I knew the twins were hard workers and always had been. Their parents, Ole and Lena, had died separate, but tragic, deaths—a whole other story—leaving the boys to run the farm, which, like so many farms in the area, had been in the family for generations.

With the help of relatives, Buddy and Buford had worked the fields while attending the University of Minnesota in Crookston, where they'd studied agriculture and business. Upon graduation, they took over the entire operation, dedicating themselves to expanding it. Of course, none of that excused Buddy's behavior. But it may have explained it.

The wind whistled, coaxing another strong breeze, complete with dirt, into my face—and my eyes. No doubt, I needed to head back to the car. I wouldn't be missed. After all, I hadn't contributed to the discussion. Not that I'd planned to. Nope, I wasn't about to get involved.

It didn't matter anyhow. Guy knew nothing substantive about the crime or the suspects. And clearly his partner never had much on his mind. Yep, the way I saw it—that is if I could have seen—we were—I mean Barbie was—gaining little by hanging around.

Barbie must have agreed. "If that's all you bozos have for us," she said, "we're taking off. We haven't eaten supper, so we're going to Hot Dish Heaven. Margie's testing new recipes, and there's one I definitely want to try. It's called Sauerkraut Hot Dish." She licked her lips.

"Yeah, Margie's 'broadening her horizons,' culinarily speaking." Barbie fluttered her eyelashes at the made-up word. "And as her primary taste tester, I'm broadening my hips." She flung them from side to side, coming awfully close to sending skinny Jarod with a "J" into the next county.

ABOUT HALFWAY BACK TO TOWN, I broke the silence that had descended over the car. I did it in small part because I had questions I wanted answered but in large part because I needed to divert my attention away from Barbie's erratic driving. With darkness settling in, her unpredictability behind the wheel had my stress level soaring to new heights. "So," I said in a shaky voice, "those two deputies aren't very bright, are they?"

Barbie didn't seem to notice my tentative tone or my fragile emotional state. "To be honest, Guy's not as dumb as he looks." She glanced at me. "Then again, how could he be?" She chuckled as the wind howled, heralding the arrival of snow. Heavy with moisture, the first flakes hit the windshield like BB pellets. "Jarod's another story."

She accelerated along a straightaway, and I gripped the sides of my seat, babbling in an attempt to distract myself. "Yet, he's in law enforcement. Hard to believe. You wouldn't think he'd meet the requirements. Not that I'm an expert on what they are. But I'm sure . . ."

Barbie flipped the wipers on, leaving them to squeak while smudging snow across the glass. "Their mothers are the sheriff's sisters. There's no way in hell he'd cross those two by laying off their sons. So their jobs are safe in perpetuity. To be fair, though, they come by their stupidity naturally."

"Huh? How so?"

Barbie clicked on the defroster, then the air conditioner. I did a double take. It was the air conditioner all right. "No one in their family is particularly bright." She bounded over the railroad tracks, and I believe I actually caught air. "Take the whole Two River thing, for example." She barely slowed for the approaching intersection. "That's a river up here. It was supposedly named by their great-great-great-grandfather based on the number of tributaries."

"And?" While passing under a street light, I snagged a glimpse of my hands. My knuckles were white.

"It has three," Barbie said, veering onto Highway 75. "The Two River has three branches."

I had to peel my fingers from the seat to wipe my runny nose. "So can you take anything they say seriously? Do you really think the sheriff's after Buddy Johnson?" I shoved my tissue back into my pocket.

"Oh, yeah." Barbie jerked the car to a stop across the highway from the café, and I offered a silent prayer of thanks for our safe return. "While those two may only have the intellect of basic garden tools, they know their boss." She doused the headlights, switched off the engine, and along with it, the air conditioning. That prompted another prayer of thanksgiving. "He's no fool in spite of what I might say. And he hates Buddy Johnson. He'd love to arrest him for anything."

"Hmm." I'd met Sheriff Halverson while laid up during my last visit. With his bulging muscles, barrel chest, and crew cut, he came across as a drill sergeant. And he treated me like an unwanted recruit. Under the guise of investigating that earlier murder, he made one condescending remark after another. And no matter what I said in return, he merely muttered, "I see," when clearly he had no inclination to do so.

"Is that how Randy got his negative impression of the twins?" I asked. "From Sheriff Halverson?" Deputy Randy Ryden didn't care for Buford and Buddy. As a matter of fact, he'd almost convinced me they were responsible for that other homicide. Of course they weren't, though they did get hurt by it.

"I think so." She pulled the key from the ignition. "Then again, Randy and the twins have had lots of issues over the years. Primarily because of his relationship with their sister."

My heartstrings tied themselves in knots. Yes, my jealousy was irrational. The man was thirty years old. He was bound to have been in a few relationships prior to meeting me. And I was fully aware he had dated the twins' sister. I also knew they were pretty serious before things fell apart. I just didn't like hearing about it.

"What's more," Barbie said, "the twins used to get into their share of trouble, especially after their mom died. And since Randy's a cop, that caused some tension. But you already know all that. Besides, they've changed a lot over the past couple years. Much to Sheriff Halverson's chagrin."

We eased from the car, the wind whistling at us like a chorus of construction workers. "Why does the sheriff dislike them so?" An especially strong gust practically swept the words from my mouth.

"Something that happened a few years ago," she shouted in an effort to be heard. "He just can't seem to forgive or forget."

Before I could follow up, Barbie started across the road, and I scooted after her, the sharp, ice-like snowflakes stabbing my cheeks.

Chapter Eight

The commingled scents of melted cheese and baked bread drifted throughout the cafe. Margie was behind the counter, preparing a fresh pot of coffee, when Barbie and I plunked ourselves down on the stools opposite her.

"Is it gettin' nasty out there?" the café owner asked.

"Oh, yeah." Barbie rubbed her hands together. "I better get back to Hallock, or my hubby will worry about me." She wiggled her eyebrows. "And I certainly don't want to be late. It's date night."

"Gee whiz," Margie muttered.

"What are you two talking about?" I combed my fingers through my hair. It was ripe with static electricity, not to mention snarls. I was sure it stuck straight out, and "Pippi Longstocking" had never been a good look for me.

"Sex," Barbie said. "We're talking about sex. Tom and I end every date night in bed. And our sex is so good that when we get done, even the neighbors light cigarettes."

"Gee whiz," Margie repeated.

"Before I go, though, I want to taste some Sauerkraut Hot Dish. I also want to find out what you learned from the folks in there." She bobbed her head toward the middle room. The beet banquet was well underway. I heard the murmur of voices and the occasional heightened sound of laughter.

"The weather's been the major topic of conversation," Margie informed us. "I don't think anyone will be stayin' very long. If they had their druthers, they'd probably be at home right now."

She filled a coffee cup and handed it to Barbie. "That oughtta warm ya up." She then glanced my way, the implicit question in her eyes.

"Yes, please," I answered.

"Do you mean to tell me you didn't find out anything about Raleigh Cummings?" Barbie sounded surprised if not altogether disappointed.

"I didn't say that." Margie gave me a mug of coffee, and I wrapped my hands around it, hoping to thaw them out. "I asked around," she said, "and some people were more than happy to talk about him. But since he wasn't from around here and only drove on the night shift, the day folks didn't know much."

She added to me by way of explanation, "Beet harvest takes 'round-the-clock work. Ya don't stop for nothin' other than too much heat, too much cold, or too much rain. And since ya always encounter some of that, ya gotta move fast when the conditions are right. So all the beet farmers run two shifts during harvest—a day shift that works from noon to midnight and a night shift that goes from midnight to noon."

She leaned back against the service counter and crossed her feet at her ankles. "I talked to Dinky Donaldson." She honed in on Barbie, who didn't appear all that impressed by her source of information. "Did ya know he and his brother sold their beet stock last winter?" She dipped her chin. "Well, they did. So as it turns out, they were able to drive beet truck for Buford and Buddy this past week." She glanced at me. "See, flu season started early this year. Workers were droppin' like flies, leavin' the farmers scramblin' to find fill-in help." She sidled up to the wall and rapped her knuckles against the wainscoting. "Knock on wood I don't get sick. That flu bug sounds awful."

Barbie slurped her steaming coffee. "It makes sense they'd help out, doesn't it? You're all related, right?"

Margie returned to her stance against the back counter. "Yeah," she said slowly, "if I remember right, Arlene Donaldson—that'd be their grandpa's sister—married Gus Johnson, my grandpa's uncle on his father's side." She squished up the left side of her face. "Or was he my grandpa's first cousin? Hmm, I always get that mixed up." She snapped her fingers. "No, I got it now. He was my grandpa's nephew. That's right. He was the oldest son of his youngest brother. Yeah, I remember. He married—"

"Stop!" Barbie pounded her head against the counter. "I should have known better than to say anything. With you even the most innocent question about family turns into a genealogy lesson."

Margie shrugged. "I like knowin' how everybody around here's connected. That's all."

She looked to me, perhaps for agreement, but I saw it as an opportunity to change the subject. Having no family to speak of, I'd never found genealogy particularly interesting. "Margie, what did you mean when you said the Donaldson brothers sold their beet stock?"

With a swing of her ponytail, Margie shifted from the subject of ancestors back to farming. "Not just anyone can grow sugar beets, ya know. Ya need stock. And if ya don't have any, ya hafta buy or rent some from someone else. And if ya can't find any, well then, you're out of luck. No beets for you." She stopped, ostensibly to give me a chance to absorb everything she'd said. "That's how the growers regulate the amount of sugar produced and, ultimately, the price." She stopped again. "Well, that and they own the processing plants." She chuckled, and a renegade gray-blonde hair came to rest on the lashes of her right eye. It flitted when she blinked.

"Yah," she continued, "even though sugar beets are still a darn good crop, financially speakin', some growers are sellin' off their stock." More blinking. More flitting. "They're afraid what Congress might do in the way of decreasin' subsidies and all. So they wanna get out while the gettin' is still good." I think my eyes were glazing over. It was way too much information to process at one time. Besides, that flitting thing was hypnotizing.

"Anyways," she said, "what I was gonna tell ya was that Dinky went over to the city office this past Tuesday afternoon, after he got done in the field. And before he even got to the door, he heard Raleigh Cummin's arguin' with Janice."

She again paused to provide me clarification. But this time she spoke a little faster, apparently suspicious of my attention span. "Janice Ferguson's our city clerk. Has been for some time. Does a darn good job too. Knows how every dime is spent. And what more could ya ask?" She didn't wait for an answer. Then again, she probably didn't expect one. "On the flip side, she can be a real pain in the keester. She's set in her ways. More stubborn than hammered iron, as William Shakespeare said."

"Pssssh." Coffee spewed from my mouth and squirted out my nose.

Barbie threw her head back and let go of a guffaw.

Margie stiffened her spine, set her shoulders, and with a righteous amount of indignation, demanded, "Now what in the dickens is so funny about that?" She glared, first at Barbie, then at me. "I may be a small-town café owner, but I can read."

I yanked a napkin from the dispenser in front of me and tended to my face. "I'm sorry, Margie. It just seemed out of character. I didn't know you were fond of Shakespeare. You don't seem the type."

"Well," Margie huffed, tugging on her tee-shirt, "that'll teach ya not to pigeonhole people." She stepped toward the cash register, grabbed the tube of Chapstick tucked alongside it, and outlined her thin cracked lips. "Durin' the last couple months, I've been tryin' to broaden my horizons. And not just in the kitchen." She replaced the cover and returned the tube to its resting place.

I felt terrible. Hurting Margie was the last thing I wanted to do. "Margie, I'm truly sorry."

She brushed aside my words and hopefully her anger. "Anyways, Dinky said . . ." She let her voice trail off as she peered at me with one eye, the other tightly closed. "I think ya met Dinky and his brother, Biggie, when ya were here last."

While never formally introduced, I remembered them as the guys who had driven an old tractor to town. They'd lost their driver's licenses due to excessive DWIs. But since a license wasn't required to operate farm machinery, they didn't seem concerned.

I suspected their carefree attitude ran in the family. Grandpa Donaldson, who was pushing ninety, if not dragging it behind him, recklessly drove a golf cart all over town, refusing to listen to anyone who urged him to hang up his keys. During my last visit,

I'd spotted the cart in his front yard, the front end leaning into a hedge, the rear wheels hanging on a garden timber. A bumper sticker plastered on the back read, "If you don't like my driving, stay the hell off the sidewalk."

"Anyways," Margie said, "Dinky was comin' in to ask Janice about gettin' a delay in tearin' down that shed he owns on the southeast end of town there. It got condemned by the city, and rightfully so. But, of course, Dinky wasn't thrilled about spendin' the money to demolish it. See, those Donaldson boys are tight unless they're playin' poker or buyin' booze. Yah, they're worth millions. Still, for the most part, when either one takes a five-dollar bill out of his wallet, Lincoln is temporarily blinded by the light."

Margie snickered while picking up her coffee cup, only to set it right back down again. "Anyways," she said for the umpteenth time, "Dinky told me that Janice and Raleigh were goin' on about garbage bags, if ya can imagine that. See, Raleigh was stayin' in the house his cousin Harvey had been rentin' here in town before his heart attack.

"Now I'm not sure if Raleigh didn't know ya had to use special garbage bags or simply didn't care. But either way he failed to put his garbage in the official orange bag, so his trash didn't get picked up. It was left at the curb, and some dog got in it, and he had to clean up the mess. Which made him madder than a wet hen. So he went on over to the city office and accused Janice of never explainin' about the official bags." She took a break but only long enough for a deep breath. "Personally I find that hard to believe considerin' how seriously she takes that aspect of her job."

Another deep breath. "Ya know, Dinky told me he actually turned sideways along the door frame to keep Janice and Raleigh from seein' him." She borrowed one of the snorts I'd been saving up. "Like that would make a difference." She added to me alone, "If ya remember, Dinky and his brother are each the size of a Mack truck." She paused, peering over her shoulder, as if checking the time.

"And?" Barbie prompted.

"And . . ." Margie repeated, visibly struggling to recount exactly where she'd left off. "Oh, yah . . . Raleigh called Janice some

God-awful names. But she just hollered back, 'Are ya always a pain in the ass, Raleigh, or is today a special occasion?'" Margie rubbed her large, rough hands. "Oh, that Janice can be a real wise alec. And even though I think she's pretty darn funny, not everybody agrees. Nope, some folks don't get her sense of humor at all. And I'll admit, it's an acquired taste. Still, Raleigh went too far. He actually threatened her. And that's when Dinky walked in."

Margie crossed her arms and tucked them under her breasts. "Raleigh left right away then. And when Dinky asked Janice if she was okay, she told him that Raleigh didn't scare her one iota. She said, if need be, she'd take care of him for good." Margie allowed us to consider that remark for an extra moment. "Dinky told me that in spite of Janice bein' small, he had no doubt she'd do it too. He saw it in her eyes."

"Margie, do you really believe Janice would kill Raleigh Cummings over garbage bags?" Barbie drew in her thick lips and bit down. I got the sense she was doing her best to stifle a giggle.

"Accordin' to Dinky," Margie answered, "there was a bunch of trash dumped on the steps of the city office on Wednesday mornin'." She stopped for a beat. "Yeah, that would of been yesterday." She allowed another beat to pass. "Dinky didn't see it himself because he was in the field. But Biggie saw it and told him about it." She glanced at me. "Biggie was workin' the day shift, so he didn't start till noon."

"And?" Barbie tapped her index finger on the counter. Once more she appeared to be urging Margie along. Or perhaps she was trying to keep her on point. Either way I figured she didn't stand much of a chance.

"And," Margie repeated, "guess who was cleanin' up the mess?" She answered herself in the same breath, "One very angry Janice Ferguson."

"Hmm." Barbie's expression was an odd mix of humor and impatience, as if she didn't know whether to laugh at what Margie had told her or dismiss it as so much malarkey. "I don't know. You got your information from Dinky Donaldson, not an especially credible source. And while Janice may not be the most principled person in the world, I don't believe she'd kill over garbage bags."

"I'm not sayin' she did. In fact, I'm prayin' she didn't. I like her, and we need her on our curlin' team this winter." Again, to me, she explained, "We have a pretty good shot at goin' far this year. But only if Janice is on board. She may be small, but she's as strong as an ox. And by golly, she can sweep a rock like nobody's business." She turned back to Barbie. "I'm just repeatin' what I was told."

Barbie tapped the tips of her short fingernails against her dark red lips. "Do you really think she'd be strong enough to move Raleigh's body to the scale pit? Remember, he wasn't killed down there."

Margie thought about that. "Like I said, she's strong. Besides, if she couldn't do it by herself, she could probably get help."

Barbie didn't appear persuaded. Yet, she said, "Something to consider, I suppose."

Margie stood straight. "How about considerin' it while ya eat some Overnight Hot Dish?" She peeked across her shoulder. "That's all I've got left on the stove. The rest of the hot dishes, includin' two different sauerkraut ones, are out in the banquet room. One recipe's from Darla Hanson, and the other is from Linda Kutzer. And I don't know which I like better. Anyways, the boys decided to set the buffet tables up in there, so there wouldn't be so much traipsin' back and forth. And God only knows what'll be left when that crew gets done."

She leaned her head sideways, evidently listening for something. "Ya know, it's soundin' quieter. Maybe folks are headin' out. Wanna wait and see? Or ya wanna go with the Overnight Hot Dish? It's a new recipe from Jill Fedo. She's mostly known for her bakin'. She's won more state fair ribbons than ya can shake a stick at. But I'm wagerin' she's a decent cook too."

"Oh, I guess I'll go with the Overnight Hot Dish." Barbie's tone conveyed her disappointment. She really wanted to try something with sauerkraut. "I'm so famished I suppose I could eat just about anything."

Margie balled her fists. “Well, I certainly don’t wanna force anythin’ on ya.”

Recognizing her mistake, Barbie began backpedalling. But it was too late. The damage had already been done. Margie was irked.

Being no dummy, when Margie looked at me, I played the role of Switzerland by saying, “I don’t want to cause any problems, so I’ll just have whatever you think is best.” In truth, while hungry, I really didn’t want to hang around the café for fear of meeting up with the twins—Buddy in particular. Nevertheless, I added, “Overnight Hot Dish would suit me just fine.”

As I said, Margie was an easy-going person, at least where I was concerned, but I’d annoyed her once already, and I wasn’t about to press my luck.

Chapter Nine

MARGIE WENT TO THE KITCHEN to dish up some hot dish for Barbie and me. And while she was gone, Barbie sat quietly, most likely mulling over everything we—I mean she—had learned about Raleigh Cummings and his death. As for me, I was thinking about food. Yeah, I did that a lot. Some might say too much. And I was making a concerted effort to change. At present, for example, I had a second portion of my brain fretting about the possibility of running into Buddy Johnson, while a third was stewing over what Randy must have said about me to Tweedledum and Tweedledumber.

Oh, yeah, I was also upset about this latest murder. I enjoyed this area and, for the most part, the people in it, so I didn't want bad things to happen here. And because I'd always been a fair-minded person, I didn't want anyone—including Buddy Johnson—prosecuted for a crime unless actually guilty. But from what I'd gathered, Sheriff Halverson wasn't like minded on that particular subject. He wanted to solve this case quickly, and he'd prefer to do it on the back of Buddy Johnson. Naturally that bugged me.

When it came right down to it, though, unraveling this murder wasn't my cause. I was a mere guest in town. Tomorrow forenoon I'd get my new recipes. Then I'd meet up with Deputy Randy Ryden. And if he could adequately explain away the attitude of his fellow deputies, we'd go on to have a great weekend at his place, despite the weather or Kennedy's current crime wave. At least that's what I'd hoped.

"Hey, Emme Malloy!"

The force of the bellow practically blew me off my stool. And while I didn't need to raise my eyes to verify its source, I did just the same.

It was Father Daley, the Irish priest who ministered to the few Catholics who resided in this corner of the state. Like me, he was an oddity here. Then again, he probably would have been an oddity anywhere.

He was a sixty-something clergy who enjoyed beer and wine and was a fierce competitor at bowling, golfing, and curling, not to mention poker and whist. He laughed hard and often and was known to frequent the VFW in Kennedy as well as the Eagles in Hallock. He wasn't particularly tall, but what he lacked in height, he made up in girth and volume. His hair was black, curly, and streaked with gray. He always wore black pants and shirts, his religious collar barely peeking out from under his double chin. As customary, a toothpick was lodged between his jaws. Tonight his normally bright blue eyes were tired, rimmed in red, with dark shadows beneath them.

"Hello, Father." I stood for his embrace. Father Daley was a hugger. A big hugger.

"I heard you were planning to visit us, lass." He stepped back after nuzzling me. "I just wasn't sure you'd make it in light of the weather." He spoke with an Irish brogue that sometimes was more prominent than others. I suspected it changed to suit his needs.

"The threat of a storm couldn't keep me from dropping in on all of you."

Margie placed a plate of food in front of me and another next to Barbie, while the priest squeezed my arms with his big bear paws and asked, "So how are you feeling?"

When I was laid up here, Father Daley had stopped by every day. I'm sure he did it primarily because of his friendship with Margie. Since he spent considerable time with her in the café, I suppose it didn't take too much effort to trudge upstairs to "visit the sick." Still, it was nice of him to break the monotony of my days, even if I was exceedingly uncomfortable around him at first.

I had no idea what an older priest and a young wayward Catholic woman with a bump on her head would discuss. But it didn't end up being a problem. As Margie often said, "We talked up a storm." He also recited poetry and told pitiful jokes. And not once did he question my religious practices, although, in the end, that also caused me guilt. You see, while not a particularly good Catholic, I'm a Catholic nonetheless, and we're born with more than a lifetime worth of guilt, especially about our faith.

"I'm doing fine, Father. Just fine."

He narrowed his eyes while using his tongue to slide his toothpick to the opposite corner of his mouth. "Are you sure, Emerald?"

When I'd first met Father Daley, I feared he—and all priests, for that matter—could see into my soul. It was a notion imparted on the students at my elementary and middle school by Sister Helen, the most frightening person to walk the face of the earth. Even in the lower grades, I knew better than to put any faith in what she said. Yet I found myself steering clear of clergy whenever possible. And when not possible, I did my best to avoid eye contact. The practice flourished in high school. And now, while I was doing my utmost to put a halt to the silly habit, it was tough going, mostly because Father Daley was extraordinarily perceptive. Despite an inability to see into my soul, he seemed to have little trouble otherwise reading me, as he was doing at that very moment.

"Well, I suppose I'm still struggling." I forced myself to meet his gaze. "But I'm certainly doing better than I was."

"Aye," he replied, "and now that you're among friends, you'll grow even stronger. See, Emerald, the support of others is important to overall well-being." He winked at Margie. "As is laughter from a good joke." He eyed Barbie. "And believe it or not, I happen to have one!"

Both Margie and Barbie dropped their heads and groaned, but the priest grinned, exposing a set of square white teeth that resembled so many piano keys.

Now trust me, Father Daley wasn't the only person in the area who told jokes. Ole and Lena jokes, recited in memory of two of the town's most beloved residents, were as common as "snow in January," as Margie said. And given the number I'd heard during my last visit, I could attest to that.

"Emme," the priest said, his weary eyes conjuring up a tiny sparkle, "don't pay any attention to those two. Just sit and enjoy."

He steered me back onto my stool while remaining standing at my side. "I got this one from Jodi Johnson. She and her husband farm just west of Hallock. True, they're Protestants. But they're nice folks just the same." He chuckled at that.

And Margie repeatedly cleared her throat.

"Okay, okay," he said, dismissing her impatience with a wave of his hands before hitching up his pants. "One day Ole was driving along, when he got hit by a truck. So he sued. And while in court, the truck driver's lawyer asked him, 'So, Ole, did you report to the police officer at the scene that you were just fine?' And Ole replied, 'Well now, I'll tell ya what happened. See—'

"The lawyer interrupted. 'Your honor, I'm trying to establish that Ole's a fraud. First he said he was uninjured, but now he's suing. So please instruct him to answer my question!'

"The judge, obviously intrigued by Ole, said instead, 'I'd like to hear more.' And Ole replied, 'Tanks, your honor. Well, I'd just gotten my favorite cow, Bessie, into my truck and was drivin' down da road, when dat udder truck came thunderin' through da stop sign and hit me. I was thrown into one ditch, while Bessie was thrown into da udder. I was hurt bad. But worse den dat, I could hear old Bessie moanin' in pain. And when da officer showed up, he went on over to Bessie, saw her sufferin', took out his gun, and shot her right between da eyes. Den he crossed da road, his gun still in his hand, and said to me, 'Now, fella, how are ya feelin'? So I ask ya, what would ya of said?'"

Margie and Barbie moaned, while Father Daley snickered as he scratched his belly.

I did the same—the snickering, not the scratching. "Hey, Father, what are you doing here on such a terrible night?" I asked the question after concluding I didn't dare encourage another joke, even though I got a kick out of them. "I assumed you'd be tucked away at home in Hallock."

Snatching his toothpick between his stubby fingers, he picked his teeth. "I had to come to the beet dinner."

Margie echoed, "Had to?"

"Yes," the priest replied emphatically. "I wasn't about to let bad weather keep me from getting a free meal out of you and your nephews. I deserved this banquet. I worked hard."

"What?" I repeated the remark to myself before I spoke out loud. "You worked in the beet fields?"

"Of course. I may be old—"

Margie cut him off. "Eh, there's no maybe about it. You're so old your Social Security number is 'one.'"

The priest bit his lip, visibly working to stifle a grin. Just as I'd remembered, Father Daley and Margie thrived on kidding each other.

"Yes, Emerald," the priest said, playfully turning his back on his friend, "I operated a beet cart on the day shift. I've done it for years. And the good Lord willing, I'll do it for many more. Working the earth is good for the soul." He expelled a lung-clearing breath. "However, at my age, doing both farming and preaching on a daily basis is tough on the body. Thankfully beet harvest only lasts a few weeks. Although because of the rain and the cold, it dragged on much longer this year."

Barbie, who'd been eating, let her fork clamor against her plate. "Father, since you were on the day shift, I suppose you didn't get to know Raleigh Cummings, the guy who was murdered, did you?"

While a question, she asked it as if she already knew the answer, so the priest surprised her with his reply. "I met him once. This past Tuesday, as a matter of fact. Right after his shift ended. And I suppose you could say we talked." He settled on the stool next to me.

"How did that come about?" Margie wanted to know.

Indecision flickered in the priest's eyes. "I don't know if I should say . . ." He wrung his thick hands as he sputtered, "But . . . umm . . . since he's deceased . . . And . . . umm . . . considering I've already told the sheriff . . . Still . . ."

"Hey, Padre," Margie squawked, "let me know when you're done arguin' with yourself." She stepped into the kitchen, only to return about five minutes later with four plates of Lemon Meringue Pie. She placed one in front of each of us, keeping the last for herself.

I was awestruck by what looked to be confectionary perfection. Margie had made a variety of pies for the beet banquet. When she told me this particular Lemon Meringue Pie was the best she'd ever tasted, I knew I had to try it. "The recipe's from Irene Stellon, over there in Drayton," she had said. "It's been a family favorite of theirs for generations."

"So what did you mean you 'could say' you talked to Raleigh Cummings?" It was a good question on Barbie's part, but I wished she'd waited with it. I didn't want anything affecting my pie experience. I was hoping to engage all my senses.

"Well," the priest replied, "he was so angry I couldn't really get a word in edgewise. He just kept on ranting."

"Ranting? About what?"

Father Daley picked up his fork. "Margie's niece, Little Val."

Chapter Ten

THE PRIEST FORKED A SIZEABLE chunk of Lemon Meringue Pie into his mouth. "Buddy asked me to speak with Raleigh about his . . . umm . . . inappropriate use of the field radio." He licked his lips. "Margie, this is delicious. Definitely one of your best." He helped himself to another big bite. "He thought a warning from me might carry some extra weight." He glanced down at his paunch, then up at Margie and winked.

I turned back to my own slice of heaven. And after finishing it off in record time—thank you very much—I ate more of my dinner, alternating mouthfuls of hot dish and Jell-O.

Normally I avoided Jell-O salads and desserts. But I was hungry. And this Jell-O salad was good, even if it consisted of little more than Jell-O and Cool Whip. It was called Lime Jell-O Salad.

Earlier, Margie had handed me the recipe card, noting that the dish was perfect for the paper's next spread on "church cuisine." And now, while perusing the short list of ingredients, penned in her barely legible handwriting, I eagerly took another bite of the final product, only to stop short of swallowing.

The priest was staring at me. I felt his eyes boring into the side of my head. The sensation left me with no choice but to rest my fork on my napkin and meet him eye to eye.

"See," he said, once he had my full attention, "each machine used during harvest has a radio so everyone on that particular farm can communicate. You know, the guys driving the trucks can talk to the person manning the lifter back in the field and so on. But whatever is said by one is heard by all. And there's the rub."

"What's that got to do with Raleigh being mad to Little Val?" Barbie pushed aside her empty dinner and dessert plates.

"Well, even though the radios are mainly for work, folks also use them to shoot the breeze. And usually that's not a problem. But this past Tuesday morning Raleigh Cummings used it to tell a joke that was totally inappropriate. And he did it while Vivian was operating the rota-beater, and Little Val was on the lifter."

"Huh?" I'm sure my eyes nearly popped out of my head. "Did you say Vivian?" That was almost impossible for me to fathom. I'd met Vivian. She was Margie's younger sister and the mother of Little Val. She talked nonsense—literally. She routinely mixed metaphors and jumbled her words. Half the time no one had a clue what she was saying. On top of that, she was utterly full of herself. I couldn't imagine her consenting to work anywhere, much less in the beet fields.

"Oh, she didn't do all that much," Margie was quick to point out. "She only helped those last few nights 'cause Vern got the flu." Margie seldom gave Vivian credit for anything, in spite of being quick to come to her defense if anyone else criticized her. "She wanted to keep on his good side." She said for my benefit, "She'd finally convinced him to drive down to Arizona early this year, and she didn't want him havin' any second thoughts. They're scheduled to leave right after Thanksgivin'. Other years, they've waited 'til after the first of the year. But Vivian says that's too late. She gets too cold."

Margie cocked her head. "Yah, they're snowbirds. Every winter they stay in one of those RV camps near Phoenix." She shuddered. "I don't care how nice the weather is down there, I'd go crazy with so many people crowded into such a small area."

She switched back to the subject of farm work without so much as a breath. "Anyways, while Vivian doesn't really do diddly squat on the farm, Little Val has pretty much run the place—the whole kit and caboodle—just as good as any man, ever since her dad lost his arm in that farm accident a few years back. Oh, for sure, he offers her 'a hand' every now and again."

She chuckled at her "one arm" joke. They were her favorite jokes to tell. And oddly enough, Vern didn't seem to mind being the butt of them. To the contrary. He actually was flattered when she renamed her signature meal at the cafe "One-Arm Hot Dish," noting on the menu, "It's so easy to make even Vern can do it!"

"Oh, yah," Margie added, "Wally—that's Little Val's husband—tries hard too. But even though he's got all four limbs, he's not much of a farmer. Not that I'm criticizin', mind ya. I'm just sayin'." She wrapped a stray strand of hair behind her ear. "And make no mistake about it, he does a good job drivin' beet truck every year, and he works darn hard at that job of his in Hallock. He sells crop insurance, don't ya know. And he makes decent money and gets family health benefits to boot. So, by golly, things could be a whole lot worse there."

Margie kept on talking while she poured Father Daley a cup of coffee. "Durin' harvest, though, we all hafta pitch in to make sure everythin' gets done." She handed it to him. "That means Buford and Buddy work with Little Val on her farm. Then visa versa. Like I said, even Wally helps out. And if absolutely necessary, Vivian too." She flapped her hand in the air, motioning to the space around her. "Since I can't leave this place, I prepare all the lunches and such."

I set my fork on my plate and rested my forearms on the counter. "Isn't Little Val pregnant?" During my last visit, I'd seen her perform in a band alongside her husband, Barbie's husband, and Buford and Buddy's sister.

"Ya betcha, she is," Margie answered. "She's due in less than three weeks. That's why Vern and Vivian aren't goin' south till the end of next month. They wanna be here for the birth. The first of the next generation." She smiled wistfully for a moment.

"Since Little Val's been feelin' fine, she just keeps on workin'," she then went on to say. "I guess that's not quite true. She feels good, but she's had a devil of a time sleepin'. That darn baby has its days and nights all mixed up." The twinkle in her eyes belied her harsh tone. "That's why she opted for the second shift durin' beet harvest this year."

Father Daley shook his head at Margie, a look of exasperation lined with humor on his face. “Well, as I was saying about an hour ago—before old windbag here got going—Little Val was the first to get on the radio and give Raleigh a piece of her mind about his so-called joke. But when she finished, most of the crew followed suit. As you might expect, Raleigh got really angry and started going on about how field work wasn't meant for women. Again, right over the radio. And I guess he made some terrible cracks about Little Val in the process. Though pretty much everyone on the crew came to her defense. Which only made the guy more furious.” The priest rocked his head in disappointment.

“I wasn't aware of that.” Margie's features were pinched. “But it doesn't surprise me.” Although it clearly annoyed her that no one had bothered to inform her about the fuss in the field. Margie, you see, prided herself on being “in the know,” especially about family. “Little Val has always spoken her mind,” she then said in a manner that suggested the slight didn't upset her, even if her pursed lips told a different story. “And now that's she pregnant, she's even more blunt, if that's possible. Oh, yah, it's as if she's gotta set the whole world straight before her baby's born into it.” She shook her head. “I pity the soul who doesn't fall in line.”

Father Daley finished his coffee. “As it happens, Little Val and Vivian weren't the only women on that crew either. One of the twins' best truck drivers is a devoutly Christian woman from over by Lancaster. She's been hauling for them for years. She was there too.”

Margie's face relaxed, her aggravation easing at the mere mention of that other woman. “She's as nice as can be. And, uff-da, what a worker!” She shook her finger at me, the movement in sync with her words. “She just had a baby two months ago, but that didn't stop her from harvestin'. No, sir-ree. She simply took that little guy right along in the truck with her.” She nodded, as if to assure me she wasn't telling a tall tale. “He slept in his car seat next to her. And since she did most of the diaper changin' and nursin' when she was waitin' to get loaded and unloaded, it caused no problems whatsoever.”

"Yep," the priest said, "in the words of the great poet Bob Dylan, 'Times, they are a changin'."

"Yah, for sure, Father," Margie murmured. "And it's about time."

The priest offered his friend an agreeable nod. "When Buddy heard what had happened between Raleigh and Val, along with the rest of his crew, he called me. He wanted me to talk to Raleigh and, if possible, settle him down. With only a couple days to go in the field, he and Buford didn't need anyone causing trouble. And since he and Raleigh didn't get along, he figured it wouldn't do any good for him—or Buford, for that matter—to say anything to the man."

He pulled a napkin from the dispenser and wiped his thick hands. "When I first met Raleigh, I assumed he was simply on edge, like a lot of people get by the end of harvest from too much work and too little sleep. But the more we talked, the more he started going on about how a field radio was no place to be exchanging recipes or discussing the trials of breastfeeding and menopause."

Margie interjected, "Barbie, that's why you'll never be asked to work in the field. All you ever do is whine about menopause."

Barbie set her shoulders. "I can't help it. Between the bloating and the hot flashes, menopause has just about done me in." She pulled the front of her jersey away from her neck and blew down her chest. "The truth is I'm so hot right now I could strip down—"

"Enough!" Margie barked with laughter.

The priest zeroed in on me, ignoring both Margie and Barbie. And who could blame him? "I told Raleigh I'd ask the twins to get the women on the crew to refrain from that kind of chatter. But that wasn't enough." He plucked his toothpick from his mouth and tapped it against his plate. "He was livid with Little Val. And I couldn't do anything to appease him."

"I suppose Wally gave him an earful too." Margie circled toward me. "He's always so protective of Val."

The priest arched his brows. "Oddly enough, from what I understand, Wally didn't say a word. Nothing at all. Not to Little Val or to Raleigh Cummings."

"Really?" Margie seemed shocked.

"That's what I was told. Although when I talked to Raleigh, he had no trouble coming up with a few choice words about Wally. But none of it made much sense to me." The priest paused. "I believe he'd been drinking. I thought I smelled alcohol on his breath."

Barbie pulled a napkin from the dispenser and wiped her mouth. "Tell me again, Father, when did you talk to him?"

"Around noon on Tuesday. He was coming off his shift, and I was about to start mine."

Less than a second passed between the priest's answer and Barbie's next question. "Do you know if he and Little Val—or he and Wally—exchanged words later?"

The priest chewed on the question as well as his toothpick. "I don't know. Until tonight in there"—he pointed toward the middle room—"I hadn't seen either Wally or Little Val for quite a while." He held his hand up. "I take that back. I saw Wally in Hallock Wednesday afternoon." He thought about that for a moment. "Yeah, that would have been yesterday. I was waiting my turn at the car wash. I was behind Hunter Carlson. He was washing that pickup of his—inside and out—and taking forever. But, no, I didn't get a chance to talk to Wally. He was in his old Jeep. He just drove by. He appeared to be in a hurry."

"Was he alone?" Barbie wanted to know.

"Yep."

"Hmm."

The priest twirled his stool around to face Barbie and me. "When it comes right down to it, I don't think any of this matters."

Hard lines of worry marked Margie's face. "What makes you say that?"

"Well," the priest replied, checking out the hallway before lowering his voice, "the sheriff came into the middle room a while ago to question Buddy."

Margie groaned. "If that don't take the cake." She pounded the counter with her fist. "He always assumes the worst of that boy.

I swear that ever since Harold Halvorson became sheriff, most of the time he hasn't known whether to wind his butt or scratch his watch."

And with those words hanging in the air, I attempted to finish my dinner.

Chapter Eleven

I WALKED BARBIE AND FATHER DALEY to their cars. The sky was dark. Snow was coming down hard. And because of the blustering wind, visibility was poor. Both the priest and the newspaper lady were confident they'd make it back to Hallock without any trouble. Even so, they promised to proceed in a caravan. I'm sure they only wanted to placate me, but I didn't care. Driving didn't seem like a good idea, particularly for Barbie, who, storm or not, was a menopausal maniac behind the wheel.

As for me, even though I hadn't planned on traveling anywhere, my car still posed a problem. My overnight bag was in the back seat, and the sleet that had fallen earlier had formed a sheet of ice over the entire vehicle, freezing the doors shut.

With only the light slanting from a couple of street lamps, I chiseled along the door handle with a pen I'd found at the bottom of my purse. After that I scraped ice with one of my credit cards. I warmed one hand in my jacket pocket, then the other. I hadn't thought to bring gloves. It was only October, for God sake.

True, I could have asked for help from someone in the cafe. But I didn't want to chance a run-in with Buddy Johnson. Not a particularly friendly thought considering, at the moment, he was being grilled by the sheriff. But there it was. And, as penance, I was forced to struggle with my car door all by myself.

Finally, after swearing under my breath and jerking the handle repeatedly, the door cracked open. With hands so cold they burned, I snatched my bag and rushed across the highway, a gust of wind nearly knocking me to my knees. Recovering with the grace of a drunk, I stumbled to the sidewalk, pushed through the door, and retreated to my rented room upstairs.

It was a small and drafty space but just about perfect as far as I was concerned. With its white iron bed, antique dresser, and drop-leaf table, it reminded me of my own room growing up. This room, however, had an adjoining bath.

Before turning in for the night, I showered, mostly to warm my cold limbs. I also took a shot at combing my hair. Being it was incredibly curly—think old-time telephone cord—combing it was always a lesson in patience and, quite often, futility. Especially after subjecting it to a hard-driving wind, like the one blowing outside. I gave up shortly, choosing instead to slip into my flannel nightie and wiggle beneath the blankets on the bed. A draft was sneaking through the cracks along the windowsill, so I nuzzled deeper and pulled my quilt higher before switching off the bedside lamp.

Lying there in the dark I heard the faint murmur of voices downstairs. There were only a few of them now, the lone female voice undoubtedly being Margie's, and the male voices, very similar to one another in timbre, surely belonging to the twins.

As they spoke, I tossed and turned, knowing full well I should have stayed in the café and showed some courage by facing Buddy. After all, did I truly believe I could spend three days in a town the size of a bus shelter and not see him?

Last time I was here I'd chalked up my jumpiness around him to the fact that he oozed testosterone and recklessness. And, admittedly, his brooding dark eyes and bad-boy smile still sent me reeling. But deep down I knew the primary reason for my current angst when near him was my failure to apologize for my part in the demise of his family. That lapse had left me feeling terribly guilty because I knew what it was like to lose family due to others. I also knew the anguish of having those responsible fail to express regret for their actions.

I threw my pillow aside and buried my face in the mattress. Apologizing was hard work though. It was much easier, even if undeniably childish, to avoid Buddy, claiming I was protecting myself from a gorgeous scoundrel, who, if allowed to get too close, would do me wrong. Which, on one hand, was true. But only on one hand. One itty, bitty hand.

I snatched my pillow and slapped it over my head, unsuccessfully hiding from the guilt that assailed me. Flipping on my back, I groaned. I had to apologize. I didn't want to. But I had no choice.

Emme, isn't it strange how in the dark of night truth and right can shine so brightly you can't ignore them?

"Yeah," I mumbled to the irritating voice in my head, "I might start sleeping with the lights on."

❧ ☙

I woke to an overture of clanging dishes and muffled voices accompanied by the aroma of coffee. The coffee alone should have excited me—made me glad I was alive—but it didn't.

I leaned up on my elbow and checked the clock on the bedside table—7:30 a.m.—in glowing red. I moaned and fell back against my pillow. Who was I fooling? I wouldn't go to sleep again. I hadn't done much of it during the night. And daylight certainly wasn't likely to change that.

I threw the covers back and got up, my toes cold against the hardwood floor. I tapped-danced to the window and gazed outside. The sky was dusky and the wind, spooky sounding. With high-pitched screeches, it blew the snow horizontally into banks that buffeted the buildings and vehicles and hid the highway in low drifts that reminded me of sand dunes—terribly misplaced sand dunes.

I flipped on the lamp and got dressed, starting with my socks. Next came my jeans and a navy cable-knit sweater over a red turtleneck. I finished with my trusty red tennies. I don't adhere to the fashion rule that redheads shouldn't wear red. I love red. It makes me happy. And that particular morning, I needed happy. My fitful sleep had left me unsettled, much like the weather.

I dug out my makeup and applied just enough to feel stronger. More put together. A swipe of mascara on my lashes and some blush along my freckled cheekbones. Then another attempt at taming my curls. But even when feeling strong, I'm no match for my hair, and I soon called it quits.

I straightened my bed covers, brushed my teeth, and checked my phone. No calls. From anyone. Not even Randy. I did, however, have another text from Boo-Boo. I deleted it without so much as a glance. Nonetheless, worry tripped along my spine. I should have been able to dissuade him by now. What was wrong with me? Why couldn't I get him to leave me alone? I'd have to try harder. And I would. As soon as I returned to Minneapolis.

Chasing Boo-Boo from my thoughts, I switched off the lamp and headed downstairs, the stairs creaking, old and achy, beneath me. While still upset with Randy for what he must have said about me to Tweedledum and Tweedledumber, I found myself eager to see him and, if completely honest, a little disappointed he hadn't reached out to me.

With a toss of my head, I shook off my discontent and hopefully the insecurities that incited it. I was being silly. There was no reason to hear from him. Our plans were made. He'd be back in the afternoon, and I'd see him then. As Margie routinely said about almost everything, "That should be good enough."

As I entered the café, I discovered the lights on, yet the place itself empty. Margie's voice echoed from the middle room, but I opted to postpone joining her until after an infusion of coffee. Yes, Margie's coffee was notoriously weak, but it was sixty miles to the nearest Starbucks. And on this particular morning, the trip would require a dog sled, which I'd left at home, next to my winter jacket, gloves, and head-bolt heater.

In the kitchen, I claimed a standard restaurant-style coffee cup from the shelf above the sink before twirling around and nearly smacking into Buddy Johnson. He stood directly in front of me, only inches away. I yelped and dropped the cup.

"Mornin'," he said. His hair was tousled. His eyes were sleepy. And his naturally sun-kissed cheeks were covered in a whisker shadow. I had to remind myself to breath—but not to pant. The man was definitely too handsome for anyone's good.

He stooped to pick up my cup and its broken handle, tossing both into a nearby trash can. Next, he grabbed two mugs from the shelf. "Sorry if I scared you." With a heavy-lidded gaze, he offered me one of the mugs.

"Umm . . . no, you . . . I mean yes, you . . ." I seized the mug and clutched it to my chest. "Umm . . . no, that's not right. I mean no, you didn't scare me. And . . . umm . . . yes, thanks for the cup."

Hey, Emme, that was almost as smooth as when you learned to drive a stick shift.

I think I actually heard the voices in my head high-five one another over that little joke.

"Shut up," I mumbled.

"Excuse me?" It was Buddy. Thankfully he had moved to the coffee station out front, in the dining section of the cafe. "Did you say something?" His voice was slightly raised so I could hear him.

"Umm . . . no."

He stepped back into the kitchen, the coffee pot extended. "Want to finish this off?"

"Yeah . . . umm . . . thanks."

He poured the last of the coffee into my mug and set the pot on the metal prep table. He grabbed a stool and motioned me to follow suit. "I was surprised to see you here last night," he said. "I didn't know you were coming up."

"Well . . . umm . . ." I sat down. "Well . . . umm . . . we're doing another funeral-food spread, so . . . umm . . . I needed more of Margie's recipes."

He chuckled. "That could be interesting considering this new kick she's on. 'Expanding her horizons' and all."

"Uh-huh." This wasn't going well. I had to apologize. And I had to do it soon. It was the only way to restore my self-respect and, with it, my ability to think and speak. Sure, it would have been easier to phone it in, but I hadn't gotten around to doing that. So now I had no choice but to look across the table and tell Buddy Johnson—face to face—how sorry I was for everything that had happened to his family.

That's right, Emme. Apologize. If you don't, you'll continue to be pestered by guilt. And when that happens, you not only turn into an idiot, you search for comfort at the bottom of ice cream cartons and among the crumbs in brownie pans. And you really don't want to do that, do you?

I wasn't about to admit it, but the voices in my head were right. At that very moment I was practically consumed by cravings for Black Bottom Cupcakes. I'd spotted some on the kitchen counter the night before. Margie said the recipe was from Nancy Peterson Lundberg. She also said, "They're gall-darn tasty." I gave the room a quick once-over but didn't see any. *Damn! I mean darn!*

With a resigned sigh, I folded my hands and rested them on the steel table in front of me. "Buddy?" I attempted to inhale deeply, but my chest was too tight for anything more than a shallow breath. "I'm sorry about your family." I pushed the statement out fast, on a single exhale, afraid I'd chicken out if I paused at all. "I didn't mean for things to turn out the way they did."

"It wasn't your fault." Buddy shifted uncomfortably. Clearly, he didn't want to talk about the incident either. But now that I'd committed myself to this particular act of contrition, I couldn't turn back, even if that's what he would have preferred.

"Well . . . umm . . . in truth," I stuttered, "I was only supposed to gather hot dish, Jell-O, and bar recipes. Nothing more. I wasn't . . . umm . . . assigned to dig into an old murder case. Even so, that's what I did." I swallowed over the lump in my throat. "See, I wanted to be . . . umm . . . a hero. I wanted to become an investigative reporter. I really didn't give much thought to how my ambitions might hurt other people."

In spite of what folks may claim, unburdening yourself doesn't feel all that great. At least not initially. And Buddy was no help. He didn't say a word. He merely raised his head and stared at me, his intense dark eyes giving nothing away. And the silence stretched on between us.

I hate silence. It leads to obsessive thinking. Usually about painful experiences: My parents' death, my uninspiring job, my past relationship with Boo-Boo, this frightful confession. So I fill silence whenever possible.

"See, Buddy, I tried to . . . umm . . . crack the case to advance my career. But I'm not particularly good at investigative work. The truth is I only stumble along. Solving that murder was a fluke."

"Emerald, I understand. Let's just leave it at that, okay?" Nope, he wasn't any more thrilled about rehashing that other murder case than Margie had been.

Maybe Barbie was right. When I'd asked her to explain Margie's reluctance to "talk things out," she said that Scandinavians usually keep their problems and disappointments to themselves. Which was probably true. But I was Irish. Stubborn. A talker. And I was going to finish what I'd started.

"Well . . . umm . . . I just wanted to apologize, Buddy, and say that I'd do anything to make it up to you." I glanced all around the room but not at him. "Truly I would."

I sucked in a deep breath and waited. But believe it or not, the world didn't end. I'd done a very hard thing. I had taken responsibility for my actions. I'd even apologized for them. Still, the earth kept spinning. So I summoned all the courage I had left in me and forced my eyes to meet his. And when that didn't tilt the planet right off its axis, I indulged in a big gulp of coffee, feeling awfully smug.

At the same time, Buddy flashed me one of his half smiles, where just the right corner of his mouth ticked upward. Then, with a wink, that same smile morphed into what could only be described as a leer. "Really?" he said. "You'd do anything?"

I gagged on my coffee. There was enough suggestive inflection in his voice to choke a horse. "What did you say?" I knew full well what he'd said, but I had to ask again because I didn't want to believe my ears. Buddy Johnson had propositioned me! Just when

I was ready to cut him some slack, he proved what a creep he actually was.

I was angry and embarrassed. And I was pretty sure I wanted to go home. This trip had been doomed from the start. First, Randy had called to say he wouldn't get back until Friday afternoon, so I'd have to stay with Margie Thursday night. Then, I was late leaving Minneapolis because one of my tires sprang a leak. On top of that, there was this new murder investigation, which I desperately wanted to avoid. And now, Buddy turned out to be the sleaze Randy had warned me about. Could things possibly get any worse?

Ya betcha, Emma. Just wait and see.

Chapter Twelve

BUDDY LAUGHED AS HE patted my back. "I was kidding, Emerald. Just kidding."

With my coughing winding down, I wiped the corners of my mouth with my fingertips. I wasn't sure if I believed him.

"In all seriousness," he continued, not appearing especially serious, "I want something from you. But it's not what you think." He stopped for a two count. "I'm not interested in you in that way."

I dropped my eyes. I couldn't look at him. *First he comes on to me, only to deny it. Then he assures me he doesn't find me the least bit desirable. What a jerk!*

"Emerald," he said, "I need your help."

Unless it involves me shoving my foot so far up your ass I'm able to tie my shoes through your nostrils, you shouldn't count on it.

"See," he continued, oblivious to the snide commentary running through my mind, "I'm having a problem with the sheriff."

"What?" Although I heard him, I was still too humiliated and confused to make sense of his words.

"He's decided that I killed Raleigh Cummings." He combed his fingers through his hair. "Margie told me you know the story. She said you and Barbie were out at the piler, talking to Guy and Jarod while they stood guard, waiting for the body to be picked up."

My breath hitched, prompting another coughing episode.

Once again Buddy patted me on my back.

"The body . . . was still . . . down there?" With all my hacking, my words ended up staggered in phrases that sounded like really bad rap.

Buddy seemed perplexed. "Well, yeah."

Oh, God! I was standing on top of a dead guy! Another shiver ran along my backbone, while several others fanned out to my legs and arms.

"Anyhow," he said while scratching the whisker stubble that covered his chin, "despite what you claim, I know you're good at solving mysteries. So how 'bout it?"

"Huh?" I couldn't process his words.

"Emme, I don't want to go to jail, particularly for something I didn't do."

I massaged my temples and concentrated on slow, steady breathing. Eventually his words resonated, causing me to lurch forward. "Whoa!" My hands instantly made the international sign for "no way." And when I was certain I'd gotten my point across, I added out loud, "I'm not a detective. You need to hire a professional."

He canted his head toward the front window. "It's storming. I wouldn't be able to get anyone out here for at least a couple days. By then the sheriff will have me bound and gagged. Once I'm in jail, I won't be able to do much." His eyes pleaded with me. "I need to figure things out now. And to do that, I need your help."

"But I can't." I had to stay strong. I couldn't get tangled up in another murder investigation. "I don't know how—"

"Emerald." He leaned across the table, a curly lock of his hair falling across his forehead. "What happened to wanting to do whatever you could to make things up to me?"

"I wouldn't be aiding your cause. You need . . ." An idea limped forward from the back of my brain. "You need . . . the BCA guys. Yeah, they can help you."

Buddy set his right elbow on the table and rested his chin against his fist. "Maybe, when they get here. But who knows when that'll be. The interstate's closed at Alexandria. There's no air travel between here and St. Cloud. And unless we do something soon, the sheriff will tie the crime to me. Then by the time the BCA guys do show up, it'll take them forever to sort everything out. And all the while, I'll be stuck in jail. And I can't handle that."

I twisted my hair around my finger. “What about Buford?” Even as I said it, I knew it was a dumb idea. Buford knew farming, but otherwise he wasn’t a deep thinker. Barbie had once told me he could only identify major cities by their professional hockey teams.

“Emerald, I don’t want my freedom dependent on Buford.”

I didn’t want his freedom dependent on me either. I couldn’t be responsible for him. I could barely manage my own life.

“I’m not asking you to strike out on your own.” He spoke as if he understood my concern. “I’m just asking you to work with me. Let me bounce ideas off you.”

“But it’s already Friday. And I’m scheduled to go home on Sunday.” I gathered some much-needed gumption to add, “And . . . umm . . . I have plans beginning this afternoon.”

A bemused expression overtook his face. “There’s no way lover boy’s going to make it back today, if that’s what you’re thinking. This storm’s out of the northwest. He’s stuck in Williston.”

My heart sank so low that if not for my stomach it would have ended up in my lap. Sure, Randy and I needed to work through the whole Tweedledum-Tweedledumber thing. But I was pretty sure we could. At least that was what I was hoping.

“Wait a minute.” Buddy studied my face, his own features slowly revealing understanding. “He hasn’t called or texted you, has he?”

He may have wanted an answer, but I wasn’t about to volunteer anything. See, I had tried to assure myself that Randy’s failure to call was no big deal. But in truth, his disregard hurt. Apparently, while not as needy as I’d been earlier in my life—or even earlier in the year—I still required reassurances. Then again, a measly phone call wasn’t exactly “reassurance.” It was just common courtesy, right?

I gazed at my reflection in the surface of the metal prep table. My distress was apparent to me, and Buddy must have recognized it too because he switched gears, now speaking in a passive voice—the kind you use with a child or an adult you find pitiful. “Hey, the more I think about it, phone reception out there might be spotty with the storm and all. Hell, it's spotty here when the weather's good." He waited, possibly hoping I'd laugh at his attempt at humor. When I didn't, he rocked back on the rear legs of his stool. "Yeah, he probably called and just couldn't get through."

I bit down on my bottom lip. I was a loser of such monumental proportions that even the grand poobah of the local womanizer's club felt sorry for me. Tears stung my eyes. But I refused to let them fall.

"So?" He settled his stool, stood up, and stretched his arm across the table. He lifted my chin with the tip of his finger. "How about working with me?" He sat back down, his eyes showing so much compassion that it almost made me sick with humiliation. "You'd be helping me out." He waffled, obviously hunting for something more to say. "And it would keep your mind off . . . I mean . . ." The words stalled on his lips. He hadn't intended on mentioning Randy or his apparent decision to forget all about me. As a result, he now found himself at a loss. "Well . . . umm . . ." he sputtered. "Who knows? It might be fun."

I deadpanned, "You're accused of murder, Buddy? What part of that might be fun?"

He smiled that half-smile of his—the nice one—the one that makes his dark eyes shine like polished stones. "Oh, come on. Do this for me." He once more bent across the table, this time invading my personal space. He covered my hands with one of his own. "Please."

While his palm was calloused and his fingers, rough, his touch was soft and soothing. And for someone who had undoubtedly slept in his clothes and hadn't yet cleaned up, he smelled good. I caught the scent of musk along with a hint of something else. Baby powder perhaps?

I pulled my hand free as soon as I realized I had absolutely no desire to do so. "Did you sleep on the pool table last night?" A change of subject was definitely in order.

"What? Where did that come from?"

"Well, you smell like baby powder. You know, like people use when shooting pool. Plus, I'm guessing you didn't go home." I wagged my finger up and down, pointing out his rumpled appearance, which included the same clothes he'd worn the previous day. "And since I slept in one of the bedrooms upstairs, and I assume Margie took the other, you and Buddy were left with the booths or the pool table. And you're too tall to stretch out in a booth, so you must have slept on the pool table. Am I right?"

He regarded me with appraising eyes. "You are good at deduction."

He arched what must have been a sore back. And as his torso stretched and his tee-shirt climbed, I couldn't help but sneak a peek at his abs. "I flipped Buford for it," he said, relaxing his midsection. "I got the pool table. He got stuck on the bar."

"The bar?" I mentally scratched my head, determined to keep my thoughts trained on his words and nothing else. "Isn't that a little narrow for sleeping?"

"Well, you don't want to do a lot of tossing and turning, that's for sure." He settled back on his stool, his half-smile again in place. "On the flip side, you're close to all the bottles if you get thirsty before morning."

I found myself chuckling. It was easy to do around Buddy Johnson. My impression was he didn't take himself too seriously.

"So what do you say?" He tilted his head. "Will you hang out with me for a while? At least until Dudley Do-right shows up?"

I stopped chuckling so I could scowl.

"Sorry, no more snide comments about the esteemed deputy." He flashed me the Boy Scout hand signal. "I promise."

"Yeah, right." A grin betrayed my terse tone. "Like I'm going to believe you were ever a Boy Scout."

He adjusted the cuffs on his flannel shirt. "How dare you doubt me!" He was going for indignant, but it didn't work. "Okay, come on," he added, pretending total exasperation by my misgivings. "Let's go to my place, and I'll show you all my badges." He waggled his eyebrows.

"Does that line really work for you?"

"No, but it made you smile." He dipped his head toward me. "So? What's it going to be?"

His expression was full of expectations, which scared me, leaving my mind to jump around until, for some reason, it landed on Pudding Shots. Margie had made some to serve as an after-dinner treat for the adults at the beet banquet. From what I understood, they were nothing more than dollops of pudding in various flavors, all infused with alcohol. She said there were extra servings in the fridge. And I wondered, as I checked the time, if nine o'clock in the morning was too early to taste test a few.

"Emerald? Are you going to help me out or not?"

I sighed. I couldn't get drunk. I was on the job. Besides, I owed Buddy, given what I had done to his family. So with yet another sigh, I replied, knowing full well I'd more than likely regret my words, "Yeah, I'll help. I don't know what kind of assistance I can provide, but I'll try—at least for the time being."

"That's all I'm asking." He pushed his stool back, the legs scraping the wood floor. "How about some breakfast while we talk things over?"

"Sounds good."

He started for the refrigerator, while the chimes at Maria Lutheran began to play, just like they did every morning. On this day, though, I could have sworn the tune was something of a funeral march.

Oh, Emme, did you just make a horrible mistake?

Part Two

Survey the Buffet Table To See What's Left

Chapter Thirteen

While Buddy was in the kitchen, scrounging up breakfast, I ambled to the front of the café and grabbed a seat in one of the booths. The Community News section of *The Enterprise* was on the table, and I pulled it closer. A notation across the top of the front page encouraged folks to submit information regarding social events, group meetings, and other "happenings."

The first entry in "Social Events" read,

> Sue Kulbeik and friends drove from Elbow Lake, Minnesota, to Oakwood, North Dakota, last Wednesday for taco night at the bar.

It was followed by,

> The Hennen sisters had lunch at Bauer's Flowers, Gifts & Coffee Corner in Warren after visiting the Willow and Ivy Gift Shop and their urologist in Crookston. The lunch was pleasant. As was shopping. The urologist, not so much.

The next was a bit more dramatic:

> Unexpected guests stopped by Lyndon Johnson's rural-Hallock home last Saturday afternoon. Having nothing prepared to go with the coffee he served, Lyndon whipped up Fork and Pan Cake, which takes very little time and, as suggested by its name, requires only a fork and a pan to prepare."

Hmm. The recipe wasn't included, but I made a mental note to ask Margie about it.

I then skimmed the rest of the event entries as well as two ads, one urging folks to visit Drayton Drug for their prescription and gift needs and the second encouraging them to shop at Anderson's Pharmacy in Hallock for the same.

Buddy walked into the room and, from the large tray balanced on his forearm, retrieved plates of what he called Breakfast Pie. After setting them on the table, along with a pot of coffee, a carafe of orange juice, and a plate of buttered toast, he tossed the empty tray onto the table in the next booth and slid in across from me. "Tell me what you've got so far."

"Didn't Margie already do that?"

He held up his hand, signaling he'd respond as soon as he'd finished a mouthful of eggs. "I'd like to hear it from you," he said on the swallow.

"Well . . ." It was my turn to do the hand thing. I'd never been especially concerned about my manners, but I was making an effort to change my ways. "Well," I repeated after washing down my food with a sip of coffee, "I don't have a lot."

My thoughts stumbled over the few tidbits I'd gathered, and I relayed them to him. I explained how I'd learned about Raleigh's early-morning "joke" from Father Daley. And I reported Margie's account of Dinky Donaldson's afternoon encounter with Raleigh and the city clerk. "Plus, there's the story the deputies shared with us about you and Raleigh having it out at the Caribou in Hallock." I pointed at his black eye. "So what's your side of that?"

An engine whined outside, distracting both of us. The sound grew louder and louder before it stopped altogether.

"First," Buddy answered after the quiet had been restored, "it's not much of a black eye." He held up one finger, followed by another. "And, second, I saw Raleigh in the Caribou around six on Tuesday night, when I stopped in for supper. He was well on his way to getting hammered. When he spotted me, he started going on about how Buford and I had it so easy. I reminded him he didn't even know us.

But he said he knew our kind, and that was enough." He rubbed his hands down his face, apparently already tired of dealing with the death of Raleigh Cummings. "I wasn't in the mood to listen to that shit, so I told him that since he couldn't work drunk, he may as well consider himself done. We only had a day or so left anyhow."

He picked up his fork and poked at his Breakfast Pie. It was a mixture of eggs, sausage, potatoes, cheese, and seasoning. "Then because I'd finished my meal, I paid my bill and left. But like some damn shadow, Raleigh followed me outside, yakking about how he wasn't drunk and I couldn't fire him." He raised his eyes to mine, his expression subdued. "I tried to ignore him. But when I opened the door to my truck, he took a swing at me. He missed, but I reacted." He shrugged. "What can I say? I shoved him. He fell against another truck and slid to the ground." He loaded up his fork. "I didn't stick around to help him up."

I had lots of questions, but in the end, curiosity dictated what I asked. "So where'd you get the shiner?"

He hesitated, his fork midway to his mouth. "I told you. It's nothing."

Before I could offer a rebuttal, the café door creaked open to an odd-looking pair. They clomped inside, leading the way for a lot of cold air. Despite wearing a turtleneck and a sweater, I had to rub my arms to stave off the chills.

The taller of the two wore a black nylon snowmobile suit, black boots and gloves, and a matching helmet, complete with a dark face shield. The shorter one also wore clunky boots, thick gloves, and a helmet with a face shield. But the other clothes were different. Very different. They consisted of plaid bib overalls that looked to be wool, a knit turtleneck, and a down jacket that refused to zip more than a few inches, leaving a protruding belly exposed.

The two removed their gloves and helmets, as Buddy and I shifted to get a better look at them. It was Wally and a very pregnant Little Val. I easily recognized him from my previous visit. But she had changed considerably over the past few months.

"It's getting so damn cold around here," Little Val hollered, "we'll soon be growing nothing but snow peas and iceberg lettuce."

"What in the hell are you two doing out in this weather?" Buddy asked by way of hello.

Wally offered a resigned sigh. "She's craving Rhubarb Bars." He hooked his thumb toward his wife, who was clumsily shedding her jacket. "We didn't have the ingredients to make any at home, but she knew Margie had some down here, already done."

Without realizing it, I muttered, "Must be some good bars."

Little Val waddled by. "They are. Margie got the recipe from Heidi Auel, who's great at making up new dishes." She fluffed her curly blonde bob. "And these particular bars are gluten free, so I can eat 'em." She patted her large belly. "At this point, stomach problems wouldn't be good." She lumbered into the kitchen, each step of her heavy boots sounding like the pounding of a hammer. "I'm grabbing a plate of 'em, and if there's any left when I get done, I'll give 'em to you."

I rummaged through my brain until locating the image I had of Little Val from my last visit. She was petite back then, with just a tiny baby bump. Now, in addition to her ginormous belly, she had a plump face, sausage arms, and a butt that crowded the backside of what appeared to be men's pants.

Buddy commented on them after Wally plopped down next to him. "I haven't seen overalls like that since—"

"Don't go there," Wally warned. "She couldn't come close to fitting into her snowmobile suit. Or for that matter, any of her maternity pants. And it's too cold for the dress she wore last night." He tapped his fingers on the table. "She found those overalls in the back of the hall closet. They're her dad's. He must have forgotten 'em." Still more tapping. "She tried 'em on, and they fit after she cuffed 'em up. And since they're wool, they're warm. So now she says she won't wear anything else till the baby's born." He wouldn't stop tapping! "As soon as the storm passes, we're driving over to Young's General Store in Middle River to buy another pair. One for church, according to her."

"If you can't get it at Young's, you don't need it," Buddy replied and slurped his coffee.

Wally slumped against the booth and unzipped his snowmobile suit. Right away it rose as if attempting to swallow his head. "Whatever it takes to get through the next three weeks." He folded his collar over.

Buddy chuckled. "That bad, huh?"

Wally sighed heavily. "I guess I've got no business bitching. The wife's got it a lot worse. But since you asked, yeah, it's been hell." He thought things over for quite some time. "The pregnancy and harvest and . . . umm . . . you know, just everything." He wiped his nose with the back of his hand and extended his long legs in front of him, slouching down a bit farther and dropping his head back.

Wally wasn't a handsome man, especially from my new vantage point, which entailed seeing right up his nose. Much of the hair that had disappeared from the top of his head had found its way into his nostrils as well as his ears and along his eyebrows. And if that wasn't bad enough, his Adam's apple protruded something awful, while his eyes bulged like those of a fish.

"So, Wall-eye," Buddy said, "have you met Emerald Malloy?" I guess I wasn't the only one who saw the fish resemblance. "She's the reporter from the Minneapolis paper. The one who did that piece on Margie. The one who . . ." His voice trailed off. There was no need to finish. Everyone in the tri-county area knew what had happened while I was here last.

Wally sat up, the nylon from his snowmobile suit rustling, and stretched his hand in my direction. "No, I haven't met her, but I've heard a lot about her."

Fearing where this conversation was headed, I tensed. "I can only imagine."

A slight grin cracked the tight line of Wally's mouth. "What can I say? Vivian Olson is my mother-in-law." He let go of my hand. "And while you made mention of her and her cake-decorating business in that newspaper article you did on Margie a few months back, you didn't focus on her. So, of course, she wasn't entirely pleased."

I relaxed. Of all the things he could have said, that wasn't so bad. I seriously doubted Vivian was ever "entirely pleased" about anything.

"So, what are you two up to this morning?" Wally wanted to know.

"Well," Buddy answered, "Emerald's here to get more recipes from Margie for another newspaper article, which should thrill Vivian."

Wally grunted.

"And since she's in town, I've asked her to help me dig into Raleigh Cummings' death."

"What?" Wally's face registered concern. "Why would you do that?"

"Well," Buddy said, "after you and Little Val left the dinner last night, the sheriff stopped by. He made it clear I was his number-one suspect."

Wally shuffled in his seat, his snowmobile suit swishing. "Based on what?"

Buddy picked up his knife and rocked it between the fingers of his right hand, his eyes holding steady on what he was doing. "A beef Cummings and I had on Tuesday night."

"You mean when you fired him?"

"Yeah, if you want to call it that. It was going to be one of his last nights anyhow."

"Well . . ." Wally wavered. "You certainly weren't the only guy who bitched about Raleigh Cummings." He stopped for another second or two. "He was an asshole."

I took that as my cue to wade into the conversation. "I heard he made some nasty remarks to your wife after she called him out on the field radio Tuesday morning."

Wally swallowed hard, his Adam's apple bouncing around like a tennis ball. "Umm . . . Well . . . Yeah . . ." He glanced at Buddy. "You already know all about that."

"Uh-huh." Buddy squinted at me, clearly wondering what I was up to.

I leaned toward Wally. "He really got upset with her, huh?"

Wally appeared thoughtful, as if weighing what he should say. "Yeah . . . umm . . . he was mad at her, but . . . umm . . . I think he was mad at a lot of people. See, she wasn't the only one to get after him."

"Even so, I imagine you really lit into him." I knew better but wanted to see how forthcoming he'd be with me.

"No." He peered at me sideways, with just one eye, like fish do. "I didn't say anything to him."

"Really?" I did my best to act surprised. I'm not sure if I pulled it off. "Why not?"

Buddy kicked me under the table, no doubt commenting on my acting ability. But I wasn't in the mood to listen to critics.

"Val was doing fine on her own," Wally said. "She . . . umm . . . didn't need me buttin' in." He pressed his fingertips together, and he must have found the resulting steeple mesmerizing—perhaps soothing—because he stared at it.

While I continued to fire questions. "Didn't you want to voice your support for her like the other crew members did?" I considered it a legitimate question. But when I peeked at Buddy, I noticed his jaw muscles tighten. Just to be safe I curled my legs up onto my seat, out of striking distance.

"She knows I support her."

"Yeah, I suppose she does." I wasn't really getting anywhere, so I decided to come at him from a different direction. "Besides, you probably talked to the guy later, after work, when you didn't have everyone listening in on the radio, right?"

"I . . . umm . . . didn't see him after work. When we got done, Val and I dropped Vivian off at her house, then went home ourselves."

"And you didn't go out again?"

He looked at me straight on, frustration seasoned with a pinch of anger simmering in his eyes. "No. Not until we went back to work that night."

"How about the next day? Wednesday?" I again peeked at Buddy. He appeared to be squirming on Wally's behalf. "Did you go out then?"

Wally slapped his hands against the table. “What’s going on here, Buddy? Why is she asking me all this stuff?”

Buddy planted his hand on Wally’s forearm. “She’s only trying to help me.”

He jerked his arm away. “How? By pinning Cummings’ murder on me?”

“Of course not.” Buddy glared at me, his jaw muscles getting a good workout.

I guess he wanted me to dial it back. Be more discreet. But that had never been one of my strengths. Still, because I’d probably pushed these guys as far as I dared, I gave it a shot. “Wally, I’m sorry if I came on too strong. I’m only . . . umm . . . attempting to get a handle on how folks reacted to Cummings. So . . . umm . . . I can do what I can for Buddy.”

Wally expelled a deep sigh and shuffled in his seat. He wasn’t happy. But he was going to give me a break. After all, Buddy was family. “No, I didn’t go out on Wednesday either. Val and I got home from the field around one o’clock, ate lunch, showered, and went to bed. That was our routine most days during harvest. Pretty much the same thing day in, day out.”

“What about your job in Hallock?”

He shuffled in his seat. “Every year I take vacation during beet harvest. Lots of people do that.” He glimpsed at Buddy. “That’s what Raleigh did, right?”

Buddy grunted. “He was on paid vacation from his office job in Fargo.”

“But unlike him, I still had to go in once in a while.”

“Yet not this past Tuesday or Wednesday?” I reached for a nonchalance I wasn’t feeling and hoped it didn’t show.

“No, I was too tired.” His countenance remained guarded, indicating I probably wasn’t as good at faking nonchalance as I had hoped. Big surprise. “Plus, Val doesn’t like being left alone anymore. Now that she’s getting close to her due date, she wants me around all the time. I don’t think I’ve left her side since last Friday night.”

“So you didn’t go anywhere?”

He frowned, apparently signaling that once again I was pressing too hard. "Like I said, we slept most of Wednesday. I don't think either of us got up until it was time to go back to work at midnight. Then two hours later we were sent home because the piler got shut down due to the cold. So we went back to bed. And we didn't leave the house again until Val's doctor appointment at noon yesterday. Then, when we got done there, we went home, cleaned up, and came here for the banquet." His frown lines deepened. "Now, that should answer all your questions." He pulled himself from the booth.

"I've gotta get out of this snowmobile suit before I roast to death," he added to Buddy before tromping out of the café and down the hallway, with Buddy behind him.

Chapter Fourteen

WHILE SLOWLY FINISHING MY BREAKFAST, I read through the rest of the local paper. I especially enjoyed the Meeting Notes that focused on Margie:

> The VFW women's auxiliary from Kennedy held its fall meeting last week. At the suggestion of Margie Johnson, owner of the Hot Dish Heaven café and the group's treasurer, the women performed a team-building exercise by driving to Wahpeton, North Dakota, where they shopped and ate at Antoinette's On the River, a gift boutique and luncheonette. While most everyone ordered the chicken salad, Margie tried the Chicken Dumpling Hot Dish, insisting she needed to expand her culinary horizons. With the exception of Margie's sister, Vivian Olson, the women praised the food. And for her part, Margie was over the moon about the hot dish, noting that it was "gall-darn tasty." The business portion of the meeting went off without a hitch. And a pretty good time was had by all.

I had folded the paper and was just about done with my coffee when Buddy returned, a scowl on his face. "What in the hell were you trying to prove with Wally?" He spoke in that hissing voice that people use when they're angry but don't want anyone to hear them except the target of their wrath.

Irritated by both his expression and his tone, I matched his scowl and raised him a pair of defiant eyes, along with a snarl. "I was teasing out information."

"No you weren't. You were torturing the guy." He plopped down on the seat across from me. "Any minute I expected you to start with the waterboarding."

I steeled myself against his criticism. "I warned you, Buddy, I'm not a professional investigator."

"But you've heard of tact, haven't you?" He was getting downright pissy.

"I can quit anytime, you know."

His lips tightened like a piece of taut string. "I don't want you to do that. I just want you to be more diplomatic. He's my cousin's husband, for cryin' out loud. He's one of my best friends. And he certainly didn't have anything to do with Raleigh Cummings' death."

"Then why'd he lie?"

His face twisted into a grimace. "What?"

"He was in Hallock on Wednesday afternoon. But he said he never left his house after he and Little Val got home from the field. Not until they went back to work at midnight."

"How do you know he was in Hallock?"

"Father Daley saw him."

Doubt clouded his eyes. "Maybe the priest was mistaken."

"He seemed sure of himself. And it was only two days ago. Unlikely he'd make a mistake like that."

Buddy poured himself a fresh cup of coffee. "Maybe Walleye got mixed up. He's under a lot of pressure with the baby coming and all."

"Yeah, maybe."

I wasn't convinced. It seemed to me that stressed out or not Wally would remember if he'd spent the afternoon at home with his pregnant wife or in Hallock by himself. But rather than speculating about that, I decided to review what I knew for certain about the murderer. I also decided to do it silently. It'd give me an opportunity to calm down. Which would be a good thing because, at the moment, I still wanted to shove Buddy's Breakfast Pie right up his nose.

I glimpsed at him. He was absently scanning the newspaper, the corners of his mouth turned down, the crease across the bridge of his nose more defined. He appeared as if he needed a break from me as much as I did from him. Hard to fathom.

I sipped my orange juice and mulled over who might have committed the murder. In my view, the killer was strong and, odds are, worked the night shift for a local beet farmer. After all, he—or she—had the ability to lug a dead body around and was aware of the unplanned night-time shutdown at the piler. The killer also knew that the piler had scales serviced via underground pits—perfect for hiding bodies.

By my estimation, there were a couple hundred night-crew beet workers in the area. But as I'd learned in a journalism class on investigative reporting, I only needed to focus on those who had "motive" and "opportunity" to carry out the crime.

Granted, I was just getting started, but my mental list of suspects already included several people. First, Little Val and Wally. Because of that dustup in the field, each had reason to dislike Cummings, though I questioned if it was motive enough for murder. Next, Janice Ferguson. True, she wasn't employed by a beet farmer, but she was overheard arguing with Raleigh Cummings only a day or so before he died. The subject of the argument, however, was garbage—literally garbage. Again probably not much of a motive. And finally, there was the man sitting across from me. His fight with Raleigh was the most contentious. But if he had committed the crime, why ask me for help?

I stared at him, yet he refrained from looking up from the newspaper, even though he was well aware I wanted him to do so. "Buddy," I said, my tone stern, "are you going to explain that black eye or not?"

He meticulously folded the paper and placed it on the seat next to him. "I already told you, it's not important."

That irked me. Call me crazy, but I'd always preferred reaching my own conclusions. "Listen, if this arrangement of ours is going to work, you have to level with me."

"I am leveling with you. My eye has absolutely nothing to do with Raleigh Cummings' death." His manner suggested the topic was closed to further discussion. Another point of contention with me. In fact, it really ticked me off. I hated anyone censoring me.

"Fine!" I flung my napkin at my plate. "Forget the whole thing." Frustration and fury had sharpened my voice and were urging me to toss around a few other "F" words.

Before I went that far, I slid from the booth, and he grabbed my arm. "Hold on. I need your help."

"No you don't. At least not enough to be up front with me." I shook my arm free.

"But you agreed."

I pinned him with a glare. "Not if you're going to be less than honest."

"I didn't lie."

"Omission is the same thing. Or is that concept just too vague for you to comprehend?" See? I could get pissy too.

He halfway rose to once more tug on my sweater sleeve. "All right. All right. Sit down, and I'll tell you."

I vacillated. This was my chance to bow out with a clear conscience. I could assure myself that while I'd offered my assistance, Buddy wasn't keen on my approach or my need for transparency. As a result, I couldn't help him. End of story.

So why didn't I leave? The urge to go was so great it actually made my feet tingle. Still I remained in place. How come?

In a word—curiosity. In another—nosiness. I also could have gone with "prurience" or "inquisitiveness." All pointed to the same thing. My unadulterated shameless need to know everything in general. And in this specific situation, the story behind that shiner.

Feigning disinterest, I edged back into the booth and poured myself another cup of coffee. "Well, okay. I guess if you insist. Go ahead. Shoot."

He murmured something unintelligible.

"I can still take off, you know."

He shook his head. "No, don't do that." He fingered the corner of the newspaper. "It's just that I was surprised how . . . umm . . . aggressive you are."

"You mean pushy?"

"You said it. I didn't."

I warned myself to remain civil. I'd been called worse. And he was right. My inability to be subtle was one of my biggest shortcomings as a reporter. It was one of the primary reasons I'd been assigned to the Food section at the paper and not real news, where I'd actually have to interact with people on a daily basis. Even so, I didn't need him to remind me.

"Buddy, if I recall right, you were the one who said we didn't have much time. So I was searching for information as quickly as I could. That didn't allow much of a chance to get all touchy-feely. Sorry."

He momentarily closed his eyes. "Okay. Let's just move on."

No way. I wasn't done justifying my actions. Or making him feel bad for yelling at me. "I also had the impression you weren't thrilled about asking your family or friends the tough questions yourself."

"Of course I wasn't 'thrilled' about it."

"That's one of the reasons you brought me on board, right? To ask the tough questions? And that's all I was doing." I stopped to allow him to think about that.

"Now," I then added, "tell me about your eye." He puffed out a big breath of air. He was giving in. I mentally licked my fingertip and drew a hash mark in the air, scoring one for me.

"I got hit by a guy named Hunter. He got upset with me over his girlfriend."

I unintentionally smirked. "Why? Were you hustling her? Or was the hustling part over by the time he caught you?"

He raised his shoulders, appearing somewhat incredulous. "Why would you say that?"

I brushed my hand across my mouth but couldn't wipe the smirk from my lips. "You have a reputation for being a cad."

He leaned forward and spoke in a voice just above a whisper. Again I had no idea why, unless he suspected that Margie, Buford, Wally, and Little Val were eavesdropping on us from the kitchen. "I may like women," he said, "but I don't poach girlfriends—or wives."

I mimicked him by leaning forward and replying in a similar tone, "This Hunter guy must think otherwise."

"Not really."

"Then why'd he hit you?"

Uncertainty crossed his face, embarrassment following close behind. "Because I . . . umm . . . said he was too good for her."

"What? Why would you do that?"

He backed into the corner of the booth, bending his knee and pulling it toward his chest, his foot resting on the seat. "Because I saw her in the Eagles in Hallock last Saturday night. She was making out with some other guy while Hunter was at the bar in the next room, drowning his sorrows, as usual."

"As usual?"

"Yeah, she runs around on him a lot." He settled his forearm on his bent knee, his hand dangling. "When Hunter finds out, which he always does, he heads to the Eagles and ties one on. After that things settle down until the next time she chases after someone." He rubbed the side of his nose. "Normally she's more discreet. But for some reason that night—"

"He actually puts up with that?" I was having trouble accepting what he was telling me.

"Yep. Has for decades."

"What?" I sat up straight. He definitely had my attention.

"They've been dating since high school, back in the seventies. They're both in their late fifties now."

"Wait a minute." I had to take another run at this. "They've been dating for some forty years?"

"That's right."

"And they've never married?"

"Nope." He bit back a smile, yet the corners of his mouth twitched. "Hunter says it wouldn't be 'prudent to marry' given her 'proclivity' for other guys." He worked to keep his smile in check. "Those are his words. Not mine. And where he got them, I have no idea. He doesn't talk like that, so my guess is he's met with a preacher or a shrink or someone like that."

In an effort to clear my head, I gave it a good shake. It didn't help. "But short of marrying her, he's fine with the relationship as it is?"

Buddy offered a palms up. "That's basically what I asked him Saturday night. I'd never said anything before. Figured it wasn't any of my business. Besides, she's nice enough—to everyone else anyhow. She just treats Hunter like shit sometimes. But I always thought that was between the two of them. On Saturday, though, I decided I needed to speak up."

"And?"

"He hit me." He brushed his bruise with his knuckle. "I would have gotten mad, but he was so drunk there wasn't much force behind his fist." He shrugged. "And he's a friend."

"Some friend."

"Yeah, well, most guys in his situation would have gone a little berserk."

I gaped. "Buddy, most guys wouldn't be in his situation. Not for long anyhow." I raised my coffee cup to my lips. "Why does he put up with it?"

"That's what I asked him."

"And?"

"Well, just before he let me have it, he told me he loved her. And he said everyone should leave them the hell alone."

"Hmm." So many questions. So little time. "Did he go after the other guy? You know, confront him? Beat him up?"

"Not that I saw."

"But he must have known him. This isn't exactly a metropolis."

"Maybe he didn't get a good look at him. I didn't."

"You didn't?"

He winced. "I might have had a few too many drinks that night. I don't remember everything real clearly."

"You got drunk during harvest? I thought that wasn't allowed."

"We weren't in the field last weekend. It was raining off and on, so we were shut down."

I backtracked. "You really didn't recognize the guy?" To my way of thinking, drunk or not, Buddy should have been familiar with practically everyone in the county.

As if reading my mind, he said, "Emerald, strangers do pass through once in a while. Guys come up to work beets every fall. And construction workers move through on a regular basis."

He sank deeper into the corner of the booth and fixed a glassy gaze on some point beyond my shoulder. "I remember catching sight of her on my way to the bathroom. She was in the corner with . . ." He spoke in a quiet, modulated tone, as if narrating the scene playing out in his mind. "Then about forty-five minutes later, when I was headed back to the bar to get another drink, I saw her again. She was in the same corner, with the same guy. It was . . . It was her and . . ." His words faded as his gaze was replaced with the gleam of recognition.

"You remember, don't you?" My interest turned to excitement. "Who was it? Who was she with?"

The curl of his lip signaled near disbelief as he said, "Raleigh Cummings." He sat up straight. "She was with Raleigh Cummings."

"Really?" Prickles of excitement ran up and down my spine. "Are you positive?"

He again stared past me, apparently rerunning the events of that evening through his head. "Yep, it was him."

"Hmm." Buddy's revelation was disturbing yet fascinating in a perverse way. "And all this took place this past Saturday night?"

"Yeah, the Eagles had a dance—a live band." He shifted away from the corner of the booth. "But how is any of this related to Raleigh's murder?"

I searched the recesses of my mind for the answer to that question and came up with nothing concrete. "I don't know. Maybe it's not. But for what it's worth, we now know your friend had a very good reason to dislike Raleigh."

"Reason enough to kill him?"

"Again, I don't know." I paused to collect my thoughts. They were all over the place. "People have killed for less. But since Hunter didn't even bother to break them up, I wonder how much he really cared for his girlfriend in the first place. On the other hand, he told you he loved her, and he popped you one for criticizing her. Still . . ."

"Maybe he went after Cummings, and I just didn't see it or don't remember it."

"If there had been a ruckus, Buddy, you'd have heard about it at the very least."

"Well, I never heard a thing."

"Then I suspect nothing happened. There wasn't a fight. At least not at the Eagles." I stopped for the count of two. "We need to talk to this Hunter guy to see what we can find out."

"I don't know."

I raised my eyes and silently prayed for patience. "Buddy, we don't have much else to go on. And since you aren't keen on questioning Wally . . ."

He appeared ready to argue but must have thought better of it. "If the weather clears up," he said, his tone yielding, "there'll be a fish fry tonight at the Eagles. Hunter never misses one of those."

"Hey, guys." Our discussion had been so intense that the sound of someone else's voice startled me. I jerked my head to find Little Val waddling our way from the kitchen. Instead of a plate full of Rhubarb Bars, she held a fork and a deep-dish pie pan with only the slim remains of a Peaches and Cream Pie. "Where's Wally?" she squeaked as she clutched her stomach the best she could, given that both of her hands were full.

I know she said something more, but I was focused entirely on the tiny sliver of pie that remained in the pan. Another dessert made by Margie for the beet banquet. She got the recipe from Lillian Heine, who insisted it was "the best pie ever." But Lillian's daughter, Elizabeth Stellon, disagreed. She claimed her Rhubarb Meringue Pie was even better. Being someone who preferred making up her own mind, I was looking forward to testing both and deciding for myself. Now I wouldn't get the chance. I felt cheated and . . .

A scream broke my rumination. It was Little Val. She followed with another that was almost too shrill for humans to hear. And after that she dropped her fork, along with the pie pan. "I think . . . I think . . . I think I'm in labor," she yelled just before her water broke, gushing down the legs of her father's wool overalls.

Chapter Fifteen

A SHAFT OF SUNLIGHT PENETRATED the café's front window. It was early Friday afternoon, and the storm was winding down. The rumbling of snow plows harmonized with the buzzing of snow blowers and the scraping of shovels. And together they provided background music for Little Val, who was moaning and groaning her way through labor.

She was lying on the floor in the café, next to the juke box. Everything had happened so quickly we didn't have time to get her upstairs, much less to the hospital, even if we could have powered through the snow-blocked roads.

Initially we had considered laying her in a booth, but she wouldn't fit. As I said, Little Val wasn't very little anymore. She also refused to be hoisted onto the pool table, much to Buford and Buddy's poorly disguised relief. So she was making do with the floor until the ambulance arrived, which wouldn't be until later, when the roads were once more passable.

Margie and Vivian were attending to her, while I did what I could to help, from fetching pillows and blankets to sterilizing everything that wasn't nailed down. As for Little Val's husband, Wally, he shifted between kneeling next to his wife and hiding out in a booth, depending if at that particular moment, she "needed him" or wanted to "kill him" for "doing this" to her.

Buddy and his brother had excused themselves early on, claiming they had to go upstairs and get cleaned up since "they were crawling with germs." Apparently they kept extra clothes up there because the next time I saw them, they were showered, shaved, and hightailing it out of the café in fresh shirts and jeans, professing the need to shovel out the vehicles buried in the snow. *Chickens.*

Little Val's father wasn't any better. Ever since he and Vivian had arrived, he'd been outside, supposedly clearing the sidewalk. But as I mentioned before, the man was missing an arm, so he couldn't shovel any better than he could drive his snowmobile. And Vivian had to do that. No lie. After Wally phoned them, it was Vivian who made record time from the farm to the café on the Arctic Cat, Vern merely hanging on for dear life. Regardless, Vern now insisted on remaining outside, scooping snow from the sidewalk so the ambulance crew could make its way into the café. *Chicken.*

Inside, during some of her more intense contractions, Little Val begged for painkillers, assuring Wally he could buy them from the guy down the street—the one who'd just undergone knee replacement surgery. When Wally refused, she became furious, demanding that he perform a variety of solo sex acts that were either anatomically impossible or illegal in most states.

Later, after she'd calmed down or grown nearly numb from pain, she agreed to forego further demands for illegal drugs if Wally would sing Righteous Brothers tunes to her. Eager to win his way back into her good graces, he started off with her favorite, "Unchained Melody." His voice was soft and sweet and full of love. Yet when he got to the line about "time going by so slowly," Little Val screamed that if he really wanted to see time go by slowly, he should switch places with her. Needless to say, that was the end of Wally's singing.

Still, he wasn't ready to give up. He was bound and determined to provide his wife some comfort. And to that end, he plugged in the juke box and grabbed a handful of quarters from the cash register, feeding them into the coin slot and hitting the buttons. He was so nervous he couldn't think straight or, obviously, see clearly. The first song up was "Goodbye Earl," by the Dixie Chicks:

"It wasn't two weeks after she got married that Wanda started gettin' abused. She put on dark glasses, long-sleeved blouses, and makeup to cover her bruise."

"Push, push, push," Vivian urged her daughter while flashing her son-in-law the stink eye. Wally, in response, slapped more buttons, but the song played on, leading Vivian to yell, "Come on now. This isn't rocket surgery." And to that Little Val cried, "I'm doing the best I can, Mom!" Then the Dixie Chicks insisted that "Earl had to die." And Vivian glowered at Wally, making me certain that Earl wasn't the only guy in really big trouble.

After that, Margie caught Wally's attention and calmly said, "Just pull the gall-darn plug, son. Just pull the gall-darn plug." As if a light had finally switched on in his attic, Wally immediately rushed to the juke box, rounded the corner, and cracked his head on the wall. Dazed but not bloodied, he yanked the cord, and the song screeched to a halt. He smiled. Then staggered. And I gave him only about a fifty-fifty chance of remaining upright for the duration.

But who was I to talk? My stomach had pitched and rolled with each one of Little Val's contractions. And as she urged that baby along, sweat trickled down my chest. On the flip side, I was totally mesmerized by the sight of a human being entering the world. And when that little boy was delivered into his grandmother's arms, I cried at the wonder of it all. Then I rushed down the hall to the bathroom, where I threw up in the toilet.

When I returned, which may have been too early for my own good, I witnessed Vivian snip the umbilical cord with a kitchen scissor and deliver and wrap the afterbirth. Again I got woozy and had to mimic some of Little Val's breathing techniques.

Inhaling through my nose to the count of four and exhaling via my mouth to the count of eight, I stared at Vivian. I only knew her to be pretentious and self-centered, as if she were the star of life and everyone else mere bit players. Yet during the birth of that baby, she exhibited none of that arrogance. True, she carried herself with an air of authority, but that was appreciated under the circumstances. Someone had to take charge. Someone had to know what needed to be done. Even if we weren't always sure what she was saying.

Vivian carefully placed the baby on Little Val's chest as Wally stretched out on the floor beside them, a soft, buttery light streaming through the window and enveloping the new family. Wally alternated between kissing Little Val's forehead and patting the tiny boy's head, while Vivian covered both mother and child with blankets. I took a mental picture of the entire scene. A scene bathed in rich, golden hues. A scene I'd undoubtedly recall many times throughout my life.

The snapshot faded far too quickly, although it was replaced with yet another amazing picture: one of Vivian and Margie embracing. I'm not kidding. When the two of them finally allowed themselves to consider what they had done, they were astounded and delighted by it all and cackled gloriously while hugging and slapping each other on the back.

Their actions must have signaled Wally that it was time to celebrate because he jumped to his feet and sprinted to the door, bidding the guys outside to come in and meet the newest member of the clan. They did but declined all offers to hold the little tyke, though they were quick to join the debate over what to name him.

I hung back, wanting to watch this extraordinary family happening but not wishing to intrude upon it. I was happy for the whole lot of them but felt some envy and sorrow as well. Having no real family, I knew I'd never enjoy an event like this.

Those thoughts—along with a dip in adrenaline now that the birth was over—nudged me toward a melancholy state. But I dug my heels in, refusing to go.

Despite my determination, I was relieved when Margie sidled up alongside me, providing me additional strength just by being there. "Uff-da," she whispered as she redid the ponytail bound at her neck, "that there was incredible." She swept her fingers across her damp cheeks. "I never helped deliver a baby before."

"I never saw a baby being born before." I gazed at her with admiration. "You were great, Margie."

"Thanks, but most of the credit has to go to Vivian. And ya know that's not easy for me to say. But it's the truth."

I slid my eyes to my left, where Vivian and Vern had rooted themselves on the edge of a table about ten feet away. My impression had been that Vern and Vivian weren't especially fond of each other in spite of being husband and wife for twenty-five years. At that moment, however, Vern stood behind his wife, his only arm wrapped around one side of her waist, and cooed, "Oh, Mama, ya did good. Real good. What would we of done without ya?"

She relaxed her head against his chest. "Well, Papa, the thing of it is, ya didn't hafta find out." Shifting her eyes between her son-in-law and the little boy nestled against their daughter's breast, she added, "I only hope he's not a chip off the old shoulder."

I captured Margie's eyes.

"What can I say?" She continued in a hushed voice. "Somethin' happened to them recently, but I have no clue what it was. It left them nicer to each other than ever before. Sure, Vivian's still prickly to other folks, but she's sweet as pie to Vern." She leaned in closer. "The rest of us have taken to callin' them the Mamas and the Papas because that's the only way they refer to each other anymore."

"Hmm." I canted my head until it almost touched hers. "The last time I was here I thought Vivian was running around with the guy everyone refers to as the President." As soon as the words left my mouth, I wished to call them back. Margie could get vicious with anyone who spoke disparagingly about her sister. Apparently that was her job alone. "Not that anything was going on between them," I quickly added, doing my best at damage control. "I just heard they hung out together."

Margie eyed her sister but spoke to me. "I haven't seen the President around for a month or more. Sure he was busy workin' beets at the end there. But in the past that wouldn't of stopped him from droppin' by the café here, especially if he thought he might bump into Vivian. And if nothin' else, I thought he'd come by to pick up his sack lunch, being he was workin' for Buddy and Buford. But he never came by." She paused. "True, Dinky and Biggie didn't stop in for theirs either. Fact is I didn't know they were workin' for the twins until Dinky told me last night. But like he said, they only helped out for a few days at the end, so . . ." Her words dangled mid-sentence. "Yah, it's strange that the President never stopped by."

The juke box suddenly came to life, startling both Margie and me. Buford was hunched over it as Johnny Cash belted out "A Boy Named Sue."

"Anyways," Margie said loud enough to be heard over the din but not so loud that others might hear, "now that I think about it, the President may of called Vivian at her house early last Friday night." Her thoughtful expression played up the sharp angles of her face. "Someone called her cell phone, and after she answered it in the dinin' room, she hurried to the livin' room, so Little Val and I couldn't hear." She leaned her butt against the banquette behind us.

"See, I was over there for supper. Oh, yah, Vivian and I don't see eye to eye much of the time, but we're still family, so I eat there every once in a while." She blew a wisp of hair out of her face. "Little Val was spendin' the night 'cause Wally was workin' late at the office. It rained last Friday, so no one hauled beets, and Wally got to get caught up with his job in town." She rotated what appeared to be a stiff neck, probably due to the tension surrounding the birth. "Little Val and Wally live in the country. But once she started her last month, she wouldn't stay out there by herself. And who could blame her?"

Wally and Buford joined Johnny Cash for the final stanza of the song:

> "Well, I think about him every now and then.
> Every time I try, and every time I win.
> And if I ever have a son, I think I'm gonna name him—
> Bill or George. Anything but Sue. I still hate that name!"

The two of them then joked about all the odd names they could call the baby, including "Buford," teased Wally, and "Wall-eye," Buford shot back.

"Though I couldn't hear well, I could tell Vivian wasn't happy with the person on the other end of the line," Margie explained. "I also got the distinct impression it was a man. But it wasn't Vern. He uses the landline when Vivian's at home. The reception's better. Besides, I never heard her call the guy 'Papa.' Not even once."

I had a few questions, but before I could ask the first of them, the café door swung open, and the ambulance crew trudged in. The guy out front shouted to no one in particular, "Cold enough for ya?" And when no one answered, he filled the silence by stomping snow from his boots and wheeling the squeaky stretcher across the floor.

I hugged myself to keep the goose bumps at bay while watching a female member of the crew hustle toward Little Val. As soon as she reached her, she knelt down and hurriedly opened her medical bag. Then with an expression of confidence that put me at ease, she began a cursory examination of both mother and child.

Before long a man rushed to join her, his short thick legs moving like a pinwheel. As he bent over, his jacket rode up, and his pants pulled down, exposing what is universally known as "plumber butt." It was then, I'm ashamed to say, that I recognized him, not because of some prior intimate encounter but, rather, the frequency with which that butt crack had been on display around town.

The man "behind" it all was Shitty, the local plumber. I'd met him my last time in town. He was a jovial character with a beer belly so big it forced his belt to relocate south of his hips. Hence, the additional "sunshine."

Besides owning his own plumbing business, Shitty apparently volunteered on the local ambulance crew. Which was a good thing, though I couldn't help but consider the irony of it as well. I'd sterilized everything that might possibly come into contact with Little Val or her baby, and now Shitty, the plumber, was going to take over.

"Say, everyone . . ." After dashing into the kitchen only minutes earlier, Margie re-emerged with what she called celebratory fudge. "The recipe's from Peggy Pemberton, and it's the most exotic fudge I've ever made. Perfect for a special occasion."

She titled the tin in my direction, and I wasted no time choosing the largest piece and biting into it. "What makes this fudge exotic?" I asked as the chocolate melted on my tongue and oozed toward my throat.

"Well," she replied, "I believe it's the beef."

Although I heard her, the words didn't make sense, so I went ahead and swallowed. Remember, it was chocolate. And it was in my mouth.

"Yah," Margie confirmed, "it's definitely the beef."

It was only then that I realized the meaning of what she'd said. And the chocolate and beef mixture immediately skidded to a stop somewhere along my esophagus, seemingly uncertain if it should keep on its current course or return from whence it came.

Chapter Sixteen

When the ambulance took off for the hospital, the Mamas and the Papas, along with their son-in-law, Wally, followed in a borrowed pickup. Back in the café, the twins and I helped Margie clean up.

After we finished, we called the Eagles in Hallock to see if the fish fry had been canceled due to the inclement weather. "No," someone told us, "it's still on." So the twins and I climbed into Buddy's pickup and headed north.

By my silence on the subject, you might have guessed that I hadn't heard from Randy. And even though a part of me was certain his lack of communication was evidence he'd dumped me, another part held out hope it was just a terrible misunderstanding. Or absent that, he was lying in a snow-filled ditch, hurt and unable to call for help because his cell phone was dead. That part urged me to stay at the café so I'd be there if he was ever found and delivered back to Kennedy. But to that, yet another part yelled, "*No way, girlfriend! You have your own life to lead. And if he can't get here on time or call to explain why he's late or otherwise dig himself out of a damn ditch, he'll just have to catch up with you later.*" That voice was kind of feisty and seldom heard from. But on this day, when a new human being had kicked and screamed his way into the world, it seemed appropriate to listen to a little sass.

When we got to the Eagles, we pulled into the makeshift parking lot on the west side of the highway. Someone had plowed it out, the displaced snow forming a twelve-by-four-foot ridge next to the road. Many of the trucks and SUVs in the lot idled with no one inside, but when I asked Buddy about it, he merely shrugged and said, "Who likes to get into a cold vehicle?"

I shook my head. "If you left your car running unattended in Minneapolis, you wouldn't have to worry about it being cold. Just stolen."

"Yeah, but you aren't in Minneapolis anymore, are you?"

I scanned my frozen and desolate surroundings. "No, Toto, I don't believe I am."

He chuckled as he pressed his hand against the small of my back. "Come on. Let's go." And the three of us ran toward the brick building on the opposite side of the road, our shoulders hitched and practically stuffed into our ears.

"Brr," Buford shivered as we hurried through the door of the old building, "it'd be a bad night to get tied naked to a tree."

He peeked through the eye-level opening on the wall across from us. The hole was about two feet square. Years ago, when this was a private club, that "window" must have been where folks showed proof of membership. Now it simply afforded a quick look into the main bar.

"Janice is bartending," Buford mumbled to his brother.

"Janice?" I repeated, checking out the only woman behind the bar. While short, thin, and middle aged, she was clearly aiming for a more tantalizing look. She'd dyed her hair coal black and had it piled high on her head. And her droopy gray eyes were caked with thick liner and baby-blue shadow.

"Janice Ferguson," Buford replied.

"Kennedy's city clerk?"

The twins nodded as they began exchanging greetings with nearly everyone in the place, each seemingly a relative, friend, or business associate. It was plain to see they were well liked, though not particularly adept in social graces. They didn't introduce me to a soul.

I was left awkwardly surveying the place from where I stood—the nondescript pool room to my left and the kitchen and dance floor to my right. The pool table was occupied by two young men, but rather than bustling with two-stepping couples, the dance floor was crowded with long folding tables and beige metal chairs, all filling up fast with fish-fry enthusiasts.

"Janice has to work a couple jobs," Buford said once the three of us were alone again. "She has a nasty bingo habit."

I shot him a quizzical look.

"Yeah, she'll go as far as Roseau and Warroad—both more than an hour away—just to play for an evening, especially if there's a big jackpot. When she's in Roseau, she says she's shopping at Carol's Cedar Cellar. A flower shop over there. And when she's in Warroad, she swears she's checking out the deals at Dollar Savers. But she's not fooling anyone. We all know what she's really up to. Sometimes she's on the road four nights a week."

Buddy shook his head. "You're such a gossip, Buford."

I dismissed the chiding remark since the guy making it sported a black eye from sticking his nose in someone else's business and instead asked Buford, "Doesn't that create a problem for her at work? How can she be trusted to handle the city's money if she has a gambling problem?"

Buford squinted at me, a befuddled expression on his face. "She doesn't have a gambling problem. She just plays too much bingo."

"But, Buford, bingo is . . ."

Buddy nudged me into the buffet line, muttering in my ear as we moved, "Save your breath. To him it's not gambling unless you're in a casino or at the track."

Uncertain I could make sense of that, I put all thoughts on hold except those pertaining to the food heaped on the plate handed to me: deep-fried fish, French fries, and coleslaw. While the smell hanging in the air—a mix of fish, grease, and stale beer—wasn't particularly enticing, that food looked "gall-darn tasty," as Margie would have said.

After insisting on paying the bill, Buddy motioned me to the bar, while Buford headed toward a table full of young women, mouthing that he'd catch up with us later.

I turned to Buddy. "For a minute, I thought you and Buford had nothing in common. I see now, at a minimum, you share one trait."

"Yeah, yeah." Buddy prodded me along by bumping the rim of his plate against my back. "Didn't your mother teach you that when someone does something nice, like buys you dinner, you thank him, not make fun of him."

I laughed as I set my plate on the bar and hiked myself onto a stool.

"Hey, Janice," Buddy called, "a Bud Light when you get a chance." He slipped his eyes in my direction, and I nodded. "Make that two," he called.

He laid some cash on the counter, and after Janice plopped down two longneck bottles, she grabbed it and made change, placing the excess back in front of him. "How's your eye?" she asked in the coarse voice of a heavy smoker.

"It's fine." He quickly changed the subject. "Did you hear Little Val had her baby?" He didn't wait for a response. "This afternoon. Right there in Hot Dish Heaven."

"You're kidding!" Janice wanted all the details, so Buddy supplied them the best he could. She especially enjoyed the part about Little Val delivering on the floor, next to the juke box. Hearing that, she let out a cackle that finished with a dry smoker's cough.

"Yep," Buddy said after introducing her to me, "with Emerald gathering recipes for the Minneapolis paper, Little Val giving birth in the café, and Raleigh Cummings getting murdered, it's been a crazy few days around here." He added without skipping a beat, "Did you know him, Janice?"

Janice barely moved her head. "Yeah, I knew him."

"Well," Buddy said, "I'm not all that broken up by his death."

Janice blinked her blue-shadowed lids. "Oh?"

"We shouldn't have hired him in the first place. He was trouble right from the start."

With vein-fanned hands, Janice patted the sides of her updo, as if trying to keep it from falling over in either direction. "I wouldn't know about that."

"Huh? You mean as city clerk, you never had any issues with him?" Buddy stuffed more fish in his mouth, and I did the same.

Janice forced a chuckle, followed by an involuntary hack. "Well, I did have an argument with him this past Tuesday. Dinky might have told you about it. He caught the tail end."

"What happened?" Buddy's tone and countenance were equal in their innocence. No doubt about it, the guy was slick. It made me wonder why I was with him. Did he really need my help? I didn't think so.

"Oh, it didn't amount to much. But as he was leaving, Dinky came in, and if looks could kill . . ." She stopped short, puckering her mouth, tiny smoker's lines picketing her upper lip.

"I know who Dinky is." I'd decided it was time to earn my dinner by asking a few questions of my own. "He seems like a nice enough person. Why was he upset with that Cummings guy?" While I knew the answer, I still did my best to mimic Buddy's carefree tone.

"From the little I heard," Janice replied, "Dinky owed Raleigh money, and Raleigh wanted to get paid pronto."

Someone shouted for a drink, leading her to move to the other end of the bar, somewhat reluctantly from what I could tell.

"Why would Dinky owe Raleigh Cummings money?" I asked of Buddy. "I thought he was like you, a rich Red River Valley farmer." I'd learned early on it was fun to tease Buddy because he was easy to get riled.

"We aren't 'rich,'" he grumbled. "Most of our money is tied up in equipment and land."

"So you're saying Dinky's so cash poor he had to borrow money from a fill-in truck driver?"

Again the answer was slow in coming because Buddy had gotten waylaid by someone. As they spoke, Buddy's friend peeked over Buddy's head and smiled at me, a glint of curiosity, then approval, in his eyes. Naturally I was flattered and quickly cleared my throat in anticipation of the conversation that was sure to follow. But when the guy got the drink he'd ordered, he simply moseyed away, leaving me with nothing to occupy myself but the fish on my plate, while Buddy chatted up the curvaceous blonde pair who'd taken the guy's place. Like the man before them, they also took stock of me. But rather than smiles on their lips, they had fire in their eyes. Apparently they didn't appreciate me dining with Buddy Johnson, even if we were only bellied up to a bar.

"I wasn't suggesting that Cummings loaned Dinky money," Buddy said once the ice princesses had left. "My guess is that Dinky lost some to him in a poker game." He raised his empty beer bottle, signaling to Janice he was ready for another. "See, Dinky's a high-stakes gambler, and I heard he got taken to the cleaners in a game last Friday night."

I ran my finger up and down my beer bottle, making squiggles through the condensation. "Wasn't he hauling beets Friday night?"

Janice set Buddy's fresh beer in front of him. She had an odd expression on her face and lingered while making change from the small pile of cash in front of us.

Buddy refrained from speaking until she left. "No. Remember, it was too wet."

"So, instead, Dinky played poker with Raleigh?"

"Could be. Dinky has a hunting shack out by Lancaster. He and his brother, Biggie, have games out there on a regular basis."

"You ever play?"

Buddy snorted. "Not with those two. They play for big bucks."

"And what? You're too poor for that?"

"No, too smart."

We both returned to our food. And after I'd consumed all the fish I could possibly eat, I wiped my hands and wadded up my napkin. "That was . . ." I struggled to find just the right word. "Scrumptious," I decided. "Simply scrumptious."

"Glad you liked it." Buddy had a determined look in his eyes. He was going to eat everything on his plate.

"So who else was there?"

"What?" His attention was on his food alone.

"For the poker game last Friday night? Who else do you think was there?"

He speared his last piece of fish. "I don't know. But I wouldn't be surprised if Hunter was. He hardly ever misses one of those games."

"Is Hunter another rich farmer?"

Buddy dropped his fork onto his empty plate. "We aren't rich farmers! Hunter doesn't even own any land." He was truly exasperated, and I couldn't help but smile.

"But he still plays poker?"

"Yeah. He's good at it. He doesn't lose very often."

"Hmm."

"Hmm," Buddy echoed. "What does that mean?"

I rested a forearm on each side of my plate. "It means we now have possible connections between Hunter Carlson, Raleigh Cummings, and Dinky Donaldson. The three of them may have played poker together last Friday night."

"So?" He wiped his own hands. "You're grasping at straws, Emerald."

"Maybe." I considered that for a moment. "Then again, maybe not." I bent toward him and lowered my voice so no one within earshot could hear. "Janice said that Dinky and Raleigh argued, quite possibly about poker. Maybe that argument led to a fight that ended in murder."

Buddy followed my lead by leaning in close. Too close. His face was a mere inch or two from mine. I recoiled, and he grinned that lopsided grin of his. He knew full well he'd unnerved me. "Dinky's no killer."

"Well . . . umm . . ." I stammered, desperately searching for the composure I swore I had only moments earlier. "H-How about Janice? What do you think about . . . umm . . . the argument Dinky heard between Raleigh and her?"

Buddy gulped more beer before he spoke. "Dinky's a gossip. He and my brother are like a couple of old hens. They listen to every story out there, then they're quick to pass them on. And while they might not lie during the retelling, they damn sure stretch the truth for effect. To my way of thinking, if Margie was looking for dirt, Dinky was probably more than happy to provide it, embellishing as he went."

I mentally replayed Margie's account of the confrontation. "Are you saying there wasn't anything to that argument?" I finished off my own beer. "Even though Raleigh was angry enough to dump garbage on the steps?"

Buddy didn't hesitate. "Hey, Janice!" She was stooped over, mixing drinks, at the other end of the bar. "Did someone throw garbage on the office steps earlier this week?"

"Yes!" She straightened and cackled, ending with a cough so violent it forced her to turn away from everyone. "It was me," she added over her shoulder when finally able to speak. "And I didn't exactly throw it." She turned back around. "I just overstuffed the bag. Then when I went to carry it out to the dumpster Wednesday morning, it got caught on the door handle and split wide open. Why do you ask?"

Buddy shook his head, letting her know it wasn't anything important. And to me he telegraphed a look that read, "I told you so."

In response, I muttered, "If Dinky was only gossiping, he's a jerk. He could have caused Janice some serious trouble."

"Ready for another?"

I nodded, and he lifted my empty bottle, once again beckoning Janice.

"She can take care of herself," he assured me. "And most people around here know better than to put much stock in what comes out of Dinky's mouth."

Janice set my beer in front of me, and following Buddy's example, I avoided saying anything until she'd moved on. "Margie seemed to take what he said pretty seriously."

Buddy chuckled. "My Aunt Margie is almost as bad as Dinky and Buford when it comes to gossiping. Truth is she may have done some exaggerating of her own. She doesn't usually let facts get in the way of a good story."

I felt foolish. "What about Barbie?" I wanted to save face. "How do you explain her interest?"

"She runs the paper. The paper depends on news. And news, especially in a small town, is fueled by gossip. Hell, this whole area is fueled by gossip—gossip and the Farm Bill."

"Come on, Buddy. Barbie has a responsibility to print facts."

"And she does. But she'll be the first to admit she shifts through a lot of gossip and hearsay to find a few kernels of truth." He tipped his bottle back. "Did she actually say she believed Dinky's story?"

"Well . . . umm . . . no. Not exactly." I recalled Barbie's skepticism regarding what Dinky had supposedly seen and heard at the city office. It didn't take me long to conclude that Buddy didn't need to know about any of that. "So . . . umm . . . now what?"

Chapter Seventeen

Buddy glimpsed past me, toward the entrance to the bar. "Let's do what we came here for." He jostled my forearm with the back of his hand, prompting me to glimpse over my shoulder. "See that guy over there?" he asked. "The one with the camouflage hat and jacket?"

"Uh-huh."

"That's Hunter Carlson."

"What? That little man is the 'friend' who gave you the black eye?"

Buddy scowled. "He's not that small."

"Yes, he is. I think I could take him."

"No, you couldn't."

"Well, if I couldn't beat him up, I'm pretty sure we could share clothes. He can't be any more than a size six, petite."

Buddy eased off his stool. "Small guys can still be strong."

"If you say so."

I slid off my stool and paraded after him, attempting to fix my focus on Hunter. It took some doing. I was a bit tipsy. Granted, I'd only consumed a couple beers, but that was about half again as much as I should have had. Yep, I was a poor drinker by any measure and a downright disgrace by Irish standards.

I swallowed a hiccup and whispered to Buddy, "Hey, would your little friend get mad if I told him that, even though he's wearing camouflage, I can still see him?" I hiccupped again, this time out loud.

Buddy glanced over his shoulder, annoyance and amusement fighting for top billing on his face. "Just keep your mouth shut unless I ask for your help, all right?"

Yeah, like that was going to happen. Nonetheless I pantomimed locking my lips and throwing away the key. But two seconds later, I murmured, "Where's his girlfriend? I want to meet her."

Buddy once more spoke to me across his shoulder, "You already have."

"Huh?"

He circled and nodded at Janice. "That's her behind the bar."

"Janice?"

He didn't answer but instead extended his hand to his little friend. "Hi, Hunter."

"Hey," Hunter muttered. "Cold enough for ya?" He followed with a bob of his head. "Sorry again about the eye."

Buddy waved it off. "Like I said before, I deserved it. I shouldn't have said anything."

Hunter shrugged.

"Have you eaten?" Buddy asked.

"Just finished."

"Then let's grab that booth and have a drink."

Again Hunter shrugged, which must have been some kind of male sign language for "okay" because Buddy ushered me into the empty booth, scooting in next to me, while Hunter slid in along the other side.

"This is Emme."

Hunter lifted his chin.

"I hear Dinky had a hell of a card game at the cabin last weekend." Buddy was fishing for information, but it didn't come across that way.

"On Friday night." Hunter repeatedly glanced at the bar. "That Raleigh Cummings cleaned us out. But I was positive he was cheatin'. I just couldn't figure out how."

The waitress appeared, setting bottles of Bud Light in front of Buddy and me and a dark mixed drink next to Hunter. "So you got taken too?" Buddy slipped her a few bills.

"Yeah." After tasting his drink, Hunter slouched against the bench back. "But I'll never have to pay him." He smirked.

Hmm. During the ride to Hallock, I'd promised myself I wouldn't make snap judgments about the people I met. I had a tendency to do that, and it ultimately interfered with my ability to reason objectively. Still, I decided right then and there I didn't like Hunter Carlson.

I studied him closely, hoping to uncover enough wrong with him to justify my feelings. Right off the bat I checked off beady eyes, a hawkish nose, and the smell of cigarette smoke permeating the air all around him, as if emitting from his pores themselves. But that's as far as I got before a waft of cold air put a shivering end to my assessment.

I craned my neck and saw that the bar's front door was propped open, inviting a draft to wind its way down the hall, along the booths, and up my pant legs.

"Hey," some guy yelled from a stool at the bar, evidently experiencing a chill of his own, "Shut the damn door! Were you born in a barn? For Pete's sake, it's cold in here!"

Those among the growing crowd in the entry ignored him, preferring instead to hoot and holler at what I could only assume were outrageously dressed adult trick-or-treaters stopping by the bar one night too early for Halloween. But, of course, I needed to find out for sure. So I stretched across our table, coming precariously close to falling into Hunter's lap. "Oh, excuse me," I mumbled, avoiding his eyes while clumsily settling back down by Buddy. "I was just trying to catch a glimpse of what was happening out there."

Buddy and Hunter said nothing but followed my eyes, while a few other burly bar huggers took turns ordering that the "damn door" be closed. It was then that the door squeaked shut, and the crowd slowly parted like the Red Sea.

Some folks moved left while others went right, leaving a gap in the middle where two men stood all alone. Neither man spoke. Nor did anyone around them. Then, as if someone had shouted, "Ready, set, go," the duo took off. And every man and woman in the Eagles went wild!

The two were capped in black snowmobile helmets with tinted face shields, rendering them Darth Vader look-alikes, at least from the neck up. They also wore thick nylon gloves and heavy black boots with metal buckles that tinkled as they darted around the pool table and across the dance floor turned banquet area. But other than that, they were bare. That's right. Buck naked. Just a couple of streaking masses of dark curly hair and less-than-firm body parts.

"Fee Fon!" some woman shrieked as they ran past her.

Unsure whether to laugh or scream as they headed our way, I ended up gurgling some strange kind of noise. I also admittedly glanced at their mid-sections or perhaps a smidge lower. And regrettably Buddy followed my gaze.

Determined not to be embarrassed, I offhandedly said to him after the men had exited by way of the back door, "I don't know what all the excitement was about, if you get my drift."

He threw his head back and guffawed. "That's not fair, Emerald." There was a sexy pitch to his voice. "I'm sure you've heard of cold-induced shrinkage."

"Of course." I did my best to keep a straight face, and I hoped it wasn't flushing red. "I've just never heard of men voluntarily flaunting it."

Naturally everyone in the place had ideas regarding the identities of the masked men. Some even hinted that one of them was Buford, which prompted Buford to stand up next to his table toward the back of the dance floor and offer to prove that neither looked anything like him. He followed by unhooking his belt to a chorus of cheers and jeers before sitting back down.

A couple other names got bantered about too. But in the end most folks concluded that the men were probably from Canada. Canadians often visited the area and almost as often got blamed for any unseemly activity that occurred, notwithstanding the evidence.

With the mystery more or less solved to everyone's satisfaction, most folks returned to what they had been doing before the floor show, which meant Buddy refocused on Hunter. "How'd you get away without paying Raleigh the night of the card game?"

Hunter played with his swizzle stick, bending and twisting it until it broke. "No one had enough money to pay him that night.

Raleigh won right from the start. And he was such an ass about it, nobody but Biggie was willin' to quit. The stakes just kept gettin' higher and higher."

I felt the pull of Buddy's eyes and got the distinct impression he wanted my help in questioning his friend. But I wasn't sure I could. In addition to being a tad inebriated, I was a bit disconcerted from the all-male review I'd just witnessed.

Buddy must have sensed I wasn't going to come to his aid because he blew out a disgruntled sigh and moved on solo. "Why didn't Raleigh come for his money right away the following day? On Saturday?"

Hunter was forced to yank his gaze away from the bar, where it had been trained on Janice. "I told him he'd hafta wait till I got paid for haulin' beets. I wouldn't have the full amount 'til then. And he wanted it all at once." With that he went back to tracking his girlfriend's every move, his eyes oddly filled with both sorrow and longing.

I realized then I may have misjudged the guy.

Big surprise there, Emme!

I now had the strong sense that Hunter adored his girlfriend but was disillusioned with her all the same. In other words, he probably wasn't a jerk. A fool, yes. But not a jerk.

"So," Buddy said, "Cummings was okay with waiting to get paid?"

Hunter tugged his droopy face away from Janice and offered up a shrug. It seemed to be his favorite expression. In this instance, however, he managed to supplement it with a few sentences. "He didn't have much choice. But, yeah, he bitched about it the whole way back to his place. See, I rode with him. He didn't think he'd find Dinky's cabin on his own. Too bad for him he did." He chuckled, then coughed.

"Don't sound so happy when the sheriff talks to you," Buddy warned. "He might decide you had a motive to kill him."

Hunter sipped his drink. "I'd never kill anyone over money. What's more, almost everyone else at the table, includin' Dinky, did a lot worse than me." He glanced around the room, then leaned forward. “Between you and me, Buddy, Dinky ended up owin’ Cummin’s about eight grand. And Wall-eye? Well, he and the President got taken for close to ten thousand each. Yeah, Wall-eye was a crazy man.” He looked at Janice but talked to us. “I didn’t even know he played poker. Then again, considerin’ how bad he was at it, maybe we shouldn’t call what he did ‘playin’ poker.’” He chuckled at that, ending with his own take on a smoker’s cough.

For his part, Buddy slouched against the back of his seat. He appeared stunned. “Like a deer in headlights,” as Margie might say. I had no idea what had caused the sudden change in him. But I did my best to help out by stepping in and asking what I presumed was the most logical follow-up question. “Who else played in that game?”

Hunter turned my way, while sucking down the rest of his drink, the ice cubes clinking against his empty glass. “When Wall-eye showed up, Biggie bowed out. So for most of the night it was me, Dinky, the President, Wall-eye, and that asshole Cummin’s.”

After he ticked the five names off on his fingers, he said to Buddy in a confidential tone, “We don’t usually talk about our games. But Buford just told me you were gettin’ hassled by the sheriff. So I figured you deserved to know how many other guys hated Cummin’s too. And some owed him big money.” He motioned toward Buddy’s black eye. “I figured I owed you that much.” He slapped the table. “Now I gotta go outside and have me a smoke.”

Once Hunter left, I spoke up. “At least we now know who all played poker last Friday night.”

Buddy remained silent. And distant. I couldn’t tell if he was even listening to me. I decided to pose a question he’d have to answer. “I can’t remember. Why is that one guy called the President?”

Staring straight ahead, he spoke in monotone. “He thinks his ancestor and namesake, John Hanson, should have been considered the first president since he was president under the Articles of Confederation.”

“Oh, yeah. I forgot. He’s nuts.”

I was certain I’d get a chuckle out of him, but I didn’t. He merely polished off his beer, then hollered for another. “Want one?”

"No, I haven't even started on this one." I pointed to the full one in front of me. "Besides, I've had enough."

He sniffed. "I haven't."

"Are you sure?"

He scowled.

Now some people might have considered a scowl proof I'd pushed too far. But I was not deterred. I continued to nag. "Buddy, shouldn't you keep a clear head about you?"

"My head's perfectly clear. Too clear, in fact."

I chewed on the inside of my cheek until it hurt before I gave up and asked, "What's going on? What's got you so upset?"

Buddy's eyebrows climbed his forehead. "Emerald, weren't you listening? Didn't you hear what Hunter said? Wall-eye was playing poker on Friday night."

"Yeah, I heard. And that means he lied to us. He didn't go to his office to catch up on work when Little Val was at her parents' house. He went to Dinky's cabin, where he lost around $10,000 to Raleigh Cummings."

Buddy handed a five-dollar bill to the waitress, told her to keep the change, and guzzled about half of his fresh beer. "It's worse than that," he mumbled when he finally came up for air.

"How so?"

Buddy twisted his torso until he was sitting sideways in the booth, his arm resting on the back of the bench. "Wally's a compulsive gambler." He spoke so quietly I could hardly hear him over the chatter around us. "He's been in Gamblers Anonymous for years. Before he and Little Val got married, she warned him that if he ever gambled again on anything, she'd leave him."

"Oh." Images of Wally and Little Val and their baby boy flashed through my mind, the trio huddled together on the floor of the café, the afternoon sun bathing them in soft light. "I didn't know that."

"Well, it's not something we're going to talk about. It's private." He paused. "Yeah, he's really stuck on Little Val. I think he'd do just about anything to keep her from leaving him."

"But . . ." I covered Buddy's hand with my own. "He must have known he'd never keep that card game secret. Not with a bunch of other guys involved too."

He once again angled himself forward and downed more beer. "You're assuming he was thinking straight. But from what I understand, thinking isn't his strong suit when he's gambling." He peeked at me. "No pun intended."

I gently nudged his shoulder. "Let's get out of here. We need to talk this over somewhere quiet."

"I doubt there's much left to talk over, Emerald. He lied about last Friday night. And he probably lied about where he was Wednesday afternoon too. Which could mean . . ."

Chapter Eighteen

"Okay," Buford said, "I'll tell you one more joke. Then you have to leave."

"Yeah, yeah," Buddy answered after swallowing the last of his sixth beer.

Buford gave me a palms up, and I offered him an eye roll in return. What a night!

"So, anyhow," he began, "a collector of rare books heard that Ole had an old Bible. So he went to check it out, only to have Ole tell him he'd thrown it away. The collector was appalled. But Ole assured him, 'Oh, dat ol' book wasn't worth nothin'. It was printed by some guy named Guten-somethin' or udder.' And the collector gasped, 'You mean Gutenberg?' And Ole answered, 'Oh, yah, dat's da name.' The collector screamed, 'You idiot! You threw away one of the first books ever printed. A similar copy recently sold at auction for $2 million.' Ole simply shook his head. 'Well, mine wouldn't of been worth a plug nickel. Ya see, some guy named Martin Luther had scribbled all over it.'"

Buddy chuckled. "That was pretty good. You get that one from Father Daley?"

"Yep," Buford replied. "At the banquet last night. He and some other priests have some kind of blog where they share jokes for sermons and stuff."

"Well, I'll be." Buddy's expression was vague.

"Now you have to leave." Buford said to him. "You promised to take Emme back to the café."

"What about you?"

Buford looked at the women around his table, all three watching him doe-eyed.

"Umm . . ." Buford uttered, trying to signal to his clueless brother what was going on, "I . . . umm . . . need to finish a few things here. But I'm sure I can catch a ride home later with someone."

Buddy shrugged. "Okay. Whatever." He headed for the door.

And I moved to follow, but Buford intercepted. "You're driving, aren't you?" he asked.

"I'll try."

He gave me a brief hug. "Don't worry. Everything will work out fine."

"Buford, your brother's a murder suspect."

"Only according to the sheriff. And he doesn't count." He winked. "But thanks for caring."

ꕤ ꕤ

"Give me your keys." I made the request of Buddy once we'd stepped out of the Eagles, onto the sidewalk, the words forming on white puffs of Arctic air. I followed by extending my hand.

He shoved his own hands into the front pockets of his jeans. "I'm okay to drive."

"Maybe, but why take any chances?" My teeth were chattering, but I suspected he got the gist of what I'd said. Still, he ignored my outstretched arm and stalked across the highway, not even checking to see if I was trailing after him.

"No one drives my truck but me," he shouted over his shoulder.

I tugged on my light-weight jacket. "Then I guess I'll see you around."

He spun in my direction. "What?" He planted his feet about three feet apart and his arms akimbo.

"I'm not going with you unless you let me drive." I mimicked him by fisting my own hands to my hips but just as fast went back to holding myself close. I was really cold.

He stood on the far side of the highway, while I remained on the opposite curb, bouncing from one cold foot to the other. It was a standoff. And after a silent count to ten, I turned back toward the bar, either retreating or calling his bluff, I wasn't sure which. I really didn't care. I just wanted to go somewhere warm.

"Okay!" he hollered before mumbling something I couldn't make out. "But if you do anything to my truck, I'll . . ."

"What could I possibly do to your precious truck?" I rushed toward him and plucked the keys from his hand, a wide-eyed look of innocence painted on my face. "I hardly ever grind the gears or ride the brakes. Ask anyone."

He leaped at me. I dodged him. He snarled, and I raced for the parking lot, laughing and breathing cold air until I coughed like Janice.

"Serves you right if you choke," he muttered, settling into the passenger seat.

I got behind the wheel and stuck the key into the ignition, the smell of exhaust and leather filling my nose. Buddy had started the truck remotely before we'd left the Eagles, but it was still cold, so I turned the heater on high, right along with the seat warmers.

"You should let the engine warm up before you do that," he warned.

I didn't answer. Nor did I turn anything down. And two seconds later I pulled out of the parking lot, onto the highway.

"D-Did the President work the night shift?" My teeth were chattering worse than when I was standing outside. I blamed it on the cold leather seats, urging the seat warmer to hurry up and do its job.

"Yeah, he drove beet truck for us the last couple weeks."

"H-How 'bout Hunter?"

"Drives semi for John Deere every year. John farms the land next to ours."

"D-Does everyone up h-here have a nickname?"

"What do you mean?"

I held my breath, willing myself to stop shaking. "Well, there's S-Shitty and Wall-eye, D-Dinky and Biggie, the President and John Deere . . ."

"John Deere isn't a nickname. That's the guy's real name. Like I said, he farms next to us, and he's the president of the beet growers' association."

"I know who he is. I met him in the café last time I came to town. But you aren't going to convince me his real name's John Deere. I'm not that gullible."

"I'm not lying." While I couldn't see him in the dark confines of the truck, I knew Buddy was smiling. I could hear it in his voice. "Not everyone around here is an Anderson or a Johnson. Deere's a common last name too. And a couple of them are actually called John."

"Whatever." I wasn't sure if I believed him but decided to let it go. We had far more important things to discuss. "You know, everyone who lost big in that card game worked the night shift during beet harvest. That means they all knew when the piler was unexpectedly shut down. And they probably knew about the underground areas beneath the scales." I stopped to categorize my suspicions. "In other words, Dinky, Hunter, or the President could have murdered Raleigh Cummings just as easily as Wally." My breath hitched. "Sorry. I shouldn't have phrased it like that."

Buddy let a lungful of air escape in a discouraged-sounding sigh. He was stressed out. He needed to clear his name. But he didn't want to do it at the expense of his relatives. "Emerald, don't you see? It's really bad for Wally, even if he didn't kill Cummings."

I slowed for the "S" curves, as Buddy had referred to them earlier. While the pavement appeared clear, he'd warned that the drifts near the shoulders often hid ice.

"Buddy, why don't you tell me more about the President. We haven't talked much about him." I didn't see the point of wringing our hands over the bleak-looking future of Wally's new family. It made far more sense to focus where we might have an impact. "From what I remember, he's self-important and not particularly well-liked."

I waited for Buddy to take over. It was a long wait. For a while I was afraid he'd fallen asleep. "He's single and lives in Hallock," he said at last. "He owns a couple businesses there but also has interest in a few over in Karlstad. He inherited his money but has done a good job of making it work for him." He laid his head against the head rest before adding, "And he and Vivian have been a force on the school board for years. Though something happened a month or so ago."

"And?"

"No one has seen much of him lately. He didn't golf this fall. And from what I heard, he didn't say a word at the last school board meeting, which was really strange since he usually dominates the discussions." I heard him fidget in his seat. "And even though he worked for us the last week or so of harvest, he never took to the radio to correct people or offer advice. Also unusual for him. Nice for everyone else. But unusual for him." More fidgeting. "On top of that, he didn't say a word when Raleigh went after Val over that whole joke thing. I figured he'd do that for sure, if for no other reason than to impress Vivian. Remember, she was working that night."

"So nobody has any idea what happened between Vivian and him? No one's asked Vivian about it?'

Buddy sniffed. "You don't ask Vivian personal questions."

"What if her answers could save you or her son-in-law jail time?" I let him ponder that. "From what I understand, Buddy, your Aunt Vivian loves her daughter and Wally, along with you and your siblings, more than anything in the world. That's what Margie says anyhow."

"Well, that may be. But most folks would rather stick a fork in their eye than question Vivian."

"How about talking to the President?"

"Won't happen. He's a very private man. He's never been particularly close to anyone but Vivian."

"But he needs to be checked out."

"Nope. Won't happen."

"Buddy!" I was getting annoyed with him again.

"Why should we talk to him, Emerald? What's your theory? My aunt dropped the President for Raleigh, then the President found out and killed the guy?"

"How can you make light of this? You're a murder suspect!"

"I might have heard that somewhere."

It was a good thing I was wearing my seatbelt. I couldn't get close enough to slug him. Instead, I could only silently count to ten. Then do it all over again before I asked, "Are you sure Vivian and the President were romantically involved?"

"You mean did I actually see them do it?"

I flung my right hand out in his direction. Even if I couldn't hit him, it felt good to try. "You're an ass, Buddy. I understand that you're upset about—"

"Sorry!" He shouted the word, so I suspected it was said more to shut me up than to seek my forgiveness. "No," he continued in a much quieter, but still frustrated voice, "I don't know for sure. Although I have my suspicions."

"Yet you let him work for you?" *Oops.*

It was probably a good thing he, too, was buckled up. Otherwise he might have flung the door open and jumped. "Emerald, we needed help to finish up with harvest, and he was available to drive truck. He'd never worked for us before, but he had driven for others, so he knew the routine. He didn't really want to. But in the end, he agreed."

"Why?"

"I don't know." He shifted uncomfortably. "I suppose it could have been because he thought he might run into Vivian."

I sat up straighter in my seat and gripped the steering wheel a bit tighter. "So you put business ahead of family?"

Sometimes, Emme, you just can't help yourself, can you?

"Sorry," I said, and I really meant it. I had absolutely no desire to argue with Buddy Johnson. "I didn't mean to sound so sanctimonious. It's none of my business how you and your brother operate your farm."

"Believe me. It wasn't an easy decision. We simply had no choice."

And with that we rode on in silence, each left to our own thoughts, mine apparently far more judgmental. Yep, just one more flaw to work on. One more flaw keeping me from . . .

Chapter Nineteen

EMERALD? JUST SO YOU KNOW, I called a lawyer before we went to the Eagles."

"And?"

"I have an appointment with him first thing Monday morning."

I slowed as we neared town. "And until then?"

"We continue to poke around. I'd like to have as much information as possible when I see him."

"Yeah, well, about that." I swallowed hard. "I think . . . umm . . . I'm going back to Minneapolis tomorrow afternoon, after I get my recipes from Margie."

"What? You're not going to stay and help me?"

I shook my head, then remembered it was dark inside the truck. "You don't need me. You're perfectly capable of finding out what happened to Raleigh Cummings on your own."

"Maybe. But it's nice to have someone to talk things over with. Especially since friends and family are involved. Like you said, it's hard to be objective where they're concerned."

"I . . . umm . . . I just don't think I can stay. I don't want to . . ." I couldn't bring myself to finish. It was too embarrassing.

"I get it. You don't want to run into Randy. But you don't even know if—"

"Stop!" I couldn't let the County Casanova pity me anymore than he had already. "If you say anything else about him, I'll run your truck into the ditch."

"No, you won't."

I swerved toward the shoulder.

"Okay!" He held his hands in the air, their silhouettes glinting in the approaching light. "I won't say another word. Just don't hurt my truck." He then muttered, "He's an idiot."

"Buddy!"

"Okay. That's it. Not another word. I promise."

"Good. Now we still have the rest of tonight. Do you think Margie would mind if we brewed some coffee in the café and went over what we've come up with so far?"

"No, she wouldn't mind. She's probably not even there. After staying over last night, I bet she was more than ready to go home tonight."

Kennedy's Main Street was deserted except for my car, which was parked across from the café. Courtesy of Buford and Buddy, it had been shoveled out of the snowbank. Yet it remained all alone. And with patches of snow left on its hood and bumpers, it looked forsaken. And that made me sad. Alone and forsaken in the cold and dark. I grew sadder by the moment. Alone and forsaken, just like its owner, nosy and judgmental Emerald Malloy.

Oh, my God, Emme, get a grip!

I swung around the corner, shadows tripping across the dashboard as we passed under one street light, then another. "I think my blood sugar's low. I better have something to eat with my coffee."

"Why? Are you diabetic?"

"No, moody. And I'm starting to feel really sorry for myself." I turned down the alley. "I need some sugar to raise my spirits."

"You eat a lot for a skinny girl."

I angled into the parking lot shared by the café and the VFW. "I have a high metabolism."

I switched off the truck and asked Buddy about the other three cars in the freshly plowed space. He informed me that the rusted-out Ford pickup was Jim's, the bartender at the "V," though he couldn't imagine why he was still there since the place was dead. And the two sedans, parked off to the side, belonged to Margie and John Deere.

"They're at the 'V' too?"

I could see Buddy just fine now because of the light glowing from the fixture high above the back door of the café. He appeared smug. "I doubt it."

"What do you mean?"

He shrugged noncommittally. "I shouldn't have said anything."

I stared at him, deliberating what he had said as well as what he had refrained from saying. I worked to make sense of it all. It was kind of like a riddle. Though the solution was way more exciting. "Really?" My voice may have been a bit shrill. "There's something going on between Margie and John Deere?"

He rubbed the area alongside his nose, doing his best to hide a grin. "I didn't say that."

"When did all this happen?"

"Emerald, I didn't say—"

I slapped the steering wheel. "That explains the whole 'expanding her horizons' thing, doesn't it?"

Buddy puffed out his cheeks before letting a long breath pass between his lips. "Well, John did graduate from MIT or someplace like that. And he was a big shot at Boeing. He's traveled all around the world. And he only came back home about twenty years ago to take over the farm after his dad died."

"And," I continued for him, "Margie's never left Kennedy for anything more than a short vacation. As a result, she's feeling insecure."

"That about sums it up."

"Who told you?"

"Little Val. She said Margie came clean with her and Vivian last Friday night, when she had dinner with them out at her folks' place."

I glanced at the cars. Then at the café. And finally back to Buddy. "What do we do now?"

He scratched his upper lip. "I doubt they're up to anything, knowing you rented a room for the night."

"She gave me a key and everything." I handed Buddy his truck key and dug into my jeans' pocket for the key to the café's back door. "But . . . I really don't want to walk in on them."

Buddy opened his door. "Come on. I'm sure we won't."

I made an effort to reassure myself. "Yeah, if they were going to do anything, they'd go to her house or even his house, right?"

"Well, I doubt Margie would want John's car in her driveway overnight. And he lives in town too . . ."

"So what do we do?"

He eased from the truck. "Don't worry. It's not like they're hormone-crazed teenagers."

I couldn't help but add, "She's related to you, isn't she?"

He slammed his door. "You're a regular comedienne."

"I try."

"To be on the safe side, close your door really hard. Let them know we're here."

I did. "If they're inside, I suppose we can't have a snack. That would be too intrusive, huh?"

The corners of his mouth tilted up in a barely suppressed grin. "They won't care if we make something to eat."

"Good, because after some dessert, I'd like more of that Breakfast Pie, if there's any left."

He slung his arm around my shoulder, and we headed toward the building. We were just about there when a humungous pickup thundered down the alley. It was unlike any other I'd ever seen. It stood tall, the chassis riding at least four feet off the ground. And it was extra wide, like a Hummer. The cab featured four heavy-looking doors, while the truck bed was covered by a windowless topper that appeared as if it could withstand Armageddon. And if that wasn't enough, it moved along on rubber tracks instead of tires.

"What in the world is that?"

Buddy shook his head. "The sheriff got some anti-terrorism money from the federal government. He used it to buy that truck and track system. They're manufactured in Karlstad, at a company called Mattracks."

"What's the purpose?"

Buddy had to think about that. "According to the sheriff, those tracks allow him to chase terrorists and other desperados regardless of the terrain." There was vibrato in his voice, enough to make clear to me that he considered the sheriff an idiot.

"And there's a big need for that up here?"

He sighed. "He insists we 'remain vigilant.'" More vibrato.

The truck rumbled into the parking lot, its bright lights now shining directly in our faces. While impossible to see anything, I heard the truck door open and a voice call out in one decibel shy of a roar, "Buddy Johnson!"

"Oh, shit," Buddy muttered before raising his own voice to be heard over the truck's grumbling engine. "Yeah, sheriff, what do you want?"

"You!" The sheriff slammed his door and trooped through the light, into view. "Hands against the building and feet spread, mister. And, miss, step over there, out of the way."

I did as he said. After all, he looked as if he'd spent every free minute during the past decade lifting weights. Not that I had any illusions of fighting him. I'm just stating a fact. The man was built. And did I mention his gun? Yeah, he had a gun. It remained in its holster. But his right hand was wrapped around it.

He swaggered toward Buddy, his feet crunching against the snow. At the same time, another truck door opened. Again the person was invisible, hidden by the blinding light.

"Buddy, don't get any ideas," the sheriff warned. "I have backup." Really? As if that actually mattered. Remember, he had a gun. My guess? That's all the backup he truly needed.

Without a word, Buddy raised his hands and slowly turned toward the building. He pressed his palms against the clapboard exterior, spread his feet about a yard apart, and stared straight ahead.

Meanwhile, I shook with fear, although a little part of me rebelled by saying over and over in my mind, *Buddy's right. The guy's an idiot.*

Part Three

Spoon a Discreet Amount of The Dish You Want Most of All

Chapter Twenty

AFTER BUDDY GOT CARTED away in handcuffs, I called his lawyer in Crookston, like he had asked. The guy assured me he would talk to Buddy first thing in the morning. Beyond that, he said, there wasn't much anyone could do until Monday, when Buddy would make his first appearance in court. If he needed an investigator, he'd hire one then.

I disconnected, stuffed my cell phone into my purse, and entered the café. The place was pitch black and eerily quiet except for the hollow pounding of the furnace as it kicked in against the cold. I was pretty sure no one was around. If they were, the noise and lights accompanying the arrival of the gestapo would have rousted them. Just the same, I slipped off my shoes and stealthily climbed the stairs and padded down the hall to my room.

I got undressed, shimmied into my nightshirt, and tucked myself in bed. With my teeth chattering and my thoughts on the loose, I attempted to warm myself while developing a plan of action. It was tough going on both fronts. I raised my knees to my chin and wrapped my arms around my ankles, while my mind jumped around as if I'd spent the evening downing cappuccinos.

I may have drifted off. I'm not sure. But sometime during the night, I heard commotion, first downstairs, then in Margie's bedroom. Whispering and laughing. Followed by bedsprings creaking. And after that, the crooning of Barry White.

I didn't trust my ears at first, certain it was nothing more than a Motown dream, prompted by one of those late-night, thirty-minute television ads for CD collections. But it wasn't a dream, though undoubtedly a CD, from which Barry White sang in his sexy baritone, "Can't get enough of your love, babe."

For a moment I considered pounding on Margie's door and blurting out everything. But for what purpose other than to silence Barry White and the giggling and bed squeaking? And I didn't really want to ruin Margie's night, did I? After all, we couldn't do anything about Buddy till morning. Besides, I was finally warm, all cuddled up in bed. And while I wasn't sleeping soundly, I was resting. So I simply clicked on my bedside radio and cranked up the volume. Giggle, giggle. Squeak, squeak. "Can't get enough of your love, babe." Really loud.

THE SUN WAS RISING when I woke to the commodities' report and a terrible headache. Despite my fitful sleep, the ruckus down the hall, and the blaring radio, I'd managed to come up with a plan. It wasn't a great plan. But considering the conditions I'd been operating under, it wasn't a bad plan either. It consisted of two parts. Part One: I'd remain in town for another day or so to do what I could for Buddy, even if it meant running into Randy Ryden. Part Two: I'd ask Barbie for assistance because she'd know more about the case than anyone other than the police. And . . . Well . . . That was it. My entire plan.

Switching off the radio, I was confident in the knowledge that wheat prices were holding steady, while corn and beans were dropping. Beyond that, I wasn't confident about much, especially solving this murder. I wasn't a real investigator. What did I truly know about finding a killer? Thankfully, when I called Barbie, she said she had some ideas, and she'd share them with Margie and me when she arrived, within the next hour or so.

By eight o'clock, I was washed, dressed, and sitting on the edge of my bed, writing some notes about the case and waiting for Margie's overnight guest to take his leave. The two of them were in the hallway. I wasn't eavesdropping. Yet I heard him say he'd call her later. I also caught her reminding him about the Halloween party. She explained that she'd be in the café, cooking for the supper crowd and handing out candy to the kids until around eight o'clock, when she'd lock up and head next door to the bar. He wanted to know what she was wearing for a costume. But she wouldn't give him so much as a hint. And with him still guessing, they headed downstairs.

Now don't get me wrong, I liked John Deere—if, indeed, that was his name—but encountering him "the morning after" would have been awkward. So I remained tucked away in my room until I was positive he was gone. Only then did I venture downstairs.

I spotted Margie on a stool at the metal prep table in the kitchen. She was sorting through recipes, her old, wooden, recipe box positioned in front of her. A couple notebooks were scattered off to the side. And near the far edge of the table rested a hammer, a few small nails, and a beautifully painted plaque about four feet wide and one foot tall.

Margie hummed along as Kenny Rogers and Sheena Easton sang "We Got Tonight" on the juke box. "We got tonight. Who needs tomorrow? We got tonight, babe. Why don't you stay?" Oh, brother, Margie was in love.

When she noticed me, she lowered her eyes. But that didn't stop her cheeks from pinking up. "Umm . . . I thought . . . umm . . . I oughtta get these recipes together for ya before I forget."

"Thanks."

"Yah, I have Tammie Cuddihy's Pudding Shots recipe and Nichol Berg's Breakfast Pie recipe. I also have one from Wendy Wheeler for Pineapple Cheese Hot Dish. Have you ever heard of that? She got the recipe from an old romance novel written by Heather Graham Pozzessere."

I pulled out the other stool and sat down. I wasn't sure how to begin telling her about Buddy. I'd auditioned several lines upstairs, but none of them sounded right. So I'd decided to wait until I got down here, then open my mouth and see what spilled out. Sure, it was a risky way to proceed, but since it required no forethought, I'd resorted to it on numerous occasions and was familiar with what to expect. "Umm . . . you're not open for business this morning?" Okay, that wasn't even close to what I thought I'd say.

"Nah, I'm not openin' till late this afternoon. And then, just for supper."

"Oh."

"Because of the storm, I ended up stayin' closed last night too."

"I see."

"Yah, it's given me a chance to collect your recipes, along with time to start my cookbook there."

"What? You're writing a cookbook?"

Margie did one of those non-committal shrugs. "I'm not positive, but I think so. That's why I've been gatherin' all these different recipes. Remember, man cannot live on Tuna Noodle Hot Dish alone." She snickered. "Yah, I've already settled on a name. I'm goin' to call it *Fifty Shades of Hot Dish*." She worked her mouth from side to side while searching my face for approval.

"Catchy," I replied. I really didn't think so, but who was I to say?

"Oh, yah, it worked for that other lady, so I figured it might work for me."

"But, Margie, her book was all about sex."

"Yah, I know. I read it."

"And yours will be about—"

"Hot dish." She fanned the recipe cards she held in her hand. "I considered weavin' in some sex. But I couldn't figure out how."

I opened my mouth but let my criticism die on my tongue. Margie was so happy I didn't want to dampen her spirits.

"So . . ." she went on to say, "did ya ever hear from Randy?"

Ugh! Margie was in love, and a part of me wanted to bite her head off because of it. Of course, I didn't really begrudge her romantic happiness. Mostly I was irritable because of the news I had to break to her. And because of my lack of sleep. Oh, yeah, and because people in new relationships always seemed compelled to pry into everyone else's love life—or lack thereof. "No, Margie, I never heard from him. And I don't—"

"I think the weather's still pretty darn bad out there. And bad weather often causes chaos with the phone service."

"Margie, I don't want to talk about Randy."

"What? Why not?"

I pursed my lips. "Well, I don't know. Do you want to discuss your personal life?" I raised my eyes to the ceiling, in the general direction of her bedroom.

Margie blushed. "Emme, I really like him. But I'm not ready to answer a bunch of questions."

"Fair enough." I fiddled with a recipe card. "Just give me the same consideration. That's all I'm asking."

She hesitated but finally said, "Fine then. But I'll tell ya one thing. If Randy ends up missin' the party tonight, he'll be none too happy. He really likes our Halloween parties."

"And I'll tell you another thing. You're great just the way you are. You don't need to re-invent yourself for anyone."

That got her flustered. "Well . . . umm . . . I'm not so sure about that."

"I am."

She screwed up her mouth thoughtfully. "Sometimes challenging yourself can be a good thing, Emme. Otherwise you might fall in a rut."

"True enough. As long as you're doing it for yourself."

She shook her head. "All this readin' and studyin' has made me feel more alive than ever. If that makes any sense." She hesitated. "Even so, I'm not ready for the teasin' I'm goin' to get from Barbie. Teasin' about my new interests as well as you-know-who."

"Well, she won't hear about either from me."

"Good."

I nervously wiggled my toes in my shoes. Then I sat on my hands. There was no point delaying the inevitable. While Margie didn't need any more grief in her life—and who did?—she deserved to know what had happened to her nephew. "So . . . um . . . Margie . . . um . . . tell me about that plaque?" Okay, I'm pitiful. I'll do just about anything to avoid hurting my friends or causing myself any anguish.

"Well," she replied, retrieving the wooden panel from the table, "this is an art piece from Ingebretsen's Scandinavian Gift Shop down in Minneapolis there." It featured a flowing flower design painted in shades of blue, orange, and green. "It's called rosemalin'. It's a form of folk art. For sure you've seen—"

"Yeah, I'm aware of what it is. I was just wondering if it was a gift or . . ." I didn't need to finish my question. Margie's flushed cheeks had provided her answer.

"I'm not sure where to hang it," she rushed to say in a clear attempt to talk away yet another embarrassment. "I might take it home. But it's so pretty. And since I spend most of my time here, I . . . well . . . I dunno."

"I'm sure you'll find the perfect place for it."

"Yah, I suppose I will." She set the piece down and fell silent.

I did the same. There wasn't anything more to add to our discussion about rosemaling, self-improvement, or cookbooks. There wasn't even anything else to say about good old what's-his-name. Yep, we'd talked about everything except the one subject I had no desire to broach. But there wasn't any way around it. So with a dry swallow, I began, "Margie . . . umm . . . I've got something important to tell you."

She must have noted the concern in my voice or felt the tension in the air because she quickly gathered her recipe cards, stacked them on the table, and folded her hands in her lap. "Okay, I'm listenin'. What is it then?"

I closed my eyes and slowly began my story, speaking with as little emotion as possible, for her sake as well as my own. Part way through, I peeked to find her eyes filled with unshed tears, and seeing that, my own grew moist. Yet I continued. In rote fashion, I reported everything from the poker game and Wally's involvement in it to Buddy's arrest and my subsequent conversation with his lawyer.

When I was all done, Margie said, "Well, if that don't beat all." She rubbed her red, dry hands together. "On the plus side, I know everythin' will work out. On the minus side, I don't wanna wait for the BCA folks. We need to get Buddy out of jail sooner rather than later. Ya see, Emme, he'll go berserk in there."

A lone tear escaped her right eye, and she rushed to wipe it from her cheek before any of the others noticed and decided to follow its lead. "He was accidently locked in a farm shed when he was young, don't ya know. He was stuck in there for more than twenty-four hours. It was in the fall and really cold out. There weren't any lights. Rodents were runnin' around. Uff-da, he was only eight. When we finally found him, he was 'traumatized.' At least that's what the doctors called it. And they were probably right because, ever since, he's been unable to handle bein' confined in any way."

"I didn't know."

"Well, it's not somethin' he's goin' to talk about." She made an apparent effort to find her bearings by redoing her ponytail and straightening her tee-shirt. "I suppose we all have things—secrets and such—that we'd rather not admit to."

"Yeah, I suppose we do." Thoughts of Boo-Boo immediately sprang to mind. I hadn't shared with anyone—not even my therapist—the details of his recent and increasingly insistent efforts to renew our relationship. To my way of thinking, I should have been able to deter him on my own, without involving others. I felt foolish that I hadn't succeeded. And I couldn't help but wonder if I was unknowingly doing something to encourage him.

"Anyways," Margie said, thankfully scattering my Boo-Boo-related concerns, "do ya have any idea how we can help him?"

I recounted my pathetic, two-point plan. "No, nothing specific, but I promise I'll do whatever it takes." I then informed her that Barbie was on her way.

As if on cue, Margie's cell phone rang. "It's Barbie." She answered but didn't say much other than an occasional "oh, for sure" and "ya betcha." The call was short. And when it ended, she reported, "Change of plans there. Barbie wants ya to go and meet her for breakfast at the Caribou in Hallock. She said there's more information we need from the police. And since Guy and Jarod never miss breakfast or their mornin' whist game at the Caribou, the two of ya should start there, while I do a little phone work from here. Then we'll get together and compare notes."

I rose from my stool and patted my friend's forearm. "We'll get this all ironed out, Margie. I promise."

She made an effort to smile, but it fell short. "Yah, we will. But I can't help but worry about the damage that'll be done along the way." She shook her head. "Uff-da, what a mess."

"Well, I better get moving if Barbie's waiting for me."

"Before ya go, wanna little somethin' to eat? Ya never know, the Caribou might not have anythin' good on the menu. And I've got some Orange Jell-O Salad. It has fruit cocktail, bananas, and mandarin oranges in it, so it's good for breakfast. Ruth Hennen gave me the recipe. I think it's a lot like one of those smoothies some folks always insist on in the mornin'. Only way thicker. And not nearly as expensive." She winked.

"No, thanks. I'll take my chances at the restaurant."

"Ya sure?"

"Yeah, I'm sure."

"Well, wait another minute then. I want ya to wear that parka over there." She jabbed her finger toward the gray down jacket that hung from a hook by the back door.

"I can't take your coat, Margie."

"It's an extra. I had it upstairs. I keep a fair amount of clothes up there. Ya never know when someone will need somethin'."

"Thanks."

"I should of given it to ya earlier, but I forgot."

I grabbed the jacket and slipped it on. It was so big a friend could have joined me inside.

"My word. A bit big, isn't it?" Margie often stated the obvious.

"It'll be fine."

"Well, ya don't hafta wear it if ya don't—"

"Margie, it'll be fine."

"If you're sure then." She scraped her chair back and ambled over to me. "I guess it's always better to have a little extra room to move around in." She zipped the jacket and pulled the fur-lined hood over my head. It practically consumed my entire face. "There, now, ya sure ya don't wanna little somethin' for the road?"

Chapter Twenty-One

When I walked into the Caribou Bar and Grill, I spotted Barbie right away. She was hard to miss. She was wearing a bright orange sweater and waving her arms high in the air, motioning me toward her booth. Feeling a bit like a plane taxing down a runway, I slowly proceeded in her direction, tossing my borrowed jacket on the glossy wooden bench opposite her and sliding in after it.

She reached across the table and handed me a menu. "All the food here is really good." I couldn't help but think how disappointed Margie would have been to hear that. "Order whatever you want," she added. "It's on me."

I scanned the laminated card, made my decision, and laid the menu on the table. "Have you come up with anything new since we last spoke?"

"No. As I said on the phone, first and foremost, we need the specifics on the murder. You know, time and place of death, weapon used. That sort of thing. And I'm hoping Guy and Jarod will be able to help."

"You really think they can?" I had serious doubts.

"Sometimes, they hear things. Important things. And as they demonstrated on Thursday, they enjoy sharing."

"You're certain they'll stop in here this morning?"

"Oh, they'll stop. And if I'm not mistaken, they'll be here pretty soon. They're creatures of habit."

The waitress sauntered over and set water glasses in front of us. She was a pretty high-school girl with a full figure and a pleasant smile. I ordered a ham-and-cheese omelet, while Barbie went with the special—a traditional eggs-and-bacon breakfast. Both of us asked for coffee and orange juice.

As the waitress walked away, Barbie grinned, her eyes fixed on the entrance behind me. "Well, speak of the devil," she muttered.

I glanced over my shoulder, as Barbie said, "Hi, guys! Come and join us."

Guy moseyed over, with Jarod dogtrotting after him. "Cold enough for ya?" Guy asked.

"Have a seat," Barbie replied, ignoring the question I'd heard about a zillion times since my arrival.

"I dunno if we should." Guy appeared skittish. "I don't wanna get into any trouble."

"Oh, come on. Sit down." Barbie stuck two fingers in her mouth and whistled, garnering the attention of the waitress as well as a half dozen patrons. "Bring these two their usual," she shouted to the young woman, "and add it to my bill."

I almost laughed out loud. Guy and Jarod were stuck. Barbie was buying them breakfast, so they had no choice but to sit with us.

With audible sighs, they slipped out of their brown, law enforcement parkas, throwing them in the empty booth behind Barbie. Guy then plopped down next to her, while I scooted over so Jarod with a "J" could perch next to me.

"How's it going?" Barbie asked the question in a tone that suggested we were the best of friends, simply catching up. "I bet the sheriff is depending on you two a lot these days."

I almost choked on my water.

"Well, yeah," Guy said, sitting a little taller. He just couldn't help himself. He desperately wanted to be important.

"I heard you made an arrest last night," she added.

Guy snuck a peek at me before answering, "I wasn't actually there. But, yeah, we did."

"So," she continued, "what did you guys come up with to tie the murder to Buddy? It had to be more than a measly argument in this place."

Again Guy glanced at me before training his gaze back on Barbie. "Well, I dunno if we should—"

"Oh, I'm sorry." She waved her hand as if erasing a whiteboard. "I didn't mean to embarrass you. I suppose the sheriff didn't share many of the details with you two. I get it. He's holding the really important information close to the vest, allowing only a few of the . . . more experienced deputies to know what's really going on."

"That's not true." Guy pulled on the cuffs of his tan uniform shirt. "We know everything that—"

"No, no, that's okay." Barbie played them like a couple of fiddles. "I don't want to humiliate you. If you don't know anything, you don't know anything. It's not your fault. Not really. I'll just wait for the probable cause affidavit to get filed. It won't be long now. Then everyone will know all the details anyhow."

Guy and Jarod cast their eyes on each other for only a split second before Guy said in the same authoritative tone often employed by Barney Fife of Mayberry fame, "Well, yeah, the probable cause affidavit will be filed soon, so I suppose it wouldn't hurt to tell you that the murder weapon was an ice scraper." He even sniffed like Barney. "The big kind. The ones used to scrape ice off of sidewalks. You know . . . wooden handle . . . about five feet long, with a heavy-duty metal plate on the end. They're also used to push tare out of beet trucks."

"Tare?"

Guy puffed out his chest. "The dirt and whatnot left in the truck after the beets are emptied."

"And?" Barbie said.

"And," Guy repeated, "we found it on Buddy and Buford's farm, in a ditch, not far from the house. It still had some blood on it. Raleigh's blood. The fact is the murder probably took place right there, near that ditch—and the house."

"Any fingerprints?" Barbie asked.

Guy answered, "Nothin' that wasn't smudged. It'd been sittin' in water for a while. And it was covered with about a foot of snow."

"How was it discovered then?"

"The handle was stickin' out of the snow." He smirked. "Just plain dumb luck. But we'll take it. And now we've got our man." He held out his hand and tapped a different fingertip while stating each piece of evidence against Buddy. "First, he was fightin' with the victim here on Tuesday night. Second, he fired his ass. Third, the murder weapon was found near his house. And fourth, Buddy doesn't have much of an alibi."

Barbie waded in. "Sounds circumstantial to me."

The deputies made eye contact before Guy added, "Then fifth"—he wiggled his thumb like he were playing Where is Thumbkin?—"yesterday mornin' a snowmobiler came across Raleigh's pickup in a grove of trees out there, on the twins' farm, near the river. Someone was obviously tryin' to hide it until they could get rid of it."

"Fingerprints?" Barbie posed.

"None that didn't check out."

"Buddy's?"

"Well . . . umm . . . no."

"Could the truck be seen from the house?"

Barbie was firing questions, and my intuition told me Guy was growing defensive. He rubbed his thumb over the badge on his chest as if reminding himself he was the cop here. "Well . . . umm . . . no, but it was on their property."

I didn't want Guy to clam up, so I decided to give him a break from Barbie by asking a few questions of my own. "So, deputy, do you have a definitive time of death yet?"

He gladly switched his attention to me. "We're gettin' closer. Ed—he's one of the deputies—well, he's been doin' some checkin'. Not that the sheriff asked him to. In fact, the sheriff's pissed off about it." Guy shook his head. "Anyhow, Ed found out that shortly after the fight with Buddy, Raleigh came back in here and drank some more. The bartender thinks he left around nine. And Raleigh's neighbor recalls seein' his pickup still at home around midnight, when she let her dog out just before goin' to bed. It struck her as odd since she knew he worked the night shift. But when she got up to use the bathroom around five, she noticed that the truck was gone. So she assumed he overslept and went in late. She said that wouldn't of surprised her given what a carouser he was."

"So," I said slowly, weaving this information into what I already knew, "he must have been killed sometime between the early morning hours of Wednesday and—"

"Wednesday afternoon," Guy finished for me. "We know it couldn't of been any later than that. We can tell by the advanced stage of rigor mortis."

"Really?" I presumed someone at the sheriff's office knew something about rigor mortis, but I was certain it wasn't Guy. He was only parroting what he heard.

The waitress arrived with our breakfast, and we stopped talking, distracted by our food and the aroma of fresh coffee and fried bacon.

Five minutes later, with my stomach full, though, I was itching to get back to it. "Deputy," I said to Guy, "once Raleigh was killed, his body was hidden somewhere until sometime after 2:00 a.m. on Thursday, right?"

"Uh-huh." Guy swished coffee around in his mouth.

"Any idea where?"

After swallowing, he said, "Not yet but we're lookin'."

"Around Buddy and Buford's place?"

"Primarily."

"Regardless of where it was," Barbie jumped in to say, "it was ultimately moved to the piler and stuffed down into the scale pit."

"Yep," Guy replied, unsuccessfully suppressing a burp. "'Scuse me." Another burp. "He was pushed into the back corner. Buddy must have reckoned that since harvest was about over, the scales wouldn't be inspected again until next year, so the body wouldn't be discovered 'til then—especially way back there. And by that time, our trail would be cold." Guy squared his shoulders. "But it didn't work out that way. And now Buddy has to pay the price for what he done."

Barbie set her cup down. "Whatever happened to innocent until proven guilty?"

"Well," Guy replied after forcing a mouthful of food into his cheek, "I think we proved him guilty."

"Really?" Barbie's tone was incredulous. "Just like that?"

"Darn tootin'," Guy answered. Then he and Jarod chuckled and bumped fists.

"When are the BCA agents expected to arrive?" I was hoping it would be before these guys had Buddy hanging by his toes.

"The storm's easin', so they're thinkin' tonight." Guy slurped more coffee. "But I don't see why they're botherin'. We've got this thing all sewed up." And at that, he and Jarod bumped fists one more time.

Right around then, the deputies' long-standing whist partners came in. And since we were done eating, Guy and Jarod left to join the two older men, while Barbie wandered off to pay the bill. I waited for her in the entry, where I perused the bulletin board.

In addition to the standard postings about homes for sale, upcoming auctions, and library events, I spotted a flier announcing a hot dish contest sponsored by the local volunteer fire department. Below the list of rules was last year's winning recipe, Mushroom Wild Rice Hot Dish, submitted by Pam Petron. She was quoted as saying, "It's a must for every Thanksgiving dinner."

"We need to check out that scale pit," Barbie declared as she joined me. "That's the only way we'll know exactly what we're dealing with."

"How will we do that? Won't it be guarded?"

"Probably. But since the body's been removed, it shouldn't be that big a deal. And if it is, I'll come up with some kind of lie so we can sneak a peek."

"Are you a good liar?"

"Oh, yeah, I can lie my pants off." She paused for a beat. "Not literally, of course." Another beat. "Except for once." A smile cracked her lips. "But that was a long time ago, and I probably shouldn't go into it."

"Thanks. I appreciate that."

Chapter Twenty-Two

BARBIE SKIDDED INTO THE PILER, her car nearly fishtailing into the squad car parked next to the scale shack. And me? Well, I elected to park about twenty feet away. My old Ford Focus wasn't much, but it was all I had.

When I caught up to her, she was already haranguing the deputy on duty. He was around forty and extremely tall. He wore the standard brown law enforcement parka, but both his hands and his head were bare, and his shaggy blonde hair blew in the wind.

He stood between Barbie and the yellow crime-scene tape wrapped around four poles, creating a rectangular enclosure about the width and length of a semi-truck and trailer. Three square manhole covers were evenly spaced down the middle. From what Barbie had told me, they offered access to the scale pit below.

"Ed, I have no interest in tampering with the crime scene," she said. "But I have every right to take a look at it. So you better let me. If you don't, I'll call the county attorney, who won't be happy about getting bugged on a Saturday. And he will call the sheriff, who's way too busy to be bothered by the likes of me. Then both of them will call you. And it won't be to shoot the breeze."

Ed scratched his chin. "Barbie, you're so full of shit it's a wonder your eyes aren't brown." Ed's eyes were a soft blue, much like the sky, with lines fanning out from the corners like tiny rays of sunshine. "You know damn well you're not going to call the county attorney or anyone else. You may be able to pressure and lie to Guy and Jarod to get what you want, but I'm not as dumb as them."

Barbie scuffed at the dirt before gazing up at him, chagrin painting her cheeks a ruddy red. "Sorry. It was worth a shot."

He shook his head. "Now start again. Tell me what you need and be nice about it. Then I'll see if I can help."

She squinted into the sun. "I need to see into the scale pit, so I can get a picture of it in my mind. If I don't, I can't properly write about the case."

"You can't go down inside." He towered over us, serving as a wind break.

Barbie leveled her hand across her forehead to shield the sunlight that beamed over his shoulders. "I don't have to."

"Well, if you only want to look, I don't see a problem. Go ahead."

Barbie glanced at me and back to Ed. "She's with me."

"I know who she is."

Ed needed just two long-legged strides to reach the crime-scene area. He then lifted the tape to allow Barbie and me to pass under it.

"Sandy told me you bowled a hell of a series last week," Ed said as he followed us. It was much harder for him to do the crime-tape limbo since he was at least six-foot-six.

Barbie spared a glance in my direction. "Ed's wife is on my bowling team." Then to him she said, "It was the best I've ever done. I broke two hundred twice." She grinned broadly.

"Not bad for a girl."

"Hey!"

He chuckled as he removed the manhole cover farthest away from us. "This will give you the best view of where the body was found." He set the cover on the ground. "And, Barbie, like I've told you a hundred times before, you'd get a whole lot farther with folks if you were friendlier. But you're always so gall-darn ready to pick a fight. Right off the bat, you assume we're going to try and stop you from doing your job."

"That's because your boss usually does try and stop me from doing my job."

"Well, hopefully not for long." Ed waffled. I think he wanted to say something more about the sheriff, but instead he simply uttered, "Now, no funny business."

Barbie saluted. "Aye, aye, sir."

He shook his head and walked away, this time scissoring his legs over the yellow tape. When he got back to his car, he leaned against the hood, folded his arms across his chest, and hooked one foot over the other. He then stared across the flat snow-covered field on the opposite side of the highway.

"He seems like a nice enough guy," I whispered to Barbie as we dropped to our knees, and from there, our bellies.

"Oh, yeah, most of the deputies are nice." She smiled. "Including Randy Ryden."

I was about to glower when I remembered she wasn't privy to what had transpired or, more accurately, hadn't transpired between Randy and me. So she didn't deserve my snarkiness.

"But for a few," she proceeded to say, "they really know their stuff too."

We lowered our heads and peered into the dark abyss. I wiggled around, striving for a bit more comfort. There wasn't much chance of that since we were lying on a mixture of ice and gravel. "So what's the deal with the sheriff?" I yanked a stone from where it had been poking me in the chest and tossed it across the snowy ground.

"As I said before, he's shrewd. And he's an asshole."

"How'd he get elected then?"

"Like assholes never win elections?" Barbie curled her lip. "He got voted in three years ago. And next year he'll get voted out. People realize their mistake. And a couple deputies, including Ed over there, are ready to take him on." Barbie stopped for a beat. "Ed's the deputy Guy and Jarod were referring to. The one who's actually investigating this case."

"If the sheriff's defeated, Barbie, you'll probably lose Guy and Jarod as sources of information."

"I'll manage."

Like me, Barbie wore a parka. But unlike mine, hers was neon pink, snug, and barely covered her back. "Aren't you cold?"

"Nah, not really." She bent her denim-clad legs, drawing her feet into the air behind her. Again no socks in her UGG slippers.

"Hey, Ed," she yelled, waving one arm wildly to capture his attention. He was fiddling with his cell phone. "Can I borrow your Maglite? I can't see a damn thing down there."

Ed grabbed a flashlight from his car and hauled it over. Handing it to her, he warned, "Don't drop it!"

Barbie grunted a reply, and he walked away.

"So," she said, switching on the light and waving it in the hole, "let's see what we've got here." Once again she lowered her head, and I did the same.

Surprisingly, the scale pit was only about four feet deep, although it extended sixty or seventy feet in length and about twenty feet in width. The cement that lined it was littered with dirt that must have seeped in along the edges of the platform above ground. The pit encased two rails that ran its entire length, each balancing four, evenly spaced, load sensors. That's what the police called them at any rate. And according to Barbie, those sensors determined the weight of the trucks.

Barbie wielded the flashlight around until a ray of light fell on the back corner of the pit. It too was marked by crime tape. "That's where the body was found," she pointed out. "Since it's not deep enough down there for an adult to stand up, the police believe the killer crawled or duck-walked all the way back there, pulling Raleigh's body along."

She raised her eyes. "The only thing worse than duck-walking is rope climbing. Ever have to do that in phy. ed.?"

I smiled at the odd change of subject but decided to go along with it. "Nope. But we did attend mass every morning."

"And?"

My smile morphed into a chuckle. "And . . . I'm pretty sure it beat rope climbing or duck-walking." I pulled my hood over my head, holding it away from my face with one hand. "Even though I never would have admitted it back then, I liked morning mass. I was a nervous kid, and it helped me start my days off calmly."

Barbie nodded. "Sort of like meditation, huh?"

"Exactly."

And we dropped our heads back into the dark.

"Barbie, I just don't get it." My voice echoed through the empty space. "Why would the killer go through all this work? It has to be twenty feet from here to that corner. That's a long way to drag a body, especially if you're crawling or duck-walking. Why not just dump it somewhere? Or throw it in the river?" As soon as I spoke those words, I was reminded once more of that prior murder. In that case, the victim was buried in a shallow grave, only to get caught up in flood water and washed onto the river bank, where she was later discovered.

Barbie evidently had the same recollection. "That doesn't always work well either, does it? Maybe the killer remembered that." She paused. "The police say Raleigh was murdered on the twin's farm, right down the road. My guess is he or she didn't want to leave the body there because it'd be too easily discovered but, at the same time, didn't want to take it very far for fear of getting caught."

"Which tells us the crime wasn't premeditated. The killer didn't have anything planned."

Barbie switched off the flashlight and rose to her feet. "Let's go talk all this over with Margie."

I got up and brushed snow and sand from my jeans and Margie's jacket. "I sure hope she has some sweets to munch on. I'm not really hungry for lunch, but I could go for a little something."

"I know she was planning to make a Pumpkin Roll today."

My hood fell over my face, and I pushed it back with jacket sleeves that extended well beyond my hands. "I don't think I've ever had Pumpkin Roll."

"Then you're in for a treat. It's a cross between bread and cake, and she slathers it with cream cheese frosting."

"Sounds delicious. But I won't get my hopes up. When I left, Margie looked too upset to do much baking."

Barbie snorted. "She bakes even more when she's troubled. So who knows? By the time we get back there, the café might be overflowing with goodies."

I licked my lips at the prospect. "That certainly would be good for me. I always think better when I eat."

"Yeah, I seem to remember that about you."

Chapter Twenty-Three

BARBIE AND I PULLED UP in front of Hot Dish Heaven shortly after lunchtime. We met Margie at the door. She was holding the small white dog I'd encountered when I first got to town. The one Barbie almost ran over.

"Oh, for cute." I petted the pooch. "You've got a new friend."

"I found him out here almost frozen to death. I took him in to get him somethin' to eat, but he started to whine. So I brought him back out. And now that he's done spray paintin' the snow, we'll go in and try some food again."

"Who'd leave a dog out in this weather?"

Margie cocked an eyebrow. "I think he belonged to Raleigh Cummin's. I phoned a few folks, and none of them remembers seein' this little guy prior to a few days ago. So I'm pretty sure he belonged to Raleigh. He must of gotten out of the house somehow and has been roamin' around ever since. See, he's got a collar but no tags."

The pup winched his head to lick my hand. "May I hold him?"

Margie handed him over, and he cuddled in my arms, his dark-brown eyes peeking through matted white fur. "Are you hungry, pup? Want some dinner?" He snuggled closer, his tiny pink tongue hanging from the corner of his mouth. He couldn't have weighed more than ten pounds. "Margie, after he eats, we should give him a bath. He's kind of stinky."

Barbie lifted her arms and proclaimed, "People pamper their pets way too much. If anyone's to get fed and bathed by someone else this afternoon, I think it should be me. And I have in mind just the person to do it. Only problem is he's unavailable." She extended her bottom lip into a pout.

"Oh, for cryin' out loud," Margie grumbled, "I thought ya got all that out of your system on date night?"

Barbie opened the café door, and we all shuffled in to the sounds of Faith Hill and Tim McGraw on the juke box. They were singing "It's Your Love." *Ugh!*

As I said, I was happy for Margie. Really I was. Still, I didn't want to be subjected to the musical interpretations of her romantic needs and sexual desires every time I walked into the café. "It's your love," McGraw purred. "Does somethin' to me. Sends a shock right through me. I can't get enough." *Double ugh!*

"I missed date night," Barbie reported. "The weather was so bad that by the time I got home, my sweetie was fast asleep, and I couldn't wake him up no matter what I did. And believe me, I tried." She swiveled her hips and opened her mouth.

"Please, Barbie," I begged, my hands covering my face, "no details!"

She regarded me with dismay. "You're a party pooper, you know that?"

"Call me whatever you want. Just keep your exploits to yourself."

"Your loss." She fingered her spiked hair. "Anyhow, because he's such a dedicated band instructor, he was busy at school all day yesterday. And this morning he was out the door early, taking some ensemble somewhere for something or other. I didn't really listen after he told me he wouldn't be able to meet up with me until later tonight, at the costume party. So in answer to your question, no, I haven't gotten any lovin' in several days, and it's left me a bit needy."

"Well," Margie replied, "I suppose that can happen."

"Really?" I asked. "How do you know?" I winked, and Margie scowled.

Barbie circled back around. "Did I miss something?"

Margie pleaded with me. She didn't say a word, but she pleaded all the same. It was plain to see in her expression.

"No," I answered, "you didn't miss a thing. I was just asking about the costume party."

Gratitude washed over Margie's face. "I told ya about it a couple weeks back, when we were talkin' on the phone. I said the 'V' was hostin' a masquerade party on Halloween night, just like every year, so ya needed to bring a costume."

For someone who wanted something from me—namely, my silence—she wasn't offering much in return. "I don't remember that, Margie. Though I may have heard you mention something along those lines this morning, when you were talking to—"

"No!" She clamped a hand on my shoulder and spoke with new understanding. "Come to think of it, I *meant* to tell ya but forgot."

Satisfaction warmed my face. Of course, I knew about the party. But I hadn't bothered with a costume because I had no intention of dressing up and pretending to be someone I wasn't. I hated doing that. "Oh, that's okay, Margie. Don't worry about it." I was barely able to contain my joy. "Maybe next year."

Barbie, it seems, didn't see the point of waiting. "Oh, Emme, I brought my costume trunk with me. It's in my car. I know we can find something for you in there."

"What?" Just like that—my joy vanished, replaced by a dull ache behind my eyes. "No, Barbie, there's no need for you to go to any trouble."

"It's no trouble." She clapped her hands. "None whatsoever."

"Wait!" The ache was quickly becoming an intense throb. "We shouldn't even be talking about going to a party, should we? We have work to do. We have to dig up all the information we can about the murder, so we can pass it on to Buddy's lawyer."

Oddly enough Barbie agreed. "And there's no better place to learn stuff than at a Halloween party." She did a quick dip of her head for emphasis. "Practically everyone in the county drops by, and they drink more than they should, and since they're in costume, they feel anonymous, which leads them to be less inhibited. More talkative. About all kinds of things."

"Ya know," Margie said, "that makes a lot of sense."

I glared at her until she muttered, "Sorry, Emme, but it does."

I hated to admit it, but she was right. It did make sense—in a strange sort of way. Just the same, I didn't want to dress up!

"Emme?" Margie's tone was extra sweet. No doubt she was worried I might reveal her secret about John Deere—or whatever his name was—now that she had sided with Barbie on the costume issue. "Maybe we can find somethin' in Barbie's case that you'll actually like. Something that isn't too provocative. Okay?"

Barbie giggled. "What's the point of dressing up if you're not going to be provocative?"

Margie pressed her thin lips together. "Ya aren't helpin' here, Barbie. Do ya want Emme in costume or not?"

Barbie scoffed. "It's just dress up. What's the big deal?"

I bristled. "I don't like it."

"Oh, I'm sorry to hear that." Even as she said the words, her grin stretched across her face. "Two years ago I won first prize."

"As?"

"Lady Godiva." She performed a pirouette.

"She rode a horse and everythin'." Margie attempted to sound disgusted by the whole thing, but the underlying tone of her voice revealed just how impressed she really was by Barbie's stunt.

"You rode a horse into the 'V'?"

Barbie huffed. "Of course not. I rode a horse 'through' the 'V.' Then I tied it up out back. It was much warmer than today."

Margie headed for the kitchen and returned a few minutes later with a large tray in hand. It held a carafe of coffee, a plate of sliced Pumpkin Roll, another with what she called Strawberry Pretzel Squares, three coffee cups, and a short stack of dessert plates. I also spotted a saucer of white rice and one of water. And next to them, a bone-shaped treat. At that I arched a brow.

"The rice and water are for the dog," Margie explained. "The treat too." Her smile was teamed with pride. But just a tad. "I make the dog treats, and the banker gives them out to all the dogs in town. See, they tend to hang out at the bank."

That made absolutely no sense. And because of the costume dust-up, I was feeling just contrary enough to reply, "Well, of course they do. Where else would dogs congregate?"

Ignoring my sarcasm, Margie went on to inform me that she got the recipe for the doggie treats from Mary Dodge of Park Rapids. Mary was known throughout central Minnesota as "the pie and bread lady." But apparently she could also find her way into a dog's heart. "As with men," Margie said, "it's through their stomachs."

Snickering at her joke, she headed for the stairs, her tray balanced high above her right shoulder. "Hey, Barbie," she yelled back over her head, "if it's not too much trouble, why don't ya go and get your costume trunk and meet us up in my bedroom. Maybe we can find somethin' in there for Emme that won't get her arrested."

Barbie put her hands to her hips. "I assumed she'd want to get arrested. Especially if the deputy doing the cuffing and pat-down was Randy Ryden."

Ugh!

As I entered Margie's room, I noticed it was similar to the one I rented, though from what I'd gathered the night before, hers came with an option for extracurricular activities.

The room was defined by a black wrought-iron bed and an oversized wood dresser with attached mirror. The small cloth-covered table next to the bed held a Tiffany-style lamp along with a clock-radio and CD player, most likely the source of the song stylings of Barry White. In the corner, next to the lace-draped window, sat an antique wooden chair, while the far wall featured a full-length mirror and two open doors, one to a walk-in closet and the other to a private bathroom.

Margie placed the kitchen tray on the dresser and poured us each a cup of coffee. Meanwhile, I put the dog on the floor, next to his rice and water. And Barbie dropped her trunk on the bed with a thump.

"When you find a costume you like, we'll need to make a few alterations." She opened the hard-sided case. "But that's easy to do with safety pins and Velcro."

I helped myself to a Strawberry Pretzel Square and climbed onto the bed, scooting up against the headboard. "I really don't—"

"Shhh!" She pointed her finger at me, prompting the nearly irresistible urge to offer her a finger of my own. "We already decided that a costume was necessary," she said. "Now it's just a matter of determining which one. I'll try on a few, so you can get an idea of the possibilities." She was still wearing that stupid grin. "I just love dressing up for Halloween! Always have."

Margie cleared her throat. "And while you're doin' that, we can share what we learned today about the murder. Then we'll know what we hafta find out tonight."

Margie collected a small notepad and pen from the top drawer of the dresser and settled in the corner chair, while Barbie picked through flimsy tops and tiny bottoms from haphazard piles in her costume trunk. As for me? I pondered my visit thus far.

I wasn't in jail, like Buddy, so that was a good thing. But between being dumped by Randy and cajoled into wearing a degrading costume in order to participate in an investigation I'd pledged to avoid, I wasn't having a great time either. In fact, it pretty much stunk. And that realization led me to mutter an old adage often uttered by my dad.

"What was that, Emme?" Margie asked when I was done.

Before I could answer, Barbie whistled. She was holding a piece of shiny black material about the size of a dish towel. "Oh, yeah, this will work." She glanced at me, her grin nearly wrapped around her head. "This should be great!"

"Emme?" Margie repeated. "What did you just say?"

I stared at the small slip of fabric and answered in a voice lined with gloom. "I said, 'Nothing is ever so bad that it can't get worse.'"

Margie let out a hardy laugh, her coffee sloshing over the rim of her cup, while Barbie complained, "You Irish are a cynical bunch, aren't you?" She added black fishnet stockings to the clothing collection clutched in her hand.

"Oftentimes for good reason."

"Oh, come on." She picked up a clear plastic zip-lock bag full of costume accessories. Among the many items inside was a feather duster. "I'm sure it won't be as bad as you think."

I shuddered while considering what that duster might have wiped off in the past. "It hardly could be."

Chapter Twenty-Four

Taking a break from rummaging through her trunk, Barbie briefed Margie about what we'd learned from Guy and Jarod as well as what we'd seen in the scale pit. When she was done, she headed into the bathroom, costume pieces in hand. She flicked on the light but left the door halfway open in order to hear us better.

I turned to Margie and cleared my throat. "Before we get too far along, I need to say something." I'm sure she expected me to make another pitch for going to the party in street clothes. So I probably surprised her when I said, "I realize that some of what we have to discuss may be difficult for you since it involves your family. But we need to talk about it. And we need to talk freely. Are you going to be okay with that?"

She barely moved her head. "Yah, I'll be fine, Emme."

Considering the sadness in her eyes, I wasn't so sure.

Nevertheless she positioned her notepad on her lap and stoically said, "Now, ya seem to think the most likely suspects are the men who played poker with Raleigh last Friday night. Is that right?"

I nibbled on the piece of Strawberry Pretzel Square stuck to the tip of my fork. "It's all we really have at this point."

Margie shook her head. "Not necessarily. What about Janice?"

I nibbled some more. "I suppose it's possible. But—"

"But," Barbie shouted from the bathroom, "she doesn't have a motive. Not a strong one in any case. Likewise with Little Val."

Margie blanched and Barbie peeked out from behind the bathroom door. "Sorry, Margie, I shouldn't have blurted that out. Though I'm sure you realize that since Little Val had a public argument with Raleigh shortly before he died, she's a suspect of sorts."

Margie sighed. "Yah, yah. We hafta consider everyone."

I finished my bar. "Those are really good." I licked every last speck of sugary goodness from my fork. "Margie, remember, Little Val is only a suspect of sorts. Yes, she had an argument with Raleigh. And he was really angry with her."

"But," Barbie once more shouted from the bathroom, "she was eight months pregnant when Raleigh was killed. And while she's strong, she was . . . umm . . . well, eight months pregnant. She couldn't have pulled him through that scale pit. What's more, if Raleigh was killed during the night, Little Val has an alibi. Unlike our four card players, all of whom drove beet truck and, therefore, could have slipped away from everyone else now and again, she worked in the field alongside other people."

"So," I continued, giving Barbie a breather, "if we eliminate Janice from our suspect list because garbage isn't much of a motive, and we do the same for Little Val because of her condition at the time of the murder, not to mention her possible alibi, we're left with the guys who played poker at Dinky's cabin last Friday night. That game provided a pretty good motive. And the timing seems right."

Barbie walked out of the bathroom, arms held wide, hips swaying. She was dressed as a sexy French maid, wearing a shiny little black dress with a plunging neckline and a full skirt that barely covered her bottom. She complemented it, you might say—but only if you were into trashy clothing—with black pumps, those fishnet stockings, a frilly apron, and a maid's cap.

I couldn't believe my eyes. Among its many outrageous features, the dress had a neckline that exposed a canyon of cleavage—the grand canyon of cleavage.

Even the little dog seemed flabbergasted. He actually left his plate to stare at the plus-size version of Frou-Frou Barbie, the Trampy French Maid.

"You've really worn that in public?" I knew the answer, but I felt compelled to ask just the same.

Barbie twirled around. "Cute, huh?"

"Actually," Margie said quite hesitantly, "that may be one of her more reserved costumes."

"Well, don't reserve it for me."

With a shrug, Barbie returned to her trunk undeterred and began sorting through a pile of spandex. Margie and I watched wordlessly. And the dog? He whimpered and scampered under the bed.

Two or three minutes later Barbie found something that met with her approval. "Let's see what you think of this." Her face glowed with anticipation as she grabbed another bag of accessories and headed back into the bathroom.

"Ya know," Margie said, her voice slightly raised so Barbie could hear, "Dinky couldn't of murdered Cummin's either. Based on what ya two said about that scale pit, he wouldn't of been able to move around down there any easier than Little Val. Not with his bad back and knees." She squinted at me. "Both Dinky and his brother have problems along those lines."

Barbie shouted, "And since those two only rely on each other, the idea of them hiring someone else to pull the body through the scale pit for them seems farfetched." I heard the snap of elastic. "I think you're right, Margie. We can rule out Biggie and Dinky."

I wasn't so sure. "It still bothers me that Dinky implicated Janice. Why would he do that unless he wanted to shift attention away from himself? Sure, Buddy says it was just Dinky being a gossip. But that doesn't feel right to me." I returned to the dresser, serving myself a slice of the Pumpkin Roll.

"I'll admit what he said does seem to go beyond plain old gossip," Barbie hollered. "Still, I don't think Dinky's a likely murderer. I'm not so sure about Hunter Carlson, though. He's an odd duck."

Barbie strode into the bedroom. This time she was dressed as a sexy nurse in a white spandex uniform. Again the hemline was high and the neckline was low—so low it easily could have induced a heart attack, even in a relatively healthy man.

"Barbie," I said, "I'm sensing a theme here." I placed my empty plate on the nightstand, knelt on the bed, and picked through the costumes in the trunk, careful not to touch anything with more than my fingertips. After all, God only knew where these things had been. "Sexy judge, sexy librarian, sexy soldier, sexy school girl." I leaned back against the headboard. "I don't think so."

Barbie swung her stethoscope around in the air. "You have to wear something."

I looked to Margie. "Emme," she said, "I . . . umm . . . agree with Barbie. Folks will be far more willin' to talk if you're in costume, just like them."

I pressed the heel of my hand against my aching forehead. "Okay, I'll find something. But I'll do it myself."

Barbie flicked her wrist. "That's fine. Go for it." She made her way to the dresser to get herself a bar, but it took practically forever since her dress was so tight she could barely move her legs.

Meanwhile, I searched the trunk. And I did it quickly, hoping I'd get done before the cooties came after me. I uncovered a couple items that didn't totally gross me out and laid them on the bed. "Barbie, what did you mean about Hunter Carlson being an odd duck?"

Bar in hand, she inched herself to the wall, planting her ample hip against it. "I've never been out to his house, but my hubby has—once. And that was enough. I guess he lives in a rickety old trailer in the country. It's such a hell hole that Janice won't even stay there. Of course, he's here in town with her most of the time, but he insists on keeping the trailer house."

Margie ventured to supply the reason why. "He probably needs a place to go when the two of them are on the outs, which is pretty darn often."

"I suppose." She nibbled on her bar. "But you'd think he'd keep the place up then. From what Tom told me, it's a disaster. Dirty dishes. Clothes all over. Broken windows. Stained furniture." She wrinkled her nose. "Tom said that while he was sitting on the couch, a weasel ran across the floor. So he said to Hunter, 'I didn't know you had a pet weasel.' And Hunter replied, 'Well, it's not exactly a pet.'" She wrinkled her nose again, this time adding a gagging sound. "He had to go to the bathroom but didn't dare and ended up squatting alongside the road on his way home."

I twisted my hair around my finger. "I assumed he had money. I got the impression from Buddy he was pretty good at poker."

Margie answered, "He might be good at cards. But like most gamblers, he probably loses way more than he wins."

"Whatever the case, he's strange, and I think he's getting stranger." Barbie finished off her bar. "Take last Saturday night at the Eagles, for instance. He knew full well that Janice was sucking face with Raleigh right down the hall, yet he didn't do anything to stop it." She took itty bitty steps back to the dresser, where she picked up her coffee cup. "And what about Janice? Why was she being so indiscreet about her . . . umm . . . indiscretions? Sure, she's cheated on Hunter pretty much since the beginning of time, and everybody knows it, including Hunter, but she's never done it right under his nose before. What was up with that?"

"Maybe she was mad at him," Margie volunteered, "and wanted to make him jealous."

I understood what she was getting at, but there was a flaw in her reasoning. "Margie, are you suggesting that all the other times she cheated she was actually happy with Hunter?"

With her notepad and pen on her lap, Margie pulled the binder from her hair and redid her ponytail. "Maybe those other times had nothin' to do with him. Maybe she was with those other guys because she wanted to be with them, pure and simple." She patted the sides of her hair and picked up her pen. "But last Saturday night she practically shoved her behavior in his face. That tells me she was really angry with him."

"Boy, Margie," Barbie playfully said as she set her cup back on the dresser, "you're getting so perceptive that pretty soon you'll probably find us too obtuse to be your friends."

"Just tryin' to broaden my horizons is all."

"A good thing," Barbie replied. "Better than what I've been doing lately, which is broadening my ass." She yanked on the bottom of her spandex nurse's uniform. "This thing is getting a little too tight."

Margie shuffled in her seat. "Honey, that thing passed 'too tight' years ago."

I leaned over the bed and discovered that the puppy was still hiding out. I was tempted to join him. "So why would Janice get so angry with Hunter?" I absently asked the question as I pulled the little guy out from under the bed, picked him up, and nuzzled him. "And is it at all possible that it somehow led to the murder of Raleigh Cummings?"

Chapter Twenty-Five

I WAS STILL SITTING on the bed, scratching the puppy's belly, when Margie said, "I realize neither of ya wants to do it because we're friends, but we can't leave it go any longer. We hafta consider Wally. He's a suspect too."

Barbie baby-stepped over to where Margie was seated and gave her a one-arm, shoulder hug. "Yes, sweetie, he is."

"You know what bothers me the most about him?" Margie's tone was reflective. "He didn't stand up for Little Val on the farm radio. And that's not like him. He worships that woman."

"Well, maybe he didn't dare for some reason." Barbie was concentrating on some invisible spot on the wall opposite her. "Maybe, for instance, Raleigh found out about his gambling problem and threatened to expose him if he crossed him."

I quit scratching. The dog kicked his legs. So I went right back to it. "You've been watching too many *Dateline Mysteries*, Barbie. How would Raleigh come to know something like that about Wally?"

Margie squeezed her chin between her thumb and her knuckle and answered for her. "Well, Raleigh and Wally are both from Fargo. And Wally's only lived here a few years. So maybe they knew each other before."

"Not you too, Margie!" Wasn't she supposed to be defending him?

"Well . . ."

I shook my head. "Fargo's a big place. It's unlikely they knew each other before Raleigh came here."

"But if they did," Barbie countered, her arms braced on the back of Margie's chair, "or if Raleigh found out that Wally shouldn't have been gambling or that his problem was a secret of sorts, he could have threatened to blackmail him over it."

"Then what?" I asked. "Wally hit him over the head and stuffed him in a scale pit?"

Margie flinched.

And I nodded at her. "See? It's a dumb idea. Wally couldn't have killed him. If for no other reason, he was never alone. He carpooled to and from the field with his mother-in-law, for God sake. And when he wasn't at work, he hung out with his pregnant wife."

"Except Wednesday afternoon," Barbie pointed out, "when Father Daley saw him rushing around Hallock all by himself."

I had to close my eyes and gather my composure. "Do you really believe Wally raced through Hallock to get to the twins' farm so he could meet Raleigh Cummings in their front yard and murder him in broad daylight?"

Margie's face brightened. "Of course not," she said with relief. "That's ridiculous."

"Yeah," Barbie agreed, "although I'd feel a whole lot better if we knew two things." She wiggled two fingers in the air. "One, why didn't Wally come to Little Val's defense on the radio? And, two, why didn't he tell the truth about what he was doing Wednesday afternoon?"

I agreed. "Those are definitely questions that need to be answered."

And Margie made notes to that effect on her pad.

"In the meantime," I said, "let's move on to the fourth card player, the guy everyone calls the President. No one seems to know much about him. In fact, no one even sees much of him now that he and Vivian are on the outs."

The two women exchanged shrugs before Margie said, "Well, I think he's kind of sleazy. And I'm not just sayin' that 'cause he chases after my sister."

"Yeah," Barbie agreed. "I'd never want to get locked in a room with him." She shuddered.

"What else?" I asked. "Anything more substantive?"

They both gave that considerable thought.

"Well," Margie said at last, "He's always been a loner except for golf, poker, and the school board."

"And he goes out of town a lot," Barbie added. "I assumed it was business. But I guess I don't really know."

It was Margie's turn again. "He's also lost a lot of weight recently."

"Oh, yeah." Barbie tugged at the mid-section of her nurse's uniform, as if to emphasize the point by way of comparison. "I bet he's dropped forty or fifty pounds in the last couple months."

"Really?"

"Remember him from before? He was kind of roly poly? Well, not anymore." Barbie continued to pull on her hem. "I should check with him to see how he did it. I could probably stand to lose a few pounds."

"So," I said, "are you saying he's fit?"

"What?" Barbie's was looking at her waistline, and she yanked her head up so fast it almost snapped right off her neck. "Did you just call me fat?"

"No!" I squealed. "I asked if the President was fit now that he's lost weight."

Barbie fluttered her hands. "Oh. Sorry. I might be getting overly sensitive about my weight. Does that mean I need to go on a diet?"

Margie rolled her eyes, then fixed them on me. "Emme, I don't know how fit he is. But as Barbie said, he's certainly not heavy anymore."

I'd quit scratching the puppy's belly. And now he was circling my lap, searching for the perfect spot for a nap. "Let me put it another way," I said as he settled in. "Could he duck-walk through a scale pit while pulling a dead body?"

Margie groaned. "Uff-da, this is one of the most morbid conversation I've ever been a part of."

"Yeah," Barbie agreed, "and it's about to get worse."

"How so?"

Barbie toddled over to the bed. And both Margie and I had to bite our lips to keep from laughing. True, we were engaged in a grim discussion. Still, it was hard to take Barbie seriously, particularly when she was on the move.

She sat down next to me, and her spandex skirt climbed to the very top of her generous thighs. "So far we've assumed one of the guys in that card game killed Raleigh because he was cheating or because they didn't want to pay him or because they were afraid he'd expose their secrets or something along those lines. But what if we're wrong?" She shifted her eyes between us. "What if . . . umm . . . it wasn't just one guy?" Again she checked us both out. "What if the President, Wally, Hunter, Dinky, and possibly Biggie acted together to get rid of Raleigh?"

I snorted. "A murder conspiracy? That's even crazier than your other theory."

She slapped her hands against the bed. "Just hear me out, Emme. It's clear they all hated the guy's guts. So why is it so hard to believe they wouldn't work together to—"

"Murder him?" I couldn't believe my ears.

"Don't act so shocked, Emme. Somebody killed him."

Margie leaned forward on her chair. "I can't imagine Wally bein' a part of somethin' as evil as that." She tapped her feet. "And even though those other guys get along well enough to play cards and such, I don't know if they're friendly enough to—"

"Kill someone?" The irony was apparent in my voice. "Why go that far? Couldn't they have simply agreed to deny that the game ever took place?"

Barbie yanked her head back. "Now who's talking crazy?"

I held up my hand to stop her from saying any more. "It's not like Raleigh could have proved otherwise."

Margie's eyes were wide. "Emme, doin' somethin' like that would of meant lyin' to a lot of people. Not just Raleigh."

"And, quite frankly, I don't know if that particular group of men could have pulled it off," Barbie added. "On top of that, it's very likely that Raleigh had them sign IOUs or something since it wasn't the friendliest of games."

Margie nodded. "In the movies, the losers sometimes hafta hand over their car titles or the deed to property or whatnot."

"And I've heard that guys around here *have* actually lost vehicles and land in card games." Barbie leaned back on the bed, bracing herself with her arms bent at the elbows. "But no one really carries around titles and deeds. They'd be more apt to make arrangements to turn them over on some future date. And in the meantime, if they couldn't be trusted, they'd probably have to sign IOUs."

For the first time since Buddy's arrest, I felt a spark of hope. "If the police found something like IOUs or car titles or land deeds on Raleigh Cummings' body or in his truck or at his house, it would go a long way toward shifting the blame away from Buddy."

Margie held her pen in the air. "Should I make a note to ask Guy and Jarod about that?"

"Hmm," Barbie hummed. "You'd think they would have told us if the folks from their office had found anything along those lines."

I raised my eyebrows. "Barbie, we're talking about Guy and Jarod here."

"Yah, you're right. We better ask them."

So Margie wrote it down.

"And while we're at it," I said, "we should check to see if any of our card players were late for work or temporarily missing from their shift Tuesday night—or rather Wednesday morning." Both of my friends appeared to need more details, so that's what I gave them. "See, the time of death is now estimated at sometime between those early morning hours and that afternoon. Basically a twelve-hour window. But the murder most likely occurred during the night. If it had happened during the day, someone would have seen something suspicious. So we need to account for our suspects' whereabouts during their shifts."

Barbie sat up straight. "Emme, I agree we should talk to Buford and John Deere. But remember, all of our card players were truck drivers. They could have snuck away for a little bit without it being noticed." She pulled on her spiked hair. "And if it was noticed, they could have blamed their slow return to the field on equipment problems or whatever."

My shoulders slumped. I felt dejected. My idea sucked.

"As for a murder during the day? It wouldn't necessarily draw attention," she added, as if she hadn't already damaged my pride enough. "You're from the Cities. It's crowded there. But up here you can drive for miles and go for hours without seeing another soul."

I shrugged. "Sorry. It was a dumb idea."

Barbie caressed my arm, as if soothing my bruised ego. "No it wasn't. It's always better to have information. I'm just letting you know that checking time sheets is not a fool-proof way to find our killer. But we should do it just the same."

I turned to Margie. She was making more notes. "So do you want to talk to John Deere?" I asked when she looked up. "Find out if Hunter was AWOL from work at all during the wee hours of Wednesday morning?"

Her face flushed at the mere mention of John's name. "Yah . . . umm . . . okay."

"And Emme and I will see what Buford knows," Barbie volunteered. "Since the cops are scouring the farm site and won't even let him sleep in the house, he's staying with Vern and Vivian. I expect we'll see him tonight." She winked at Margie. "Not that an entire evening with Vivian would have him climbing the walls or anything."

Believe it not, Margie chuckled, then rose, placing her pen and pad on her vacated chair. "Did I mention that this was the most disturbing conversation I've ever been a part of?" She shook her head. "I need a pick-me-up. Anyone interested in joinin' me downstairs for some Pumpkin Bars? I'll even brew a fresh pot of coffee to go with them."

"Yeah," I said. "Count me in." I scooted off the bed, the sleepy puppy in my arms. "Is this another new recipe?"

"Yah, it came from Bev Thompson. After I finished making the Pumpkin Roll this morning, I decided to keep on goin' with the whole pumpkin thing, so I made these bars too."

"I'm glad you did." I felt a smile ease across my face. "I love anything pumpkin."

Barbie got up from the bed and slapped her hips, the sound cracking through the air. "Oh, hell, let me change back into my jeans, and I'll join you."

Margie lifted her chin. "What about losin' weight?"

Barbie sighed. "I'm going through menopause!" She made the announcement as if we hadn't heard it a million times before. "Woman always gain weight during menopause. Why should I be any different?" She pursed her lips. "It's probably unhealthy to fight it."

"Yah," Margie said, her tongue poking the inside of her cheek, "it probably is."

Chapter Twenty-Six

LATER THAT AFTERNOON, I retreated to my bedroom to give the puppy a bath in the sink. He didn't care for any part of it, and as soon as I finished, he vigorously rubbed himself dry on the scatter rug next to the bed. I also tried to comb his hair, but his fur was matted, and he was terribly wiggly. In the end, my efforts were about as pointless as they'd been with my own hair.

I placed him on the foot of the bed, where he alternated between dozing and watching me slog through the various costume pieces I'd begrudgingly pulled from Barbie's trunk. Time and again, I slipped something on, only to look in the mirror and yank it back off, either mortified or guilt-ridden by what I saw. And time and again, the puppy seemed to agree with my assessment.

After an hour or so, I was totally frustrated and resorted to the white cotton blouse and nubby knee-highs I'd brought with me. I matched them with a green plaid wrap-around skirt I'd discovered at the bottom of Barbie's trunk. I was going to the party as a "school girl." But not Barbie's kind of school girl. That's why I'd left the "principal's paddle" in the trunk.

The skirt was awfully short but otherwise fit after I twisted it around my waist one extra time. I braided my hair and donned large black horn-rimmed glasses and a nylon backpack, both discovered in a bag of accessories. I also stuck my notebook and a pen in the backpack, just in case I really did come across some important information.

The puppy didn't appear particularly impressed with my final ensemble, and after one last look in the mirror, I had to agree.

But I couldn't do anything about it, so I placed the dog in his makeshift bed, filled his water bowl, and made my way downstairs, feeling very much like a school girl on her way to detention.

As soon as I entered the café, I spied Margie. She was dressed as a nun. She wore a long black habit, cinched at the waist, and topped off with a matching veil and white bib and headpiece. In spite of my years in parochial school, I couldn't remember what the bib was called but thought the headpiece was a "coif." Not that it mattered.

"Where on earth did you get that outfit?" I asked.

She breezed past me, two plates of tonight's special, Tami Boychuk's Lazy Cabbage Roll Hot Dish, balanced on each arm. With her habit billowing behind her, she headed for the booth where Laurel and Hardy and Lucy and Ethel were waiting for supper.

Upon her return, she explained, "Father Daley found it in a closet in the rectory. He's not sure where it came from. It was just the outfit—none of the religious trimmings—so he let me have it as long as I promised 'not to act like a jackass while wearing it.' His words, not mine."

She gave me the once over. "Ya look sorta like a co-ed."

I bit my bottom lip. "Yeah, I guess it'll be okay."

"Well, it's different, that's for sure."

At that moment, two men dressed as women walked in. Both wore nylon wigs—one brown, one blonde—and lots of makeup, like they had finger painted each other's face. They donned sleeveless dresses, complete with balloon-filled bras, and three-inch heels with pointy toes. Neither had bothered to shave his legs, underarms, or five-o'clock shadow.

They glanced sheepishly at Margie. "Can we eat here?" I recognized Guy from the timbre of his voice. The blonde floozy with him must have been Jarod.

"Why would ya think otherwise?" Margie's tone was a bit gruff.

"Well . . . umm . . . because of what happened to Buddy."

"Were the two of ya responsible for his arrest?"

"No, but . . ."

"Then ya can eat here. Just don't say anythin' that'll tick me off, or I'll . . ."

"Rap our knuckles with a ruler?" Jarod offered.

Margie scrunched up her mouth. "Make me mad, and your knuckles will be the least of your problems. Now go grab a booth."

They hobbled away on their heels, their ankles buckling every few steps.

Meanwhile, Margie spun toward me. "Ya wanna ask 'em what we wanted to know, or ya goin' to wait for Barbie?"

"Well, I suppose I can . . ."

The door squeaked open and in walked Barbie.

"Geez Louise," Margie muttered, which pretty much summed up my sentiments as well.

Barbie was dressed as Wonder Woman. And her Wonder Woman left the sexy French maid and the sleazy nurse looking like kindergarten angels.

She was greeted by a host of cat calls, not only from Guy and Jarod, but Laurel and Hardy, as well as Frankenstein and Dracula, who were seated at the counter. She bowed dramatically, her boobs dangerously close to falling out of her red and gold bustier.

After re-arranging "the girls," as she referred to them, she strutted over to us, her red, knee-high boots clicking against the floor like a warning. Which only seemed right. The women in town, I figured, deserved a chance to hide their young-uns and lock up their menfolk.

"Barbie," Margie said, "ya look so slutty I bet you'll get a Christmas card from the free clinic in Grand Forks."

No doubt about it, Barbie could have been mistaken for a superhero hooker in her hardly-there bustier, suntan-colored nylons, and blue, starred panties. The outfit left little to the imagination, and she appeared delighted by it.

As she fidgeted with her black wig and gold metallic bracelets and crown, she said to me, "What do you think?"

I couldn't speak.

She had no such trouble. Surveying my outfit, she advised, "You'd look a lot better if you'd stuff your bra and unbutton your shirt. You know, show some cleavage."

I folded my arms over my poor excuse for a bosom and stammered, "N-No . . . umm . . . that's okay."

She adjusted the cups of her bustier. "Emme, until today I never realized what a prude you were."

"I'm not a prude!" I made my case much louder than intended, leading everyone in the place to look my way. I yanked on Wonder Woman's arm and hissed, "I just don't have all the curves you do, so there's very little to show off."

"That's why you need to improvise."

I held back a sigh of frustration. Trust me, I wasn't jealous of Barbie's figure. She was much bigger—all over—than I ever wanted to be. Even so, it seemed unfair that I barely filled a "B" cup, while she was overflowing letters halfway down the alphabet.

"Guy and Jarod are over in that booth," Margie said, disrupting thoughts of padded bras and silicone implants. "If ya don't mind, maybe the two of ya could talk to 'em—get the answers to some of those other questions. I hafta get back to the kitchen."

"Not a problem," Barbie replied with an overabundance of enthusiasm. "Not a problem at all for Wonder Woman!" Margie and I did matching eye rolls. But Barbie didn't care. She merely turned on her high-heeled boots and sashayed across the room. I followed, and it wasn't long before I was so woozy from watching her hip action that I was desperate for a Dramamine.

Approaching the deputies, I saw their eyes on Barbie and drool on their chins. It was pathetic. Understandable. But pathetic. She slid in next to Guy, who couldn't take his eyes off her chest, while I sat down next to Jarod, who had no idea I was even there. Yep, for these two guys, at that moment in time, Barbie Jenson was indeed Wonder Woman.

"So," the superhero began, "how lucky are we to have the pleasure of your company twice in one day?" Her tone was spiked with derision, but the guys didn't pick up on it. Hell, I'm not even sure they heard her. They were in a trance. And if they didn't blink soon, I imagined we'd have to intervene, or they'd probably go blind.

Barbie smirked, fully aware of the powerful weapons she possessed. "I have another question for you two." She arched her back ever so slightly. "I should have asked it this morning, but I forgot." Guy's mouth hung open, and she reached over and chucked him under his chin in an effort to close it. "Have you searched the house Raleigh was renting here in town? The one Harvey used to live in?"

Both men continued to stare, while sweat beaded on their temples and their makeup ran down their cheeks in colorful streams. Barbie repeatedly waved her hands in front of their eyes, and at last they blinked, then rattled their heads, their long, nylon tresses bouncing. I believe they were starting to come around.

"Well . . . umm . . . we d-didn't" Guy stuttered, "search there, but some other f-folks from the office checked it out."

"Did they find anything of interest?" Barbie asked

Guy was trying to regain his composure. He messed with the balloons in his bra and tampered with his wig. And after that, he clasped his hands, twisting them out in front of him until his knuckles cracked. "No. Why? Were they . . . umm . . . supposed to?"

Barbie offered him a palms up. "Not necessarily." She did her best to convey innocence. She had a tough go of it, as you might expect. "Just wondering."

Jarod then telegraphed Guy a question, and Barbie intercepted it. "Hey! What's that about?" She demanded, glancing from one Halloween beauty to the other. "Come on. You two know something. Tell me."

Neither man spoke, so she inhaled deeply. "What's going on? What do you know that you haven't shared with me?"

One look at her chest, and they both were goners. But this time it was Jarod who spoke. And he could hardly get the words out fast enough. "When the guys from our office got to Raleigh's house, the back door was wide open. Jimmied, they said. Someone had rifled through all the cupboards and drawers inside. The closets too."

"Do you know what they were looking for?" Barbie asked.

"No," Jarod rushed to answer. "And we don't know if they found it either."

"Did you happen to find any papers on Raleigh's body?"

"Papers?" Jarod repeated.

"Yeah," I said, wanting to get in on the action. "Like car titles or IOUs. That sort of thing."

Barbie frowned. Okay, I wasn't exactly subtle. Then again, neither were her double-Ds.

"Nope," Guy answered. He pulled a napkin from the dispenser and dabbed his face. "We only found $200 in cash, his driver's license, and a credit card. All in his wallet."

He inspected his napkin and shook his head at the makeup he'd wiped off. "I don't know how you gals do it." He balled it up and tossed it across the table.

"So, nothing else? Not even pictures?" I asked.

"Nope," he said. "With Harvey dead, he had no family left."

"Nothing in his truck either?"

He looked at me suspiciously. "No. Why?"

Margie arrived with their supper. "Eat up, boys," she said, placing their food in front of them. "Holler if ya need anythin'."

Barbie slid from the booth, and I followed, only to circle around again. "Oh, just one more thing," I said, pushing my fake glasses up my nose, "Do you know if Wally and Raleigh were acquainted with each other when they both lived in Fargo?"

The deputies exchanged puzzled looks. "Wally and Raleigh? No, from what we understand, they never met until this fall, when Raleigh came up here to work beets. Why? What do you know?"

I shook my head and offhandedly replied, "Oh, nothing."

WHEN WE ENTERED THE KITCHEN, Margie rolled up the sleeves of her habit, letting them hang from her shoulders, and began stacking the dishwasher. "What did ya find out?"

Wonder Woman answered, "The killer was definitely after something. Raleigh's house was ransacked before the police got there."

"That must have been how the dog got out," I added.

"Trick or treat!" The three of us jumped, then spun around to find a medium-sized mermaid and a half-pint Cinderella standing on the threshold that separated the kitchen from the dining area. The little girls wore winter jackets over their costumes, along with knit hats, gloves, and snow boots. Nevertheless, because their jackets were open, we could see most of their costumes.

"Oh, for cute," I said. "Disney characters." While I hated dressing up for Halloween, I enjoyed seeing kids have fun with the holiday.

"I'm the Little Mermaid," the older girl informed us. She had to be around seven.

The younger one said nothing, choosing instead to stand on the side of her feet and stare at Barbie. "She's Wonder Woman," I told her. Right away, the little girl turned away. I'm not sure if it was because she was shy or completely overwhelmed by the wonder of Barbie's womanhood.

"So, where's your ma?" Margie asked the question as she plunked a large Hershey bar in each of the plastic, pumpkin baskets the girls held.

"She's out front, talking to Dinky," said the Little Mermaid. "Thanks, Margie."

"You're welcome, sweetie. I like your costumes."

The older girl beamed. "Little Mermaid's my favorite movie of all times."

"Yeah," Margie agreed, "it's a good one."

The girl peeked past Margie, at me. "What's she supposed to be?"

I stepped forward. "I'm a school girl. I have a backpack and everything." I spun around so she could see it.

"Hmm." She didn't appear impressed.

She grabbed her little sister's hand, and they headed out the room, the smaller one saying as they went, "That's not a costume."

"Shh."

Chapter Twenty-Seven

Margie shoved Dinky into the kitchen and onto one of the stools at the prep table. He wasn't in costume, but given Margie's stern expression, he probably wished he'd come as the Invisible Man.

"Why'd ya imply that Janice killed Raleigh Cummin's?" she asked.

Dinky was a big man with a wide jaw and tree-trunk limbs. He towered over Margie. Yet he cowered beneath her glare. "I didn't imply—"

"Hogwash!" Margie stabbed a finger at him. "Don't even try to deny it. Now, why'd ya do it?"

Before Margie pulled Dinky into the kitchen, the three of us had agreed to take a hardline approach with him. Barbie was certain he'd be more apt to tell us about the card game and the other players if we rattled him first. And the best way to do that, she concluded, was to scare him into believing he was in trouble for exaggerating the details of the argument he heard between Janice and Raleigh Cummings. In my opinion, it wasn't a great plan. Then again, what did I know about great plans? And since Margie didn't want us questioning Wally, and no one knew the whereabouts of the President, and Buddy and I had failed to uncover anything important during our visit with Hunter, we didn't have much choice but to question Dinky.

"Geez, Margie," he said, "it was just a joke. I didn't mean—"

Margie cut him off. "It was no joke, and ya know it."

Dinky stared at the floor. Granted, he could have up and walked away. None of us would have been able to stop him. Not even Wonder Woman. But he didn't. He just sat there, taking whatever Margie wanted to dish out. "I was wrong to say what I did," he finally confessed, his words barely audible.

"Ya bet ya were."

"I'm sorry." He whispered, his head bowed.

"Ya better be."

"Now," he continued, meekly raising his eyes, "can I get something to eat?"

Margie shook her head as if she didn't know what to do with the man. "Want the special?"

"No, not really. I don't like cabbage."

She surveyed the stove. "I have some Crouton Hot Dish. Wanna try that?"

"Yeah, that sounds good."

Margie grabbed a plate, filled it with hot dish, raw vegetables, and homemade dinner rolls, and delivered it to him. She then licked her lips, preparing for what I gathered was Round Two of his dressing down. Before uttering a single word, though, she got called to the dining area.

"Go ahead and take care of your customers," Barbie told her. "I'll handle things here."

Margie left the room, and Barbie eagerly pulled up the other stool and sat down next to Dinky. "So why'd you want to cause Janice trouble?"

Dinky asked for a glass of milk. I got it for him, then hung back.

He drank about half of it before he said, "Barbie, you know Janice. She ain't exactly a saint."

"And your point is?"

"Well, I asked her out a couple times." He dug into his food.

"And?"

He talked around the food in his mouth. "She laughed at me. Both times. Like I was some kind of slime ball or something. Hell, Hunter's no great catch, and she's been with him for years."

Barbie leaned closer, her boobs dangerously close to landing on his plate. "Let me make sure I understand. You asked Janice out.

She declined. That hurt your feelings. So you decided to implicate her in a murder?"

From the expression on his face, Dinky knew how despicable he sounded. "I wouldn't of let anything really bad happen to her. I would of spoken up before that."

"But in the meantime, you'd let her get questioned by the cops, huh?" She flung her arms into the air, her gold bracelets clanging.

Dinky pulled a bun apart and shrugged.

"That was a rotten thing to do."

He slathered it with butter, his eyes never veering from his task. "Oh, come on. No one takes what I say all that serious anyhow. Why are you getting so bent out of shape?"

"Dinky!"

"Well, I was sick of her acting like she was better than me. She's not, you know. I've got money, a farm, a nice truck."

"Dinky, you're a shithead." Barbie socked him in the shoulder.

"No, I'm not. I'm nice."

"And humble."

"Ha, ha." He swallowed a mouthful of bread. "You know what I mean."

"Yeah, but you can't force someone to like you."

"She's gone out with lots of guys. And I know for a fact she didn't like all of them. Besides, I didn't really care if she liked me or not. I just wanted her to—"

"Stop! I'm well aware of what you wanted. But, Dinky, that's downright creepy. She's old enough to be your mother." Barbie stretched her arms out in front of her. "See? Even the thought of it is giving me the heebie jeebies."

Dinky snorted. "Since when did you become such a spoilsport? Don't exactly fit considering that outfit you're almost wearing."

She slapped his arm. "There's nothing wrong with my costume. It's Halloween, for God sake." She tugged on her bustier. It was sliding dangerously low again.

Margie trudged back into the kitchen, her arms full of dirty dishes. "I think we're almost done out there." She emptied the dishes into the sink, and I began rinsing them, then stacking them in the dishwasher.

"Well," Barbie said, rising from her stool, "I wanted to wait for you before asking him about last weekend's poker game."

Dinky jerked, like he'd been shocked. "We don't talk about our games."

Sister Margie leaned over his shoulder. "You oughtta talk about this one, son. Bein' one of your players got murdered, and the rest of ya are suspects in the crime, it'd be the smart thin' to do."

"But that can't be. Buddy wasn't even—"

"Wait right there!" With him sitting on a stool and Margie standing about as close to him as she could get, they were practically nose to nose. "We aren't referrin' to Buddy. He didn't kill Raleigh. He didn't have near the motive that the players in that game did."

Dinky placed one of his big bear paws on the metal table. "Now just a minute, Margie. I didn't kill Raleigh Cummings. And neither did Biggie." He glanced from Margie to Barbie and then to me. "We had no reason to kill him."

Barbie was right. He was shook. "You owed him money," she said.

Dinky huffed. "Biggie only lost a couple hundred, and it was just eight grand for me. That's not all that much. I've lost way more and never killed anyone to keep from paying it."

I stepped in next to him, clutching one of my school-girl braids. "So you paid Raleigh?" The three of us now formed a semi-circle around the guy—a semi-circle of outlandishly dressed interrogators.

Dinky's shoulders slumped. "I didn't get a chance. I didn't have that much cash on me, and he wanted it all at once, in one lump sum. So I told him I'd pay him the following week, after I went to the bank."

I pushed my glasses up my nose. "But you still hadn't done so by the time he saw you in the city office on Tuesday afternoon."

Dinky leveled his gaze at me, suspicion filling his eyes. "How did you find out about that?" He answered his own question. "Janice told you, right?" He crimped his forehead. "She's a real piece of work."

Barbie slapped the metal table, and Dinky almost fell off his stool. "Yeah, she's a jerk for telling us that you and Raleigh argued, but you're a stand-up guy for incriminating her in a murder because she wouldn't put out."

It was Margie's turn to shake her head. "Dinky, you're better than that."

"I didn't kill Raleigh Cummings."

She patted his shoulder. "I know you didn't, son. But ya hafta tell us what happened, so we can figure out who did."

Dinky sat perfectly still, staring at the table. "I only took my time getting the money because he was such an asshole." He flinched, seemingly embarrassed about swearing in front of a nun. It actually took a minute for the reality of the situation to register. "From the start of the game, he gloated. It was enough to make me puke."

"Why'd you invite him to play in the first place?" I asked.

He wiggled around on the stool, the metal legs squeaking beneath his weight. "Well . . . umm . . . he said he wasn't much of a card player, but he'd like to try his luck if we ever got a game together."

Barbie chuckled, her fists on her blue-pantied hips. "He hustled you! You asked him to play because you thought he'd be easy pickings. But he turned out to be a card shark."

He shot Barbie a defiant look. "Hunter was pretty sure he was cheating. He just couldn't figure out how. None of us could."

"So he suckered you," I repeated. "And naturally that made you mad, which, in turn, led you to string him along about getting paid."

"But I did get him his money. I went to the bank after our shift ended on Wednesday. You can even check. Then I went looking for him. But I couldn't find him anywhere."

The questions were forming quickly in my mind now. "Did you stop by his house?"

"I drove by Wednesday afternoon and again that night, but his truck wasn't in the driveway, and he doesn't have a garage, so I knew he wasn't home."

Barbie muttered, "Yeah, by that time, his truck was already hidden down by the river."

"What was that?" Dinky was genuinely confused, which said a lot.

"Nothing," Barbie replied. "Nothing important."

I pressed on. "Dinky, at the end of the game, did any of you guys happen to give Raleigh IOUs or anything else to secure payment of your debts?"

He reared back. "How'd you know?"

"Know what?"

"That he made us sign IOUs."

"Well, you said he wasn't a friendly guy."

"He was an asshole."

"Yeah, you might have mentioned that."

He set his jaw. His teeth were clenched. "No one around here makes anyone sign IOUs. We play on the honor system. And we've never had any trouble."

"But he—"

"Had all of us sign them. All of us except Biggie. He paid him off right then and there."

I leaned to the side, resting my forearm on the table. "Has the sheriff talked to you?"

Dinky licked his teeth with his tongue. His mouth was getting dry. "No. Why would he?"

Barbie stepped up. "Dinky, you lost a fair amount of money to Raleigh. He made you sign an IOU, which he obviously planned to keep until he got paid. But he never got paid. Yet the IOU is gone."

"What?" Again Dinky was confused "What makes you say that?"

Barbie sighed. "If your IOU had been on his body or in the house or pickup, the police would have found it and asked you about it, don't you think?"

Dinky's face turned pale, and he quickly began pointing fingers. "Like I said, the other guys signed IOUs too. And a couple of them for a lot more money than mine. Besides, I tried to pay him. I just couldn't find him."

"We believe ya." Sister Margie patted his shoulder. "And we don't want ya or anyone else gettin' into trouble over this. No sir-ree. We just wanna make sure the guilty person is caught. That's why we need your help."

"Well . . . umm . . . are you sure Buddy didn't do it?" Dinky immediately shirked away. Apparently Margie's loyalty to family was well known and respected—or feared—as the case may be. "I get that you don't want it to be him," he added, "but—"

"Dinky," I said, stepping between the two of them before Margie belted him. "If Buddy was the killer, the IOUs wouldn't have disappeared. Remember, he didn't play cards with you guys that night."

We let him mull that over before Barbie asked him again about the game. "Was it filled with tension? How about arguing? Did it get physical?"

Dinky pushed his plate aside. I guess there was no point in pretending he could eat. He was too upset. "Well, like I told you already, none of us appreciated the way Cummings was acting. And Hunter made a bunch of comments about how he was probably cheating. But Cummings just kept saying over and over, 'If you think I'm cheating, show everyone how I'm doing it. Otherwise, shut up and play, little man.' Yeah, he called him 'little man.' And Hunter didn't like that one bit." He picked up his fork, only to set it down again. "This is making me nervous, you know. We don't usually talk about our poker games."

"Usually one of your players isn't murdered," I replied. "What's more, I'm sure the police will be talking to you soon enough."

He gulped some milk. "Wall-eye was jumpy the whole time he was there. I don't know why he even came. He never played with us before. And he really sucks at cards." He glimpsed at Margie. "Sorry, but he does."

"Who invited him?" I asked.

"No one. He just showed up. He must have overheard me talking to Cummings about it after one of our shifts. But it kind of worked out okay since Biggie wanted to leave. He said he was afraid he'd kill Cummings if he stuck—" Dinky's eyes got big. "He . . . umm . . . didn't really mean that, you know."

I nodded. "What about the President? What was he like during the game?"

"Well, like I said, the President got his clock cleaned. Which was odd since he's a decent player. A real blowhard, but a decent card player." He rolled his eyes toward the top of his head, as if he could actually read what was on his mind. "Of course if Cummings was cheating, that would explain it. Although . . ."

I waited for him to finish his thought. And when he didn't, I urged him along. "Although what?"

He slumped forward against the table. "I don't know for sure. But there seemed to be something weird going on between Cummings and the President. Like they knew each other or something."

"Huh?" Margie grunted. "Raleigh and the President? Are you sure?"

"Yeah." He sat straight up again. "See, we were already playing by the time the President showed up. And when he saw Cummings, he acted like he wanted to leave right away. But Cummings kept saying things like, 'Oh, come on, you don't want to leave. If you do, we'll have to talk about you. And you wouldn't like that.' And then he'd laugh."

"Did you ask the President about it? Did you ask if they knew each other?"

"Yeah. Afterwards. He said he'd never met the guy before. But he'd heard him over the farm radio a few times, so he knew he was a jerk. That's why he considered leaving. But then he decided what the hell."

"Trick or treat!" The greeting came from the front door of the café, leading Margie to grab her candy bowl and head that way with me following along.

"Hi, guys," Margie called to an eclectic group of children. There was a pirate, an angel, a cowboy, and a panda. With their winter wear under their outfits, the pirate, angel, and cowboy were a little chubby. But the panda outfit, consisting of a fur hat and suit, along with black boots and mittens, was perfect for hiding extra layers of clothing. "Are ya havin' fun?" Margie dropped giant Hershey bars into their baskets.

"Yeah, Margie," the cowboy answered, a wide, toothless grin parting his freckled face, "this is my most favorite day of the year."

"Hey," his buddy, the pirate, shouted at me, "what are you supposed to be?"

I shrugged, somewhat leery after the reaction I'd gotten from the Disney characters. "I'm . . . umm . . . a school girl. I have a backpack and everything." I made a quarter turn, just in case they truly wanted to see the whole costume. They didn't. None of them even said a word until the angel suggested they leave.

"My mom's walking us around," she told Margie. "She's waiting outside. She told us she thought we'd probably like to come in here all by ourselves. But I think she just wanted to sneak a cigarette." She bobbed her head, her tin-foil halo waving up and down. "She doesn't think we know. But we all do. Even dad."

And with that the cowboy opened the door, and the panda and angel shuffled out, followed by the pirate, who said to his friend as he passed, "School girl? Lame."

"Yeah," the cowboy agreed, "laaame."

Part Four

Gobble It Up Before Anyone Can Comment

Chapter Twenty-Eight

"WELL, LADIES," MARGIE SAID as she locked the door to the café, "let's go solve this case." She then headed down the hallway to the "V" with Barbie and me trailing after her. The three of us looked like the personification of a bad joke: "A nun, a school girl, and Wonder Woman walked into a bar . . ."

The place was already crowded with people, most in costume, although Dinky, his brother, and a few other guys were in street clothes, sitting at a table in the back corner, shaking dice. A clown sat at the bar, his face hidden behind a white rubber mask, and a woman stood on the other side of the room, dressed as a clump of grapes. She wore a green leotard and tights, with purple balloons clustered around her torso. She was talking to a hairy gorilla. He was drinking through a long bendable straw. Guy and Jarod were there too, hitting on Lucy and Ethel. Laurel and Hardy didn't seem to care. They were shooting pool.

The bar was decorated in orange streamers with black balloons. And it was noisy. Lots of visiting and laughing, all punctuated by music. At present, "The Monster Mash" blared as Frankenstein and Dracula performed some kind of bump and grind on the small dance floor.

The place was dimly lit, the neon beer signs on the wood-paneled walls and the light above the pool table providing the bulk of illumination. In spite of that, everyone noticed when Wonder Woman walked in. In fact, the gorilla jerked his head so fast his long straw got away from him and burst one of the grape lady's balloons. Barbie was oblivious to it all. At least she said nothing as

Margie snagged a table behind the clown and assigned us each a seat.

We all ordered beers, and about the same time as they arrived, so did Janice, drink in hand, purse hanging from her shoulder. She was dressed as a cheerleader, an orange pullover sweater sporting the letter "H" on her chest, her name on one sleeve, and the year 1974 on the other. Her skirt was black, pleated, and short, while the undies she flashed were orange-and-white striped. The outfit was complete with black knee highs and black-and-white tennis shoes. Oh, yeah, she also carried orange and black pom-poms. They were currently tucked under her arm.

"Janice," Barbie hollered, "I can't believe you can still fit in that thing."

Janice plopped down between Barbie and me, across from Margie. She placed her glass on the table, her pom-poms on her lap, and her shoulder bag on the back of her chair. "Why? Can't you fit into yours?"

Barbie chuckled. "The knee highs maybe."

"Huh? You're almost ten years younger than me. Surely you haven't gained that—"

"Enough!" Barbie yelled.

"I like wearing this outfit," Janice nevertheless continued. "It brings back some good memories."

"Good memories?" Barbie wrinkled her brow. "You got kicked off the cheerleading squad for inappropriate behavior."

"Exactly." Janice fluttered her gunked-up, spider-like eyelashes. "And that behavior has provided some very good memories."

Barbie snorted. "Yeah, well, from what I recall, your squad was pretty promiscuous."

"No, we weren't." Janice pretended to be offended. "And if you aren't careful, I'll tell Julie Lindegard you said that. She just came in. She's right over there. The one dressed like a lunchroom lady."

Barbie scanned the room, caught Julie's eyes, and waved. "Well, I didn't mean Julie. She wasn't like that." She playfully tapped her finger against the side of her head. "Come to think of it, you were the only wanton hussy in that group."

"Yeah, well, what can I say?" Janice twisted away to hack up a lung.

"She wrecked Hallock's Homecoming that year too," Barbie shouted at me, trying to be heard over all the coughing. "It's still a mainstay of bar talk. So I suppose I should tell you the story."

Janice didn't seem to care. While Barbie spoke, she checked the fallout of her coughing jag in the tiny mirror of her compact, retrieved from her big bag.

"The royalty included two of the nicest girls you'd ever want to meet," Barbie informed me, "as well as—"

"Me!" Janice dropped the compact to the table and snatched her pom-poms from her lap, shaking them in the air.

Barbie waved her hand dismissively at her while explaining for my benefit, "The coronation was outside, under the lights, at half-time of the football game. I remember it well because I was in fourth grade so Homecoming was a big deal to me and my friends. Oh, yeah, and because thanks to her"—she bent her thumb toward Janice—"it left an indelible impression on my psyche." Janice tipped her drink toward Barbie, as if toasting what she had done.

Ignoring her, Barbie continued. "Each queen candidate and her escort took to the field in a fancy Cadillac. Spectators filled the stands, and all the players on the team lined up along the fifty-yard line. The Cadillacs came to a stop, and the first door opened, allowing Deb and her escort to step onto the field. Next, Diane and her escort exited the second car. But when the door to the third car opened, Janice and her escort fell out backwards onto the ground. "It was quite a sight. Her escort had lost his pants, and Janice was missing pretty much everything but her Tiera."

Janice lifted a finger. "I had my panties on."

"Yeah," Barbie groaned, "around your ankles."

Janice snickered, and Barbie continued. "The crowd was aghast, and the band fizzled, except for two guys in the trombone section who insisted on playing 'The Stripper' until the band director confiscated their instruments.

"That wasn't the end of it either," Barbie added. "My mother refused to let me go to any more games until my sophomore year. And to this day, I get nauseated when I watch football. I'm always sick to my stomach by halftime of any Vikings' game."

Margie flicked Barbie in the shoulder. "That might not have anythin' to do with those bad memories. The Vikin's aren't that good. Lots of people get nauseous watchin' them."

Barbie shrugged. "It also was the end of half-time coronations. Now they take place under the lights of the school cafeteria, with the principal and janitor overseeing everything."

Janice set her drink on the table. It was pinkish-orange. Probably a tequila sunrise. "That was real entertaining and all, Barbie. But I wanna hear about Buddy. I'm guessing you know all about what happened. So tell me, did he really kill Raleigh Cummings?" Barbie elbowed her, then motioned toward Margie, leading Janice to add, "Not that I believe for a minute he did it. I was just wondering because he got into that fight with him at the Caribou. And he's a hot head. And . . . well . . . whether you want to admit it or not, Margie, your family does seem to be prone to violence, considering what happened a few months back and all."

Barbie grabbed Margie's forearm just in case she got the urge to crawl over the table and pound Janice senseless. I think the nun habit would have slowed her down enough for Janice to make an escape. But better safe than sorry.

"Buddy didn't kill anyone," Barbie proclaimed, her knuckles turning white. "And I'm sure the whole mess will get straightened out very soon." She went on to add in a conspiratorial tone, "At any rate, I'd much rather get the scoop on what happened last Saturday night. I heard you and Raleigh Cummings were making out in the Eagles, practically right under Hunter's nose. What gives?" Barbie was a smart lady. For more than one reason, it was a good idea for her to steer the conversation away from Margie's family and toward the incident in the Eagles.

Janice tapped her long red fingernails against her teeth. "Well, it's sorta her fault." She pointed a finger at Margie.

"My fault?" Margie sank against the back of her chair, and Barbie slowly released her grip on her arm.

"Yeah, because of all your talk about broadening your horizons, I decided to do the same. I told Hunter we needed to buy an RV, so we could travel the country. See some stuff. Learn a few things." She fiddled with the "H" on her chest, and I soon found myself mulling over "H" words. Hallock, harlot, hussy, ho.

"And?"

"And to raise the money for the motorhome I picked out, I promised to stop playing bingo, and Hunter agreed to quit poker."

Barbie slammed her bottle on the table, foam spilling over the top. "I can't believe you gave up bingo!"

Janice wiggled around on her chair. "I didn't exactly say I did. But that's not the point. Hunter agreed to save his money, and he didn't. I got so mad at him I couldn't see straight."

"Oh, so that explains why you were kissing some other guy," Barbie said, tongue in cheek. "You couldn't see straight. And here I thought you were just being trampy."

Janice seemed oblivious to the remark. "I really wanted to hurt him. That's why I did what I did with Raleigh right there in the Eagles. I wanted Hunter to feel bad. He knew how much I wanted to go and visit the Corn Palace in South Dakota, not to mention the Lennon Sisters in Branson and, of course, Graceland."

"So," Margie said, "ya got even with him by doin' the nasty with the guy who took his money." It was weird to hear a nun—even a pretend nun—talk about "doin' the nasty."

"I didn't have sex with him . . . in the bar. Once we got into his pickup, though—"

"Stop!" Barbie held her hands high in protest, "I don't want to hear about it."

I raised an eye brow at her.

"Okay, Emme, you're right. Everyone's got their limits."

Janice zig-zagged her finger in front of Barbie, underscoring her costume. "Yeah, right, like you're Miss Goody Two Shoes."

"It's Halloween, for Pete's sake," Barbie moaned. "Why can't anyone understand that?"

"So," Margie said, dismissing both Barbie and Janice with a toss of her veil, "did Hunter tell ya anythin' about that poker game?"

"No, not really." Janice stopped as if to reconsider. "Well, I guess he did say something about Raleigh cheating. But I was too mad at him to listen to any of the details."

"How about Raleigh? Did he talk to ya about the game?"

"Why do you ask?"

Margie shoved the sleeves of her habit up her arms and folded her hands, placing them on the table in front of her. "Like we said, we don't believe Buddy killed the man."

Janice, in turn, crossed her hands over her heart like the ingénue in a bad melodrama. "But you think Hunter did?"

"We don't know what to think," Barbie answered.

"Well, Hunter couldn't have done it. Not with his respiratory problems."

"Huh?"

Janice sipped her drink. "Raleigh was killed in a fight of some kind, right? At least that's what I heard. But Hunter has really bad lungs from smoking all these years, so he can't fight." She leaned in and whispered, "He can't do much of anything, if you get my drift." She put her fingers over her lips. "Oops, I shouldn't of said that. Well, I guess that's what he gets for making me so mad."

Barbie raised her brows. "I take it you're still harboring ill will."

Janice took another sip, this time through her straw. "A little, I guess." She paused. "Okay, the truth is I've barely spoken to him since last Saturday morning, when I found out. Can you believe it? Five thousand dollars? And he thinks he can just waltz right back into my house. No way. He can stay in that disgusting trailer of his for a while. Maybe then he'll learn his lesson."

"Yeah," Barbie said, "I'd say you're still upset."

"I can't help it. And on top of everything else, he now watches me like a hawk. It's actually kind of scary. It's gotten so I can hardly—"

"Date other men," Barbie finished for her.

"Very funny." Janice slapped Barbie on the shoulder. "I only spent two nights with Raleigh." She thought about that. "Yeah, Saturday and Sunday. Then we broke up." She leaned in. "Not to speak bad of the dead, but he was a jerk."

"In what way?" Barbie asked.

"He played the field." Janice nodded her head to emphasize the seriousness of the charge, while the rest of us sat there with our mouths hanging open. "When I got off work on Monday," she said, "I drove to his house, hoping we might have a little fun before he went to work. But he wasn't there, so I ran up to the Caribou to see if he was eating supper or whatnot. And sure enough he was there. Only he wasn't eating supper. He was doing whatnot with some skank from Lake Bronson in the backseat of her car." She sipped her drink. "Well, I gave him a piece of my mind. And you know what he did? He laughed! And called me an old hag! I got so mad I could of . . ." She stopped herself, her face turning red.

"What a jerk," she mumbled after taking another sip from her glass. "On Tuesday afternoon he actually had the nerve to come into the office and yell at me because his garbage bag got ripped open." She laid her straw on the table. "Well, I told him it wasn't my fault. And it certainly wasn't the bag. Those bags are good. Anderson Sanitation only sells the best. I know that for a fact. So I told him that damn little mutt of his probably did it."

I cleared my throat. "Was his dog a small white male?"

"Yeah," Janice muttered. "Mean little shit. Always trying to bite my ankles."

Barbie laughed. "Janice, it's hard to get too upset about Raleigh two-timing you, considering that's exactly what you were doing to Hunter."

Janice shook her head. "It wasn't the same thing at all. Hunter and I broke up Saturday morning, after I found out about the poker game." She stopped. "Well, okay, maybe we didn't officially break up. But we were definitely on a break. Still are." She finished her drink. "Besides, it's different for me." She glanced around the room, then leaned in and whispered, "I have needs. And like I said, Hunter can't . . . umm . . . perform."

Margie shook her head and chugged the rest of her beer, evidently attempting to drown those images. "Janice," she said afterward, "did Raleigh ever say anything to you about the President."

"Why?" Janice scrounged around the bottom of her bag until she found a tube of lipstick and blindly applied it to her lips, coloring just a bit outside the lines. It didn't matter. It wasn't as if her lipstick was the only issue with her appearance. Remember, she was wearing a forty-year-old cheerleading uniform. And the more she drank the more her beehive hairdo tipped to the side. After a while, we all were tilting our heads whenever we talked to her, like we were looking at the Leaning Tower of Pisa.

"Come on, Janice," Margie complained. "This is important, particularly since the President also lost money to Raleigh in that poker game."

"Do you think he killed him?" The idea seemed to intrigue her.

"I don't know." Margie was losing her patience. She'd always found Janice amusing. But she seemed to have gotten her fill of her tonight.

"Well, believe it or not," Janice said, "he knew the President from someplace else."

With our heads cocked at the same angle, we all replied in unison, "Really?"

"Yeah. In fact, he kept saying things like, 'If you only knew what I know about that guy.' But he wouldn't explain himself."

"And you didn't pursue it?"

"Margie, dear, it wasn't the main thing on my mind, if you catch my drift." She wiggled her tadpole eyebrows, and for a second, I was afraid they might actually crawl right off her face. "At any rate, I hope the police take a close look at the guy. He's kind of creepy. And I'd much rather have him be the murderer than Buddy." She offered Margie a friendly smile.

Then she put a hand on Barbie's shoulder. "Hey, wanna go to the bathroom with me?"

"What?"

"I hafta tinkle, but you-know-who is watching me. And I don't want him following me into the john."

"Where is he?"

Janice bobbed her head to the right. "Over there at the bar."

Leaving discretion far behind, the three of us—the nun, Wonder Woman, and the pathetic-looking school girl—craned our necks and peered past the clown, another guy wearing hospital scrubs, and one dressed like a referee to find Hunter Carlson. He was a hockey goalie, in full gear minus the skates and helmet. He stared at Janice but still managed to visit with the hockey player seated alongside him.

"He dresses up like that every year, doesn't he?" Barbie said.

Janice sighed. "Yeah. Any excuse to wear his old uniform and relive his glory days. I'm so sick of hearing how he single-handedly won this game or that. Like I always tell him, it's been four decades. Move on!"

Yep, that's what the nearly sixty-year-old woman in her high school cheerleading uniform said.

Chapter Twenty-Nine

JANICE HAD CONNED ME into going to the bathroom with her. And when I returned to our table, Wonder Woman was out on the dance floor, howling at the moon to "Werewolves of London.." Ed, the deputy, was her partner. He was dressed in regular clothes, obviously pretending to be an off-duty deputy sheriff.

I scoped out the rest of the place and discovered that Hunter was still at the far end of the bar, scanning the room. Apparently he couldn't find Janice. I also noticed that the clown was watching me and wasn't being very discreet about it. In all fairness, though, it's probably tough to be discreet while dressed as a clown.

"Eh," Margie said, grabbing the chair next to mine. She'd been in the café. "I just ran into Julie Lindegard, and she told me a good joke. Wanna hear it?" Margie wasn't a very good joke teller, so I cringed whenever she asked me that question.

"Well," she began, not waiting for me to answer one way or the other, which was probably just as well. "See, Ole was in the Olympics, and on the day of the finals, a reporter came up to him and said, 'So I see you're a pole vaulter?' And Ole replied, 'No, you're wrong on both counts. I'm not a Pole, and my name's not Valter.'"

Margie slapped the table. "Now I don't care who ya are. That there was funny!"

Even if Margie's delivery was weak, her enthusiasm was strong, and I couldn't help but smile—while peeking at the clown again. He wasn't watching me anymore. He was scarfing down food, his movements looking somewhat familiar.

"Hey, Margie, do you know who the clown is?" I angled my head toward the bar.

"Nope." She didn't even give him so much as a glance.

"What's he eating? He's wolfing it down like he hasn't had supper in a month."

She lifted her head in his direction. "Oh, that's Creamy Chow Mein Hot Dish. It's Jessica York's recipe. I always make a little somethin' that the bartender can serve in here durin' the party. But this year I decided to change things up a bit. So I made that and somethin' called Cheesy Chicken and Rice Hot Dish."

"Are they any good?"

"What?" Her eyes got big, and she grabbed my wrist.

Of course I was well aware that Margie was sensitive about her cooking, especially her hot dish. But I hadn't criticized her or them. I'd merely asked a question. So squeezing my hand until it tingled seemed like a bit of an overreaction.

"It's Vern and Vivian," she whispered, her face contorted. "They just walked in. They're at the other end of the bar."

"So?"

"They don't look good. They're not even in costume."

"What?" I pulled my hand free.

"They're not in costume," she repeated, only louder, as if increased volume alone would help me make sense of what she'd said.

"So?"

"They always wear costumes to this party."

She was beginning to irritate me. "Maybe they didn't want to get dressed up this year. I sure didn't." She shook her head, so I added. "They just became grandparents. Maybe they didn't have time to pull anything together."

"No, that can't be. Every year Vivian makes an elaborate costume. See, while Barbie's all about shockin' folks, Vivian goes for elegance. Last year she dressed as Cinderella. An older version, grant ya. But she looked spectacular. She won first prize. And this year's costume was supposedly even better. She said she finished it before Labor Day."

"And?"

"And ever since Vern's accident, he's worn the same costume. People have come to expect it of him. It's a pirate suit, complete with a hook for his missin' arm and everythin'. Vivian says it's in bad taste. But Vern insists it doesn't matter because it's Halloween."

I shifted my gaze to the other side of the room. Vivian and Vern stood alone at the bar, just down from Hunter. He was drinking a beer, while she was tossing back a dark cocktail. Both wore jeans and hooded sweatshirts. His was topped with a tan Carhartt jacket, and hers, a brown corduroy barn coat.

Vivian was more casual looking than I'd ever seen her, but I didn't spot anything "wrong," so I twisted back around and grabbed my own drink. At the same time, Margie seized my hand yet again, practically knocking the bottle out of it. "Don't look now," she mumbled, "but she's headed our way."

Margie abruptly looked straight ahead. "Oh, hi, Vivian." She pasted on a fake smile, "I didn't know ya were here." She patted the back of the empty chair between us. "Sit down. Take a load off."

Vivian placed two identical drinks on the table, one of them already half gone. "What a day!" She sat down and bobbed her head at me by way of hello. After that, she sucked down the rest of her partial drink, pushed the empty glass aside, and slid the full one in front of her.

Margie gawked at her as if she had no idea who she was. And now that I saw her up close, I could appreciate her confusion.

In addition to her casual attire and insatiable thrust, Vivian's blonde hair, normally twisted into a perfect French roll, was parted in a variety of directions and hanging haphazardly around her shoulders. Her eyes, meticulously lined and colored any other day, were puffy and merely smudged with makeup. And her lips? Well . . .

"Now, Vivian," Margie began, "don't take this the wrong way, but what in the heck happened to ya?"

Vivian gulped her drink, a little of it dribbling down her chin. "I 'ad a collagen treatment yesterday. I guess my lips are still numb."

"And swollen," Margie added. "They look like they've been stung by a colony of bees."

"Yah, well, I might of asked 'em to plump 'em up a little extra. Ya see, last time they deflated so fast that—"

"Oh, yah," Margie interrupted her to say, "I hate when my lips deflate." She rolled her eyes.

Vivian's eyes pooled with tears. "Margie, don't go and get after me. I don't think I can 'andle it today or forever for that matter."

"Sorry. I was only jokin' about your lips."

"And my forehead too."

"Your forehead?"

"Yah, I had 'em stick my forehead with some of those botex injections. Now I can't even raise my eyebrows." She seemed to give it a go but to no avail. Which led to more tears. "See?" She sniffed. "I can't feel my hair or anythin'."

"Is that such a bad thing?" Margie asked. "Do ya really need to feel your hair?"

Vivian glared at Margie. "Well, of course, ya do!" She gave her sister the once over. "Unless you're willin' to wear it plain, like ya do." She sniffed. "By the way there, Margie, you're sixty years old. It's time ya lose the ponytail."

Ouch! That had to hurt.

I expected Margie to retaliate with a verbal slam of her own. But she simply patted her sister's back and said, "There, there." Then, as if she suddenly got possessed by the devil, she added, "So why exactly does your hair look like ya just made your way through a blizzard?"

Vivian's face was expressionless except for the tears dripping down her cheeks. "Is it really all that bad? Or are ya just askin' a question? Like, oh, is that a new hairdo ya got goin' there, Vivian? The wind-blown look or somethin' else from nature?"

I'm not sure if Margie understood her or not. But she smartly refrained from engaging her anymore on the subject of hair. "Vivian," she said instead, "why don't ya just calm down there."

"Yah, calm down there," her sister mimicked. "Sure, ya can say that. Ya can talk 'til the cows turn blue in the face. Ya aren't all stiff and swollen. And that isn't even the worst of it.

"What do ya mean? Did ya have some other work done?" It was Margie's turn to look Vivian over.

"No, no." Vivian waved her away. "But somethin' else was sure as heck done to me."

"What are ya talkin' about?"

Vivian dropped her gaze, allowing a few of her tears to fall on the table. "It's the kids. Little Val and Wally and baby Brian." She raised her eyes again. "That's what they named him, don't ya know. Brian, with the regular spellin'." She shook her head. "I suggested Brian with a 'Y,' but Little Val said that was too 'pretentious.' Like a baby could be pretentious." It seemed as if she wanted to frown. "But ya know how Little Val can be. And ya know me. Never one to interfere. So that's what it is. Brian with the regular spellin'." She again lowered her eyes, and another tear plopped onto the table.

"Vivian, Brian's a nice name," Margie assured her. "Even if it's spelled the regular way. It certainly isn't anythin' to cry over."

"I'm not cryin' about that." She paused. "Well, okay, I might be cryin' about that a little but not too much anyways."

"And your face will relax in another day or two. Then you'll be as pretty as ever."

Vivian sniffled. "Are ya sayin' I'm not pretty now. 'Cause if ya are, Margie, that wouldn't be very nice in the least considerin' my bad day and then, too, what will be the bad rest of my life."

Margie closed her eyes, leaned her head back, and expelled a long, slow breath. "Vivian, I'm only sayin' that things sure as heck aren't as bleak as you're makin' them out to be."

Her sister's head shot up. "Oh, now I'm bein' overly dramatic, am I? Well, ya don't know the half of the whole story."

Margie glanced at me before returning her gaze to her sister. "Vivian, what else is goin' on then?"

Vivian didn't answer, and Margie and I exchanged a look of understanding. We both suspected the same thing. Vivian had somehow found out about Wally.

I scooted back my chair. "I can leave if you two need to be alone."

"No!" Margie shouted, evidently not keen about going one-on-one with her sister. "Ya might be able to help."

"Yah," Vivian concurred, "I suppose it's possible ya might be some help."

Not exactly a ringing endorsement. Nevertheless, I pulled my chair back to the table.

"Now, Vivian," Margie said, "tell us what's really got ya so upset?"

Vivian sipped her drink. "Well, ya see, earlier today, Wally called us over to the house. So of course we went, bein' asked and all. And we found Little Val cryin' like a stopped up faucet. She was goin' on about Wally losin' money in a poker game and sneakin' it out of their savin's after not gamblin' and promisin' the same."

"And?" Margie apparently believed it was best for Vivian to proceed at her own pace, which meant waiting while she drank most of her drink.

"And," she repeated while dabbing what had dribbled down her chin, "I guess Wally was frustrated with work and harvest and the baby and all and feelin' like he was burnin' the midnight oil at both ends, and he just couldn't take it. So, anyways, he got himself mixed up in a poker game. And ya know with his gamblin' problem, he shouldn't be in a card game with a ten-foot pole. No, sir-ree. Not him. And not with the winner gettin' murdered. And Buddy bein' arrested. And the sheriff questionin' Wally this mornin'."

Margie patted her sister's hand. "Vivian, I know all about that poker game. And we're lookin' into Raleigh Cummin's death. We don't think Buddy killed him. And we certainly don't believe Wally did it either. But someone connected to that card game is more than likely guilty. And we hafta figure out who. And the sooner the better. We gotta get Buddy out of jail there."

Vivian nodded. "Yah, it makes me sick to think about him in jail, practically like a prisoner or somethin'. Ya know he can't stand that."

"I know, Vivian. I know."

"So, do ya have any leads as to the real killer?" She swung her attention over to me. "Or can ya only catch folks who are related to us?"

"Huh?" I slouched against the back of my chair, stunned.

"Vivian!" Margie scolded.

And Vivian cried, "I'm sorry." The tears again fell like waterworks. "I didn't m-mean that." She blew her nose with a napkin she pulled from the dispenser in the middle of the table. "I'm just so upset about everythin' that I don't know what end is right." Her eyes veered from me to her glass, where they remained until she picked it up, tipped it back, and finished off her drink.

"It's okay," I assured her. While I wasn't shocked that she didn't care for me, I was astounded she'd had the nerve to tell me. According to Barbie, Scandinavians didn't do that kind of thing. "I can't imagine how awful you feel, Vivian. And for what it's worth, I truly am sorry about what happened the last time I was here."

Vivian waved her hand, each finger adorned with a tasteful ring and a neatly manicured nail, contradicting everything else about the woman's current appearance. "No, no. I suppose ya only did what ya had to do."

"Well, I'd really like to make it up to you and everyone else by finding out what really happened to Raleigh Cummings."

She regarded me as if I were a dunce. "He was murdered, Emerald."

"Yeah." I glanced at Margie, silently asking, *Is she for real?*

Apparently sensing I'd had just about enough of the fruitcake known as her sister, Vivian Olson, Margie stepped in. "Vivian, would ya be willin' to answer some questions that might lead us to the killer?"

Vivian stared at her, an earnest look in her eyes. "Of course, though I didn't know that Raleigh Cummin's guy."

"But ya did talk to Wally this afternoon," Margie said. "And it's important for us to know if he said anythin' about the poker game or payin' Cummin's the money he owed."

Vivian gazed off into the distance, clearly working to retrieve that conversation from her mind—not an easy job, even if she hadn't been drinking. "No . . . um . . . I don't believe he paid the man, though he did say somethin' about lookin' for him in Hallock there Wednesday afternoon, while gettin' that ice cream cone for Little Val's cravin's."

"Huh? Did ya just say that Wally admitted he was in Hallock Wednesday afternoon?" See? Even Margie had trouble making sense of her sister.

But that didn't stop Vivian from talking. "Well, of course. The Reverend Pearson came by to visit Little Val, bein' the nice man he is and givin' Wally a chance to run there to Hallock, knowin' Little Val likes her cones. But he had to get back to church for choir practice in thirty minutes. And believe me the Reverend's choir needs all the practice it can get. Givin' Wally not much time to go and come back.

"Oh, for sure," she went on to say, "Little Val had some strong cravin's durin' her pregnancy, ice cream bein' the worst, although nothin's wrong with that in moderation. At least that's what I always say to those that will listen. She also loved that Beef Stroganoff Hot Dish, eatin' it almost every day, sometimes for breakfast as well as dinner and supper, with me warnin' Wally he might hafta order a whole side of beef from Ed over there at the Farmer Store." She crunched on an ice cube from her glass.

"Anyways, she got the recipe from Margie, who got it from Juliann Armbrust, not that she couldn't get recipes from me, mind ya, I'm a pretty darn good cook, though I have lots of hobbies I prefer better than cookin'. And bein' honest, which I do my darndest most times, cookin' isn't all that hard. Just brownin' some meat and addin' a couple cans of cream soup and there ya go." She clapped her hands together, while Margie, I noticed, pressed her fingernails into the palm of her own hand until she winced in pain.

"No, it's certainly not like cake decoratin', that's for sure. Now there's somethin' that takes true talent, and I'm not afraid to say so. Although I realize ya couldn't feature my cakes in that last article ya did because ya aren't the boss and all. But, I hafta say, your paper really missed the boat comin' 'round the bend on that one."

Chapter Thirty

Vivian had returned to the bar, where she was commiserating with the Papas, her head on his shoulder except when she was sucking down booze. Which meant I actually saw her drop her head on his shoulder only once, for a few seconds. Barbie remained out on the dance floor. She and Guy and Jarod were trying to moon walk to Michael Jackson's "Thriller." Barbie was doing an amazingly good job, but the deputies' heels made it a tough go for them.

"So," I said to Margie, the two of us sitting at our table, "if I understood your sister correctly—and I realize that's a big if—Wally may not have intentionally lied to us. The trip to Hallock on Wednesday afternoon was so quick he might have forgotten he ever went."

"Makes sense considerin' the amount of stress he's been under."

"Or he could have lied since, in addition to getting Little Val's ice cream, he was searching for Raleigh so he could pay him what he owed. And he didn't want anyone to find out about that."

"That makes sense too."

"Either way, for some reason, he 'fessed up to Little Val and her parents this afternoon. Probably because the sheriff questioned him this morning."

Margie clicked her tongue against the roof of her mouth. "I don't even want to think about what's goin' to happen to that little family." She paused, looking the part of the prayerful nun, her hands folded on the table in front of her. "But at least now that he's accounted for his whereabouts on Wednesday and we know why he was so quiet around Raleigh out in the field there, he doesn't seem like much of a murder suspect. So I guess he's got that goin' for him."

"Yeah," I agreed with little enthusiasm, "I guess he's got that going for him."

Of course, neither Margie nor I truly believed Wally had much going for him at this juncture, considering what he had done to his family. But there wasn't anything we could do about it. So we simply sipped our beer until Bernie Streed ambled up alongside Margie. "Hey, Sister Margie," he said. "It's good to see you." He was dressed as Benjamin Franklin, complete with kite and key. "I've got a new joke for you."

He leaned his kite against his shoulder and, without further preamble, began, "Well, it seems that Ole and Lena decided it was time for a checkup. So Lena called her doctor and made an appointment. And the doctor said, 'Okay, Lena, I'll see you on Monday with a specimen.' Then Lena hung up the phone and asked Ole, 'Vhat's a specimen?' And Ole said, 'Vell, Lena, I don't rightly know. Vhy don't ya go on over there and ask Helga. She knows just about every gall darn thing.' So that's what Lena did. And an hour later she returned home, her hair a mess, her blouse torn, and her lip bloodied. Of course, Ole was horrified. And he asked, 'Lena, vhat in the vorld happened to ya?' And Lena answered, 'Vell, I vent to Helga's and asked her vhat's a specimen? And she said, 'Oh, piss in a bottle.' And the fight was on!'"

Bernie bowed and walked away, leaving Margie and me laughing. And after we wiped our eyes, we listened to the music and watched the folks out on the dance floor. Clearly, we both were discouraged and wanted to do anything but work the case, even though we knew that's exactly what we had to do.

"So," I finally said, "if the killer's not Dinky or Wally, should we look more closely at Hunter Carlson?"

Margie shook her head. "I'm not sure."

"Why?"

"You heard Janice. He has lung trouble. He can't exert himself."

"But Janice thinks Raleigh was killed in a brawl. He wasn't. The cops said he merely got hit in the back of the head several times with the flat side of one of those big metal ice scrapers. That wouldn't have required a lot of strength."

"But pullin' him through the scale pit would." She leaned forward and lowered her voice. "When I was in the café a little while ago, I called John, like you wanted. He confirmed Hunter has lung problems. He gets winded pretty easily. He tries to hide it, so people don't get after him about his smokin', but John knows, bein' his boss and all."

"Oh."

"Even so, I asked if he'd disappeared at all during his shift on Tuesday night—or rather Wednesday mornin'. And John said that as far as he knows, Hunter was workin' the whole time. But since he's a truck driver, he could of gone off somewhere for a little while without anyone gettin' too suspicious."

"So that means . . ."

Someone spoke into my ear. "That you have to dance with me."

I swung around in my chair to find Buford standing over me, a smile on his face. He was dressed as a cowboy, chaps included. But rather than a six-shooter in his holster, he appeared to be packing an orange water pistol.

Right away I asked, "Have you talked to Buddy?"

He frowned as he pushed his cowboy hat back on his head. "If he wasn't in jail, I'd be hurt that the first thing you did when you saw me was ask about him."

"Sorry."

He gave me a nuggie. "No, I haven't talked to him. But I did speak to his lawyer, who said he's doing fine."

He then took my arm in his as he said to his aunt in a southern drawl, "Mind if I steal this little filly for a while, ma'am?"

"Not at all. In fact, I think that's an excellent idea."

So without another word, he towed me to the dance floor, where we began the country swing to "Ghostbusters."

Like his brother, Buford was a great dancer, and it was fun to set aside all thoughts of the murder for a while, especially since we weren't any closer to solving it. We rocked back and forth, then side to side, spinning and dipping to the beat of the music.

"I talked to Wally," he said, drawing me close for the next, much slower tune. "The sheriff had just left. He stopped by to question him."

"About the poker game?"

"No, about Buddy. According to Wally, the sheriff's sure Buddy's his man."

"But wasn't he out in the field when the murder occurred?"

"Yeah, but according to the sheriff, he could have left for a while, and no one would dare say otherwise. Not if they wanted to work around here again."

I pulled my head back to search his eyes. They were partially concealed by his hat. "That's stupid," I said. "Why does he hate him so?"

Buford twirled me around, my short skirt billowing, before coaxing me back into his arms. He attempted a smile. So did I. It didn't work for either of us. We were all business again. So much for frivolity. "The sheriff has a daughter who's twenty-one or so. And not surprisingly, he thinks she's an angel. But she enjoys playing the part of the devil." He rocked me back, then forward. "What I mean to say is she runs around. A lot. Has ever since she was old enough to drive. And several years back, after she'd just turned eighteen, and Buddy was around twenty, the sheriff found her car out in the country. He also found Buddy with her in the back seat. Word is he actually drew his gun on him." He gazed down at me. "See, the sheriff was just a deputy back then. And thankfully another deputy arrived on the scene before Buddy was 'accidently' shot. Still, the guy vowed to get even."

"And that's what he's doing now?"

"That'd be my guess. It's not the first time he's arrested Buddy for something he didn't do. But this is the worst charge he's ever filed against him. That's one of the reasons Wally decided to tell Little Val everything."

"And he did," I told him. "This afternoon. Vern and Vivian too."

"So that's explains Vivian's appearance."

We moved effortlessly across the floor together. Since both of us had been dancing since we were young, we were well versed in our roles. Buford was great at leading, and I was pretty good at following—on the dance floor anyway.

"You and Buddy also scared the shit out of him yesterday morning when you told him you were poking around in Raleigh's murder. Right away he figured it would somehow lead back to that card game. So he ended up calling Father Daley and asking his advice. Naturally Father Daley told him to confess everything to Val right away. Which he was going to do, except then she had the baby. So he put it off. But after the sheriff stopped by this morning, he said he didn't think he could wait any longer. I agreed."

When that song ended, Buford insisted on one more. It was another slow song, which was just fine by me. While I had no romantic feelings for the guy, I nevertheless felt comfortable in his arms. Not surprising after the craziness of the past few days.

"Hey," I said, "have you talked to Barbie? Did she ask you if any of your folks—"

"Yeah. And I told her I didn't think anyone was late or went missing on Tuesday night."

"Even the President was accounted for?"

"Yeah, although—"

"I know. I know. Since he's a truck driver, he could have disappeared for a while without anyone noticing."

He chuckled. "Sorry, but it's true."

We danced in silence for the rest of that number. And when it was over, a cute blonde hesitantly approached, asking Buford if he'd give her a spin around the floor. From the look on his face, I figured that's exactly what he wanted to do. So with a little finger wave, I headed back to the table, where Margie was still sitting.

I relayed everything I'd learned, ending with, "So now what? Should we see what we can find out about the President? We don't know much about him."

Margie glanced toward the bar, and I followed her gaze. Vivian was headed back in our direction, each hand clutching a drink. "Well, I suppose we hafta. And since there's no one better to tell us about him than Vivian, we might as well do it now." She tilted her head close to mine. "Although I hope she doesn't need to share a lot. The less I know about that guy, the better. He's kind of creepy."

"So I've heard."

Chapter Thirty-One

"Hey, Vivian," Margie said in a cheerful voice, "I bet your chair's still warm."

Vivian's butt hardly grazed her seat before she was imbibing again. "I don't care if my chair's warm as long as my drinks are cold." She licked her blowfish lips. "Ya know, as the night goes on, Jim gets better and better at mixin' drinks. Why do ya suppose that is?" She waited for a nanosecond before answering herself. "I guess it's like anythin' else, practice makes perfect." The repeated "P" sound caused her swollen lips to putter, leading her to giggle. "P-Practice makes p-perfect," she repeated, giggling some more. "P-Practice makes p-perfect."

No doubt about it. She'd be incoherent before long. If we wanted answers, we needed to get busy and ask our questions. "So, Vivian," I said, "can you tell us about the man everyone calls the President?"

She made an effort to raise her eyebrows. "Ya mean John Hanson?"

"Uh-huh."

"I don't like talkin' about him."

Margie leaned toward her. "Believe me, I don't care for the idea either. But we hafta. He played in that poker game. And from what we understand, there was a lot of tension between him and Raleigh Cummin's."

Vivian canted her head. "And ya suspect that John killed him?" I believe she tried to whisper, but her volume control was messed up. As a result, her words left her mouth at nearly a shout.

Margie and I instantly shushed her, our fingers to our lips.

The clown was staring at me—or us—but he wasn't the only one.

"Vivian!" I said her name as quietly as possible while still sounding firm. "You need to be more careful. We're talking about murder here."

She nodded. "Okay." She lowered her head, as if that would keep her voice down. "We serve on the school board together, havin' done it for years and just doin' our part to serve and be of service. But I don't see how that's goin' to lead ya to a killer."

"Well, you're right. We aren't really interested in your professional association with the man." This was harder than I'd expected, so I fortified myself with a slug from my longneck bottle. "Umm . . . what we really want to know about is . . . umm . . . your personal relationship."

I'm not sure, but Margie might have gagged.

And Vivian? Well, she sat ramrod straight. Quite a feat considering she was half tanked. "I don't wanna talk 'bout that. Ya see, he didn't turn out to be a very nice man." She smoothed her hair away from her face.

"In what way?" Margie asked.

"Well," Vivian said, "I dunno if I can talk about it."

"Vivian." Margie's tone was much firmer than mine had been. "Your nephew's in jail, and your son-in-law, the father of your new grandbaby, could end up there if we don't get to the bottom of this."

Vivian gnawed on her swollen lips but then apparently thought better of it. "Well, ya know I'd do anythin' for the kids in our family. I love 'em. Really, I do."

Margie and I nodded with encouragement.

"But whatever I tell ya can't go beyond this table here."

We nodded some more.

Vivian opened her mouth again, but rather than speaking, she downed a long drink from her glass. "Okay, well . . . umm . . . he wanted me to be . . . umm . . . intimate with him."

I could almost see the thought bubble over Margie's head. It mirrored my own. Both read, "So? Tell us something we don't know."

"Didn't ya hear me?" Vivian seemed perplexed and a bit irked by our lack of outrage.

"Yah," Margie answered. "But we assumed you already were . . . umm . . . involved."

"Of course not!" Vivian used her most indignant voice. "I'm a married woman."

"But ya were always hangin' around him."

"I simply enjoyed his company." She sniffed before sipping from her glass, doing her best to drink like a lady, her pinky raised and everything. "He actually listened to me. And he let me have my way." She set her glass down. "Vern's not like that. Never has been." She lowered her head and her voice. "I love him, but he can be pigheaded, don't ya know. Anyways, since I married young, I never got the chance to do much on my own terms, so I missed out there. Or so the . . ." She stopped mid-sentence.

"Yah?" Margie urged her on. "Or so the . . ."

Vivian blinked at the two of us, her nerves on display. "Or so the . . . umm . . . marriage counselor says." She quickly glanced between Margie and me, watching for signs of judgment. But she wouldn't find any—not from me anyhow.

"Vivian," I said, "I've been in counseling for years."

"Really?" She sounded skeptical. "You see a therapist?"

"Yep, once a week for more than a decade now." For some dumb reason, I then decided to go for a little levity. "And see, I'm still a mess."

She bobbed her head up and down. "Well, that's true enough. From what I understand, ya don't have your act together at all."

I eyed Margie. Her expression read, "Welcome to the club."

Mine read, "I really didn't want to join."

"When did the President start pressurin' ya about sex?" Margie went ahead and asked, wincing at those last few words.

Vivian moved on to her second drink. "A couple months ago. That's when I found out he was nothin' but a wolf in cheap clothin." She rubbed her eyes. "He wanted to do some disgustin' things."

Knowing I could be psychologically scarred for the rest of my life by what she said next, I nonetheless asked the question that begged to be asked. “What did he suggest, Vivian?”

“Well . . . umm . . . he . . . umm . . . was into that swingin’ stuff. And I’m not talkin’ ’bout dancin’.”

“What?”

She took another gulp of her drink. That’s right. She was sucking that thing down like a slurpee. “Yah, and he was real insistent that I do it with him.”

Margie bristled. “Insistent? How? Did he hurt ya, Vivian?”

“Oh, no, just my feelin’s.” She rubbed her thumb through the condensation on her glass. “But I thought Vern was goin’ to kill him.”

“You told Vern?” Margie’s surprise was evident.

“Oh, for sure. He’s my husband. Besides, he’s the one who suggested we see someone about what happened and about some other things there too.” She narrowed her eyes. “But don’t say anythin’ to him. I don’t wanna embarrass him.”

Margie nodded. “So what did the President do when ya told him ya weren’t interested in . . . umm . . . swingin’?” Margie shuddered, and I couldn’t help but join in.

“I slapped his face. Then I said he was positively the most perverted person . . .” She stopped and almost smiled. She was puttering her “Ps” again. And it tickled her. Yep, even though she was in the midst of a very serious conversation, her puttering “Ps” prompted her to pause with pleasure. “After that,” she added, “I told him I never wanted to speak to him again.”

“But let me guess,” Margie said. “He didn’t listen.”

“No, he didn’t. He started callin’ me. Tellin’ me he couldn’t live without me. Said he couldn’t eat. Couldn’t sleep. And while understandable, I felt guilty, which was only natural, comin’ to find that out through the counselin’. But back then it made me crazy, so I told Vern, not knowin’ what he’d do and bein’ nervous about that to boot. Like I said, he wanted to kill the guy. But after his cooler head prevailed, he suggested we get guidance as to the best thing to do in situations such as these.”

Margie and I nodded.

"Anyways," she continued, "we began seein' a counselor down there in St. Cloud, not wantin' to go to Reverend Pearson here in town and St. Cloud havin' good services along those lines. Not that Reverend Pearson isn't good. Havin' been married, but now bein' a widower, he's probably fine at counselin', even if no one knows for sure how his wife died. Still, we went to St. Cloud and talked to the sheriff some too. The one here. Not in St. Cloud." She made quick work of finishing off her drink.

"That was a giant mistake," she said after wiping her chin with the sleeve of her jacket. "Talkin' to the sheriff. Not goin' to the counselor." She hesitated. "Anyways, the sheriff here is a friend of John's. Or, I mean, the President."

She blinked, appearing as if she was making an effort to clear her head. "I always hated that nickname because I knew people used it to make fun of him, assumin' he was a pompous ass, which he was but still . . ." More blinking. I didn't have the heart to tell her the only thing that would clear her head was about twelve hours of sleep. "And here they were right all along," Still more blinking. "Anyways . . . Now where was I?"

We were losing her. "You were talking about the President and the sheriff." I was anxiously twirling my braids.

"Oh, yeah. Well, anyways, the President financed most of the sheriff's campaign, so he pretty much has to do whatever the President tells him to do or not to do or say or . . ." She was utterly confused.

"So," I continued on for her, "even though you told the sheriff you didn't want the President harassing you, he still calls you on occasion, and nothing's done about it."

"Well, I tell him off. But I had to stop tellin' Vern about the calls, as he'd go after him. Havin' just one arm and all, he's still a good shot and bein' even handier with a carvin' knife."

Margie placed her hand on Vivian's shoulder. "Did the President call ya on your cell phone that night Little Val and I were at your house for supper? It was the night of the card game."

Vivian rubbed her stomach. "Yah. He said he wanted us to be friends again. He'd prefer bein' . . . umm . . . intimate but promisin' no undue pressure there while at the same time assurin' if I did have . . . umm . . . sex with him, he'd give up those swingin' parties in Fargo if that's what I wanted." She glanced between the two of us. "I guess that's where he goes sometimes when folks think he's doin' business of a different kind." She shook her head, then held it steady between her hands. "He said I'd never hafta go unless I wanted to, which he hoped someday I would, but again not pushin'. And even if we were only friends, he'd never see other women 'round here so as not to hurt my feelin's." She wiped sweat from her rigid brow. "I told him to take a flyin' hike."

"Vivian?" I asked, adjusting my fake glasses. "Are you sure you're okay?" She was looking a little green.

"Oh, yah, it's just hot in here." She took a slow, deep breath. "Just 'cause there's snow on the ground, folks kick the thermostat up to seventy or higher. But ya don't hafta." And with those words of wisdom, she turned to her sister and vomited in the lap of her nun's habit.

Chapter Thirty-Two

MARGIE WENT UPSTAIRS to get cleaned up. And, yes, a part of me was jealous. If Vivian had only puked in my direction, I'd be up there right now, changing out of this stupid costume. Instead, Wonder Woman was corralling me into the café.

"Did Vern take Vivian home?" she asked.

"Yep."

"So how about sharing some Buttermilk Salad while I bring you up to date on what I've learned about the murder?" She sashayed over to the fridge.

"I don't know, Barbie. Buttermilk Salad sounds . . ."

"Good. And it tastes even better. It's cool and refreshing. It has pineapple and oranges. It's a lot like a yogurt parfait."

"But I've been drinking beer."

"So?"

I sighed. "Okay, I'll give it a try."

With a smile, she served up two plates of the creamy salad squares, setting one in front of me and the other catty corner from me. "Now, dig in," she said, "while I tell you a few things."

I obliged by picking up my fork and giving the Buttermilk Salad a taste. First, a teenie weenie one. Then, after discovering how good it was, a much bigger one. "Yum."

"Told you." Barbie was using her teeth to pull a piece of pineapple off her fork. "I talked to both Buford and Ed. He was the deputy we met when we examined the scale pit."

"Well, I danced with Buford earlier and probably got the same update from him as you did. So why don't you start by telling me what Ed said."

Barbie adjusted her long, black wig and the metallic crown on top of it. "Well, he said he requested any information that the Fargo police might have on Raleigh Cummings, being that's where he lived and all. And this afternoon he received a very interesting report." She paused to yank on her bustier. After that, she began making designs in her salad with her fork.

"Barbie, don't you dare try that delaying crap on me."

She giggled and set her fork down. "Okay, okay." She jingled her hands. "Well, according to the report, Raleigh was questioned a couple months ago in connection to a house party in Fargo. The police got called by a neighbor who was complaining about the noise."

"And?"

She leaned over the table. "When the cops got there, they found folks in various stages of undress, occupying a variety of rooms with numerous people." Her eyes got bigger and rounder as she spoke. "And while there's no law against that, the police also found some drugs, mostly weed but some cocaine too. Not a lot. But enough to take down names and question those involved."

"And?"

"In the end, the whole thing got swept under the rug because, in addition to Raleigh Cummings and a few other nobodies, several big shots were there."

"Really?"

"Uh-huh. And one of those big shots had a friend with him from out of town." She paused again. She just couldn't help herself. She was born to create suspense.

"Barbie," I warned.

"Okay. Just guess who it was." She folded her hands as if in prayer. "Please. Pretty please." She was actually bouncing on her stool.

She was nutty, but I liked her. "Well, fine." I decided to play along. "Hmm. Let me think. Was it the President?"

She stopped mid-bounce, clearly dejected. "How did you know that?"

I gave her the rundown of what Vivian had told us.

"Wow" was all she said when I finished.

"So now we know the President lied to Dinky. He really did know Raleigh Cummings."

"That's right. Though Ed doesn't expect that fact to be made public anytime soon. Remember, no charges were filed in that Fargo matter. Plus, it may not have anything to do with our case, so there'd be no justification for releasing the information. On top of that, the sheriff confiscated the report and ordered Ed and everyone who'd seen it to forget they ever had."

As I'd suspected, my Buttermilk Salad was not making nice with the beer in my stomach. "He actually said that?"

"Yep."

It was my turn to say, "Wow."

"And that wasn't all Ed told me. Do you recall when Guy told us that all the fingerprints found in Raleigh's pickup were explained away?"

"Uh-huh."

"Well, according to Ed, the President's fingerprints were among them. Clear sets. Undoubtedly fresh. Yet the sheriff refused to allow anyone to ask the President about them. He said he'd take care of it. But no one thinks he will."

I pushed my plate away, out of my direct line of vision, hoping that would appease my upset stomach. "So what do you think? Did the President kill Raleigh because he didn't want to get exposed as a 'swinger'? You know, a preemptive strike? And the sheriff's covering for him?"

"It's possible. Or perhaps Raleigh was blackmailing the President, and the President got tired of it and killed him."

"You just love that blackmailing idea, don't you, Barbie?"

She smirked. "Either way he could have ransacked the house, found whatever information Raleigh had on him, along with the IOUs, and tossed the whole works."

"Well, as I've come to understand, the fact that the President wasn't noticeably AWOL from his job the night of the murder doesn't mean much. And as you reminded me earlier, the murder may have taken place during the day."

Barbie leaned her elbows on the table. "Ed doesn't think so. He agrees with you." Hearing that, I sat a little taller. "He said Raleigh was definitely killed on the farm, near the ditch, not far from the house. And it seems there was a lot of activity out there, in the shop, till close to midnight. Some machinery broke down or something. So he says the murder must have occurred during the night, when Buford and Buddy and the rest of the night shift were finishing up that last section of beets, which was more than ten miles from the house. No one would have been around the farmyard to see anything."

Frustration clogged my brain. "I don't know what to think. Who's the killer, Barbie? I have no idea." I pulled the backpack from my back and threw it on the table. I'd been wearing it all night, and I was done. I pulled my fake glasses off too, pitching them next to the backpack. "I wish Father Daley were here. He has good insight. Maybe he'd have some ideas of where we should go from here."

"Well, don't hold your breath, Emme. He never comes to these parties. He says it wouldn't be appropriate because he's a man of the cloth, and these parties get kind of wild."

I stared wide eyed at Barbie's bustier. It was sliding down again. "He may be right."

She noted the target of my focus and once more gave it a yank. "I don't remember the real Wonder Woman having this much trouble with her top."

I sniffed. "The real Wonder Woman never had that much top."

Barbie snickered. "Yeah, you've got a point."

I unzipped the backpack and claimed my notebook, paging through what I'd jotted down. Everything had been covered. Even so, as I closed the notebook a notion struck me. "Hey, why does the President allow the sheriff to go after Buddy the way he does? I realize the sheriff hates Buddy. But he is Vivian's nephew."

Barbie rested her forearms on the table. "Yeah, the President's obsessed with Vivian, but I get the impression he doesn't like the rest of her family. Most likely because they aren't real friendly to him, being he's trying to break up Vivian and Vern. You know, I have it on good authority that during the last murder investigation, the President was pushing for Vern's arrest."

"So why'd he agree to work for the twins this fall?"

"I don't have any idea. Probably something to do with his Vivian fetish. I know the twins only asked him out of desperation. They wanted Dinky and Biggy. But they were out of town at some big family gathering. Although they still ended up pitching in for a few days when they got back."

I tapped my finger on the table. "So how do we proceed?"

"I'm not sure, Emme."

I was about to say something else but was stopped by a sexy male voice. It was floating through the air, sounding much like the sensual sounds of a tenor saxophone.

Barbie formed a perfect "O" with her mouth.

The music was coming from above. But I don't mean heaven. Although Margie may have considered it that. The lyrics were soft, yet clear. "Can't get enough of your love, babe. No, can't get enough of your love, babe."

"Who on earth . . . ?" Barbie asked

"Well . . . umm . . . I believe that's Barry White."

She squinted at the ceiling. "You mean Margie?" She lowered her eyes until they met mine. "And?"

I lowered mine until they met my lap. "Umm . . . it's not my place to say." I slipped off my stool. "Now if you'll excuse me, I'm going out outside to get some air. My stomach's a bit queasy.

"Emme!" Barbie shouted as I made a beeline for the back door, "don't you dare run out on me!"

Chapter Thirty-Three

I STOOD IN THE ALLEY behind the café, Margie's gray parka hanging from my frame, my bare legs chilly beneath my short skirt and light-weight knee highs. I assumed Barbie was upstairs, pounding on Margie's bedroom door, asking her what she was doing and who she was doing it with. The thought of it made me smile. It also made me feel a tad sorry for Margie and John Deere. They'd be questioned and teased mercilessly. But mostly it made me smile.

It was dark outside, although the light above the door and the street lights along the alley provided a fair amount of illumination. I strolled back and forth in front of the parking lot, hoping my stomach would settle down and my feet wouldn't freeze to the ground.

As I walked, thoughts of Margie and Barbie and John Deere and Barry White gave way to murder. What had we missed? The President seemed to be the most likely suspect. But I wasn't sure about Hunter or Janice either. And then there was the sheriff. He was unscrupulous. But how unscrupulous?

I walked some more, but no new ideas came to me. Maybe it was just too cold for my brain to function out here. Maybe I had to go back inside. Maybe I needed something to eat. Something that wasn't sugar-based. *There's a novel idea!*

I turned toward the door, hoping I'd avoid Barbie for a little while. I didn't want to deal with her questions any more than Margie did.

As I reached for the handle, I spotted something out of the corner of my eye. Something near the far side of the building. I peered in that direction. It was a figure of some kind. I squinted. What on earth? Then I recognized him. It was the clown from inside. He was about thirty feet from me, crooking his finger, bidding me closer.

He had definitely caught me off guard. Clowns never waved me over.

He again curled his fingers. The gesture or the person making it struck me as familiar. But who would be watching me, first from the bar, then from outside? Who would be pursuing me? Teasing me to join him?

I felt a smile cut across my face as the answer came to me. Randy Ryden. Margie said he loved the Halloween party. She also said he'd be disappointed if he had to miss it.

I gave it some more thought. Margie was in on this little charade with him. She picked our table near the bar, in close proximity to him. She even pointed out our seats. It wasn't Margie being bossy. It was Margie helping Randy surprise me. Which only made sense considering she was all about romance these days.

He wiggled his finger one more time. And I was tempted to run across the parking lot, peel off his mask and smother him with kisses. I presumed we'd then go to his place, spending the rest of the night in front of a roaring fire. And later—like tomorrow morning sometime—I'd tell him about Buddy. And even though he disliked him, he'd help me clear his name because he was fair and just—as well as really hot.

But wait. I couldn't put an end to his little production just like that. He'd gone to a lot of trouble. I'd have to play along, at least for a while.

So I wrapped my arms around myself, my extra-long sleeves dangling, and padded in his direction, anticipating how he might reveal himself. Amazingly I wasn't cold anymore. Well, okay, my feet were still freezing as I shuffled across the hard-packed snow. But the rest of me was all warm, and some parts were even melting a bit.

He headed down a shoveled path toward the garden shed, and I followed. I knew that building. I was stuck in it for a while during my last visit. Consequently, I wasn't that fond of it. But I was willing to keep an open mind. With Randy in there with me, I might actually come away with a whole new appreciation for the place.

He opened the door and stepped inside, and I did the same, pulling the door shut behind me. He then wheeled around the best he could, given his gigantic shoes, and tore off his mask.

I caught my breath. I couldn't see him very well. As I said, it was dark outside, and the only light filtering through the shed's sole window originated from a street lamp in the alley. Still, I didn't need much light to see that something was wrong.

"Why?" he hollered!

"What?"

"Why do you have to stick your noise in my business?"

Right away I realized it wasn't Randy Ryden. But the question he posed didn't narrow it down much beyond that. Lots of people thought I interfered in their business.

"Who are you?" I asked.

"You know damn well who I am."

And I did. It came to me at that very moment. Which was about two minutes too late to do me any good. "You're the President, aren't you?"

"I'm John Hanson, that's correct."

"That's what I was afraid of," I mumbled.

"What? What was that?" His words were clipped, his tone, hard and angry.

"Nothing. Umm . . . what do you want from me?" I had a pretty good idea, and it was making me sick to my stomach. Or maybe it was just the Buttermilk Salad and beer. But I doubted it.

He nudged me toward the wall to the right of the door, then held me there by bracing an arm on each side of me. "Every time you come up here, you cause me trouble. Now I'm going to make sure you go away—for good."

That didn't sound promising. "So why'd you kill Raleigh Cummings." Granted, the question came out of the blue. But if he was going to kill me, I didn't think small talk was necessary. Go right to the heart of the matter.

"What?" He moved closer, his big shoes stepping on my feet, trapping them against the floor. "Are you nuts? Why would I kill him?"

"Because he was going to expose you for . . . umm . . . what you do in Fargo." It was just a guess. But it was the only thing I had on the guy.

An evil-sounding laugh slid from his throat. "How'd you find out about that?" I didn't respond. "Oh, it doesn't matter." He flapped his white-gloved hand before returning it to its place against the wall, where it crowded my shoulder. "Raleigh wasn't going to expose me. We'd just come to an understanding."

"Huh?" True, that wasn't much of a question. But I was certain I was about to be killed. I wasn't at my best.

"See, after he and Buddy had their falling-out at the Caribou, I picked him up off the ground, and we had a short talk in his pickup. I came to find out he was down on his luck, financially speaking."

"How could that be? He'd just won big at poker."

"But he hadn't been paid. And even if he got everything coming to him, it wouldn't be enough because he had developed quite a coke habit. That's why he went off on people the way he did. I was surprised that neither Buddy nor Buford recognized it. Then again, maybe they just didn't want to see it."

I tried to wiggle my toes out from under his clown shoes but couldn't, so I settled for another question. "And?"

He moved his arms closer together, squeezing my shoulders like they were in a vice. "I agreed to meet him the following afternoon to pay off my poker debt and to spot him some additional cash. In turn, at that time, he'd give me my IOU as well as his promise to refrain from talking about my out-of-town activities."

I wasn't sure if I believed him. "Why would he do that? How could you trust that he wouldn't come back for more money?"

The clown chuckled. "Well, girlie, I have friends in high places. They could cause him a lot of trouble. And after our little talk, he understood that. I also reminded him we could exclude him from future 'social gatherings.' We only allowed him in because he had easy access to good drugs. But I assured him we could get them elsewhere without too much trouble." He paused. "What's more, if I had wanted him dead, I would have had it done far away from here."

I still wasn't sure what to think. This guy was full of bluster now, but at the poker game, he'd been so uncomfortable he couldn't concentrate and ended up losing $10,000. He'd also been uncharacteristically quiet in the field. Was it simply because he hadn't yet reached an "understanding" with Raleigh? Or was he feeding me a line of bull now? And if that was the case, why?

"So if you didn't kill Raleigh Cummings, who did?" Sure I wanted an answer. But more than that, I was stalling for time to come up with an escape plan.

"How the hell should I know?" His sour breath was hot on my face, his little bird eyes seemingly telling me he'd enjoy pecking me to death. "The sheriff arrested Buddy Johnson. So . . ."

I summoned enough courage to draw myself up to my full height. "I don't believe he did it. And you're a smart man, so I doubt you do either." I'd come up with a plan, praying it was better than my previous ones. And I hoped God would cooperate, even if I didn't make it to church very often.

My idea was to play to his ego. Kill him with kindness. Or if not kill him, at least knock him out long enough to get away. "I hear you're an extremely talented gambler. So who would you put your money on? Who's the killer?"

He sniffed. "Yeah, well, I am pretty good." His features spelled arrogance, but the ruffled collar and polka-dot jumpsuit still said clown. "And I'd bet on Hunter Carlson."

"Why?"

He chuckled. "He's not like the rest of us. He doesn't have money to lose. And he was positive Raleigh was cheating, which he probably was. But it drove Hunter crazy. Then to add insult to injury, Raleigh called him a 'little man.' And little men hate being called what they are." He edged a little closer to me. "Just so you know, girlie, I'm not little at all."

My stomach churned, and I threw up a bit in my mouth.

He laughed at my obvious nervousness. "Raleigh also convinced Hunter's so-called girlfriend to shack up with him for a few days. And that had to push Hunter over the edge." He shifted his feet. "But enough about that. Let's get back to you. I want you gone. As I said, gone for good."

"But wait, I don't understand why you're so concerned about me being here?"

The clown sighed. "Because you cause problems. You're a black cat, a bad penny, a broken mirror, spilled salt, the number thirteen, a—"

"Enough!" I shouted. "I get the idea."

"Last time you were here, you interfered just when I was getting closer to Vivian. And now you're interfering again. I don't need that." He pressed my shoulder against the wall with one hand while easing a pouch from a strap on his shoulder with the other.

This was it. He was going to shoot me. *Or,* a little voice inside my head said, *he has one of those never-ending scarves, and he's going to strangle you with it. No,* yet another yelled, *it's a water-squirting lapel flower, and he's going to squirt you to death.*

The voices were cracking each other up. But I didn't find them one bit funny. Although I wasn't surprised to hear from them. Whenever I was scared beyond belief, they were there with their smart-ass comments.

"So how much will it take for you to leave and never come back?" He pulled his hand from the pouch and waved a wad of cash in front of my face.

"What?"

His features tightened with resolve. "I'm a very determined man. But I'm also a very rich man. So I'm sure we can reach an understanding. Just like Raleigh and I did."

That freaked me out. Raleigh was dead. So reaching the same kind of understanding he had didn't seem like a healthy proposition. "I don't want your money!" I hollered. "I don't want anything from you!"

With those words, I shoved him backward as hard as I could. He fell against the potting table, and because of his unwieldy shoes, he had a rough time getting up. I grabbed a large bag of fertilizer and threw it at him. It caught him in the chest, and he fell again, this time cracking his head against the shelf beneath the table. I threw another bag. It hit the table and split open, fertilizer pouring over him. At the same time, a big clay flower pot rattled off the table, landing on his head. He seemed to be unconscious. But I didn't wait around to find out for sure.

I shoved my way out of the shed, making a mental note never to step inside of it again, no matter what. I barreled down the path, hell bent on running to the "V" and, with the help of my good friend Captain Morgan, forgetting all about this investigation.

I was just about to round the side of the building that housed the café on one end and the "V" on the other when I spied something that prompted me to jump back.

Chapter Thirty-Four

I PEEKED OVER MY SHOULDER. No sign of the President. At least not yet. So I stepped forward and slowly leaned my head around the corner. I pulled back, only to look again. It was Hunter Carlson, the hockey goalie. He was now in jeans and his jersey, his jacket open. He stood alone in the parking lot, not far from the café's back door. He was forcing something into the bed of a pickup. It may have been his truck, but the vanity license plate read "BINGO," so I assumed it belonged to Janice.

As I said, there was just enough light to see that the pickup's tail gate was down, the topper flap was up, and Hunter was struggling with something that resembled a big roll of carpeting. He stopped and looked around, his shoulders rising and falling as he breathed heavily. Then he wrestled with it some more. Another break. This time he leaned against the tail gate and coughed. I stood perfectly still, hidden by the edge of the building, as he once more worked against the bundle. It was just about there. All the way in the truck. That roll of carpeting wrapped in a blue tarp.

I swallowed hard, the sound thudding in my ears. A lumpy roll of carpeting in a blue tarp? At a Halloween party at the "V"? That didn't make sense at all. No sense at . . . My pulsed quickened. And despite the cold, nervous sweat formed at the nape of my neck. It couldn't be. It simply couldn't be.

I closed my eyes, willing myself to avoid seeing anything sinister. Begging my imagination to keep from going wild. Still, a picture was quickly drawn in my mind's eye. A picture of a body. And no matter how tightly I squeezed my eyes or wished for it to go away, I couldn't erase it.

If it was a body. Whose? Surely not Raleigh's. His was in a morgue somewhere. But if it wasn't him? Perhaps it was one of the other poker players. But not the President. I'd just left him in the shed. Then what about Dinky? Absolutely not. This wasn't a king-sized tarp.

Wait. That only left Wally. And it couldn't be him. He was at home with his new family. He was dealing with the aftermath of what he had done. Wally was . . . No. It couldn't be.

I had to go inside. I needed to get help. At least I thought I needed help. But how could I make that happen? I didn't want Hunter to leave while I was gone. Although the police would surely know where to find him. But what about the body—if there was a body? Would he have time to get rid of it before they got to him? If so, it would be his word against mine. And no body.

Maybe if I hurried. He wouldn't leave yet anyhow, would he? No. Not without Janice. She was in on this with him. She was his accomplice. She had to be. It was her truck after all. And she was furious at Raleigh for two-timing her. For laughing at her. For calling her an old hag. But she was angry with Hunter too. Or was she? I scratched at my thoughts as if searching for something in the snow. Oh, yes, pretending to be estranged was an excellent way to deflect suspicion for a crime no one thought either could commit alone.

My breath quickened as it all came together. One or both of them had killed Raleigh Cummings, and together they had covered it up.

Hunter raised the tail gate and dropped the topper flap. But Janice still hadn't shown up. He lifted his hockey jersey and checked the pockets of his jeans. He didn't find what he was looking for, so he raised the topper flap and glanced around the interior of the truck. After that, he checked the ground. Only then did he hit his head with the heel of his hand. Keys! He was obviously searching for keys. He dropped the topper flap and headed back to the bar.

As soon as he was gone, I rushed to the truck. I needed to see what—or who—was in that tarp. If necessary, I'd go for help.

If carpeting, I'd amble back into the "V" and have a drink. Something mind numbing.

I pushed the long sleeves of my parka up above my elbows and turned the latch on the topper flap. Of course it wasn't locked. Hunter had no keys. I dropped the tail gate. Slowly. Oh so slowly. And there it was. A six-foot long lumpy roll of something. Wrapped in a blue plastic tarp. Secured by gray duct tape.

I peeled back a small piece of the tarp, my hands trembling. Another tug on the tape, and I swore I saw the roll move. I jumped back. Then nothing. So I unwrapped a little more. And a little more. Until I saw . . . yes . . . skin. I closed my eyes, praying it wasn't Wally. Not Wally with his new family. Not Wally, Margie's kin. I peeked out from behind my wary lids. The tarp moved again. And I may have heard a whine. I forced my eyes open and tugged at the edges. Faster. More frantic now. Tugging with all my might. Until I gasped.

My heart jumped into my throat, but I assured myself that was okay. There was plenty of room since my voice was no longer there. In fact, it wasn't anywhere to be found. It had vanished. I couldn't scream. I couldn't speak. And Janice Ferguson stared back at me, her eyes filled with fear.

Her mouth was duct taped. And with a mere nod of my head I asked if she was ready. She blinked. I yanked the tape. And she let forth a strangled sob. "He did it. Hunter killed Raleigh." She began to cry. "He d-did it because of me. Because of w-what I did." The cries came from deep within her, and they racked her body. "And b-because he humiliated Hunter. And cheated at cards. And now he's going to k-kill me because I w-wouldn't let him back into the house. He said I had to because he did this for us and—" Janice stopped, her eyes fixed on something behind me.

I shivered. But it wasn't from the cold. I knew better than that. My body was damp with sweat. I attempted a deep breath. But I didn't even come close.

I slowly circled around. Sure enough, there he was. Hunter. He held Janice's shoulder bag in one hand and a set of keys in the other. "I was going to lock the topper to stop anyone from poking around inside," he said. "Too late I guess." He dropped both the keys and the purse and picked up a curling broom from where it was lying next to Janice. "Sorry, honey." His eyes were crazed. "I realize you just bought this. And you want to break it in yourself. But I have to use it." He raised the broom, Janice screamed, and I crossed my arms in front of my face, the parka's long sleeves dangling from my hands like dead fish on a line.

ꙮ ꙮ

Other sounds began to filter in. First distantly. Then much closer. I slowly opened my eyes, working to get them to focus. The background was dark. But in the foreground, I saw shapes. Those shapes slowly transforming into people.

Buford was there, minus his cowboy hat. He was kneeling beside me, with Ed, the deputy, right next to him. Guy and Jarod, still in drag, were standing behind them.

Wonder Woman was there too. She was kneeling on my opposite side. And Margie and John Deere were behind her. Along with two guys dressed as BCA agents.

"Don't move," Margie ordered, "the ambulance is on the way."

Thoughts of Shitty, the plumber with the butt crack, flashed through my mind, and I'm not positive, but I think I might have giggled.

"Yep," Margie said, "she's definitely out of it."

Chapter Thirty-Five

IT WAS EARLY SUNDAY MORNING, and Margie and Barbie and I were in the café. Ed and his wife, Sandy, were there with us. Not surprisingly we were sitting around a table, talking about the night before. They had just finished informing me for the third or fourth time how lucky I was Janice screamed at the same time Guy stepped outside for a cigarette. Sure, Hunter still hit me. But Janice's hollering distracted him enough to throw his aim off, leaving me with only a bruised arm. A bruise the doctor said would have been a lot worse if not for the padding provided by Margie's parka.

I don't remember what happened next. I passed out. I guess I had a tendency to do that. But from what I understand, Guy came running as fast as he could in his high heels and jumped Hunter, bitch slapping him into submission. It was around then that the rest of the "V" emptied out into the parking lot.

Now, here in Hot Dish Heaven, Ed was filling us in on what they'd learned from Hunter after his arrest. As he spoke, we drank coffee and ate Blueberry Bars and something Margie called Super Rhubarb Bars. Margie didn't want to cook because she was afraid she'd miss part of the story. But it didn't take her long to convince us that since both of these bars contained fruit, they made fine breakfast food.

"On the night of the murder," Ed began, "around one in the morning, Raleigh drove out to the twins' farmstead, looking for Buddy. He was pretty drunk. That's probably why he went to the house rather than the field. I guess he wanted Buddy to let him work or pay him for the work he'd already done. But, of course, Buddy wasn't around. And after pounding on the front door and checking the garage, Raleigh stumbled into the shop."

Ed sipped his coffee. "Hunter saw it all because he was in the shop, grabbing a scraper. He'd forgotten to pick one up before leaving John Deere's place, and he didn't want to go all the way back there. He was on his way to the piler, carrying a full load. And since the twins' farm was on the way, he stopped there. He didn't think they'd mind him borrowing a scraper."

Another sip of coffee. "I guess Raleigh couldn't resist making cracks to him about his . . . umm . . . tryst with Janice, which made Hunter bonkers. But because of some kind of lung issue, he couldn't do much to stop him. So Raleigh just kept taunting him. And Hunter just kept getting madder and madder."

Ed glanced around the table and chuckled. We were hanging on his every word like a bunch of Girl Scouts listening to ghost stories around a campfire. "When Raleigh finally left," he said, "Hunter followed him outside and hit him on the back of the head with the blunt side of the metal scraper he had in his hand. He says he hardly remembers doing it. Can't even recall throwing it in the ditch."

Ed took time out to eat a Blueberry Bar, which he accomplished in two bites. "These are good, Margie," he said with a bob of his head when he was done. "You should teach Sandy to make them." He winked at Sandy.

She gave him the finger while explaining to the rest of us, "He knows damn well I don't cook or bake."

Ed chuckled. "Anyhow, Hunter found a tarp in the shop. I guess the twins keep a bunch of them 'cause you never know when you'll need a tarp. And sure enough, Hunter needed one.

"He wrapped Raleigh in it and rolled him into the ditch. He then hid Raleigh's pickup in the grove before driving his beet truck to the piler. When he was done there, he went back to the field at John Deere's place, telling John he needed to go to the shop to get a part for the truck. That wasn't unusual, so John didn't think anything of it. But instead of going to John's shop, he drove back to the twins' place in his own pickup."

"That's amazin'" Margie shook her head.

"See," Barbie added, "I told you guys he was a strange duck."

Ed sipped some more coffee. "He told us that lifting Raleigh's body into the bed of his pickup was really hard and took quite a while. So once he finally had him in there, he decided that's where he'd stay until he could figure out a good place to dump him permanently."

"Eww!" Barbie squealed. "He drove around in his pickup with dead Raleigh?"

Ed grinned. "Only for twenty-four hours or so. But since it's been cold, he didn't stink too bad."

We all shuddered.

Ed's grin morphed into laughter. "Anyhow, when the piler shut down, he got the notion that the scale pit would be the best place to bury him."

"But with his lung problems," Margie said, "he couldn't have pulled—"

"He had help."

"Who?" we all shouted like a tree full of owls.

"Not who," Ed replied. "What. He used a creeper."

"Huh?"

He rocked his chair back. "One of those little carts mechanics lay on to wheel themselves under vehicles. They're called creepers."

"And?" I wanted details.

"He backed his pickup close to the opening of the scale pit, eased Raleigh's body down inside, then slid the creeper under him and pushed him to the far back corner. There he unwrapped him because he didn't want anyone figuring out where the tarp came from. And that was that."

"What about the IOUs."

"Hunter said that on Wednesday afternoon—the day before he buried him in the pit—he parked outside of Kennedy and walked to Raleigh's house, wearing a hooded sweatshirt and a jacket no one would recognize. He used a crow bar to break in through the back door. From what he said, he first tried to check the pockets of

Raleigh's pants for house keys, but gave up because he didn't want the tarp to come loose."

Margie freshened everyone's coffee, and Ed continued on. "Once he was inside the house, he searched for his IOU. He had to move fast and said he ended up making a big mess. But he found it along with the others and took them all."

Barbie was the first to speak up. "I'm surprised nobody noticed him. Very little gets by the folks in this town."

Ed grinned. "He said he purposely went during bingo. That way almost everyone was uptown, at the Senior Center."

Barbie bobbed her head. "Smart thinking. Got to give him credit for that."

"Ya betcha," Margie agreed.

I cleared my throat. "Ed, I don't understand why he talked to Buddy and me at the Eagles. He'd have been better off keeping quiet, right? Did he say anything about that?"

"No, not really. But we got the impression he wanted to plant suspicion elsewhere as a precaution."

Margie scooted her chair back. "You know, Ed, the sheriff's goin' to take credit for solvin' this thing."

Ed smiled. "He'll try. But the rest of us will make sure the public finds out how he actually hampered the investigation. Who knows? Maybe a reporter might write a story about it." He winked at me, then raised his eyebrows at Barbie.

AFTER OUR EARLY MORNING MEETING in the café adjourned, I surprised Father Daley by driving to Hallock and attending mass. Afterward, we visited in his kitchen over lunch, him asking questions about the previous evening and me filling him in the best I could.

When we were done, I gave him a hug and promised to see him again soon. Then I returned to Kennedy, planning to grab my suitcase and the last of the recipes Margie had promised me, along with the little orphan dog I'd fallen in love with.

I had to hit the road so I'd be back in Minneapolis before it got late. I was tired. And I needed to be in my editor's office "bright and early" Monday morning. I'd already briefed him. But he wanted to hear the details.

The sun was shining in the pale-blue sky as I parked my car in front of the café. The wind was blowing as usual, so I held my hair in a ponytail as I crossed the sidewalk and stepped inside. With the door slamming behind me, I stopped to allow my eyes to adjust to the change in light. Which was just as well because I couldn't believe what I saw in front of me. It appeared to be Buddy.

"Hi, there," he said.

It was Buddy! He was out of jail and standing ten feet away from me in the otherwise deserted cafe. I was so happy to see him. And so happy for him. But I couldn't manage to verbalize either.

"So how are you?" he asked as he took two paces in my direction, causing my heart to jump up and down.

"I'm . . . umm . . . fine." I took two steps of my own.

"Thank you for everything you did for me." Another step on his part.

"It was Margie and Barbie too. And Buford and Ed and even Guy and Jarod." I managed another step forward.

"Yeah, but I want to thank you. What you did took a lot of courage and—"

"No, it didn't. I was just being nosy, like always. And I didn't want to end up looking like a fool. That's why I had to see what was in that tarp before going for help." I was rambling. But there was no stopping it. "I was scared too, Buddy. Really scared. Like I told you before, I just kind of stumble—"

"Shh." With one last step, he reached out to me, touching my lips with his fingers. "Can't you just accept a complement?" He then treated me to a gaze that made my cheeks warm and nearly set a few other parts of my body on fire. "Now let's try this again," he said. "Emme, thank you for everything you did to help me." He slowly removed his fingers from my lips.

"You're welcome." My voice was so high and squeaky I halfway expected to attract the dogs congregated around the bank next door.

"Now, was that so hard?"

"No." I smiled. "Although there's still one thing I want to know."

"Only one?"

"Ha-ha." I rested for a beat. "The joke, Buddy. What was the awful joke that Raleigh told over the farm radio that morning?"

He leaned his head to the side. "You really want to know?"

"Yeah. Like I said, I'm nosy."

"Well . . ." He took hold of my arms. "I can't say it out loud. It's too raunchy. I'll have to whisper it in your ear." He then pulled me close and did just that.

He was right. It was kind of raunchy. "No wonder Little Val got upset. Especially with her mother right there."

He chuckled. "Yeah, but they'll survive." He made no effort to release me. And I made no effort to be released. He gazed into my eyes. And I did the same in return. Then he lowered his lips and kissed me. It started out soft and tentative but soon grew deeper and more passionate. His arms slowly wrapped around my waist, and my arms found their way around his neck. And after that, I melted into him.

I wasn't aware of anything except the two of us. Not until I heard the door open behind me. "Hey, there. You won't believe what . . ." The voice sounded familiar, and my chest tightened as I broke away from Buddy and turned to find Randy in the doorway. He looked as if he'd just been punched in the gut, and I felt as if I'd been the one who'd done the punching. His eyes were full of hurt, and my heart wanted to break.

"It's not what you think." As soon as I uttered the words, I realized how pathetic they sounded. "I mean it was just . . ."

He turned away. "I didn't mean to intrude." And he walked out the door.

The End

Recipes from the Story

Carrot Bars

(the corrected version of the recipe from the first book)

2 c. white sugar
4 eggs
3 sm. jars baby-food carrots
¾ c. vegetable oil
2 c. flour
2 tsp. baking soda
1 tsp. salt
1½ tsp. cinnamon
1 c. chopped walnuts

Mix together the sugar, eggs, carrots, and vegetable oil. Add the flour, soda, salt, cinnamon, and nuts. Stir well. Pour into a greased and floured 12" x 18" pan. Bake at 350° in a preheated oven for 25 to 30 minutes. Use the toothpick test to determine when they are done for sure.

Frosting:

3 T. margarine
1 8-oz. pkg. cream cheese
½ tsp. vanilla
3½ c. powdered sugar

Cream together the margarine and the cream cheese. Stir in the vanilla. Add the powdered sugar and beat with an electric beater until creamy. Frost only after bars have cooled.

Frosted Banana Bars

½ c. butter or margarine, softened
2 c. white sugar
3 eggs
1½ c. mashed ripe bananas (about 3 medium)
1 tsp. vanilla extract
2 c. all-purpose flour
1 tsp. baking soda
Pinch of salt

In a mixing bowl, cream the butter and sugar, using an electric beater. Then beat in the eggs, bananas, and vanilla. In a separate bowl, combine the flour, baking soda, and salt. Add the flour mixture to the creamed mixture and stir with a wooden spoon. Pour the batter into a greased, 15" x 10" x 1" pan. Bake at 350°, in a preheated oven, for 25 minutes or until done per the toothpick test. (It's done if you stick a toothpick in it, and the toothpick comes out clean.) Cool.

Frosting:

½ c. butter or margarine, softened	4 c. powdered sugar, sifted
1 pkg. (8 oz.) cream cheese, softened	2 tsps. vanilla extract

For the frosting, cream the butter and cream cheese in a mixing bowl, using an electric beater. Gradually add the powdered sugar, beating the mixture with an electric beater. Add the vanilla and beat some more. Then spread over the cooled bars.

No-Bake Peanut Butter Cup Bars

½ c. butter	¼ c. butter
1¾ c. powdered sugar, sifted	½ c. milk chocolate chips
1 c. creamy peanut butter	
¾ c. finely crushed graham crackers	

Line a 9" x 9" baking pan with foil, leaving enough foil to hang over the edges. Butter the foil and set the pan aside. In a medium saucepan, melt the butter noted in the upper left column. Remove the pan from the heat. Add in the powdered sugar, stirring until the mixture is smooth. Then add the peanut butter and cracker crumbs, again stirring until the mixture is smooth. Pour that mixture into the prepared pan, smoothing it out to the edges.

Next, over low heat, melt the butter noted in the second column. Add the chocolate chips, removing the mixture from the burner and stirring until the chocolate is melted. Pour the chocolate mixture over the peanut butter mixture, gently spreading the chocolate over all the bars. Refrigerate the bars for at least 30 minutes so they can set. Finally, using the excess foil, lift the bars from the pan. Cut them with a pizza cutter. Store them in the refrigerator in an air-tight container.

༄ Vegetable Hot Dish Express ༄

1 pound ground beef
1 onion, chopped
1 c. cubed carrots
1 c. fresh peas
4 potatoes, sliced
1 can of tomato soup
Salt and pepper to taste

Brown the meat and onions. Drain the grease. Add the carrots, peas, potatoes, and tomato soup. Stir. Add seasoning. Bake at 325° for two hours. Now, if you're busy, you can substitute a can of peas and a can of carrots (16-oz. size of each), both drained, along with a bag (16 oz. or so) of frozen hash browns. Then you only need to bake it for 40 minutes or so. And that's when you add "express" to the end of the name.

Sauerkraut Hot Dish

2 lbs. ground beef
1 medium onion, chopped
2 lbs. sauerkraut
3 c. uncooked wide egg noodles
1 can cream of mushroom soup
1 can cream of celery soup
1 can cream of chicken soup
1 tsp. pepper
1½ c. of shredded cheddar cheese

Brown the beef and the onions together. Drain off the fat. Layer one-half of the beef mixture in a 9" x 13" pan that's been sprayed with cooking spray. Cover the beef mixture with the sauerkraut and top with the remaining beef mixture. Place the uncooked noodles on top of that. Combine the soups and pepper. Gently spread soup mixture over the uncooked noodles. Bake the dish for 45 minutes at 350°, in a preheated oven. Sprinkle the cheese on top and bake for another 20 minutes. This dish is great when you're having German relatives over for dinner.

Overnight Hot Dish

2 c. macaroni, uncooked
2 cans cream of mushroom soup
½ medium onion, chopped
2 c. shredded cheddar cheese
2 c. cubed cooked chicken
2 c. milk
1 4-oz. can mushroom pieces, drained
8 servings of chow mien noodles

Combine all of the listed ingredients—except the chow mien noodles—in a large casserole dish. Cover. Place in the fridge overnight or for several hours. Then, cover and bake the hot dish at 350° in a preheated oven, for one hour. Remove the cover and bake for another 30 minutes. Serve over chow mien noodles. Makes 8 servings, fewer if you're feedin' farmers. It goes great with homemade bread or rolls.

Easy Sauerkraut Hot Dish

2 lbs. ground beef, cooked
2 cans cream soup, any variety
2 c. uncooked egg noodles
1 soup can of water
Raw sauerkraut

Place cooked ground beef in a greased casserole dish. Layer sauerkraut over it. Sprinkle uncooked noodles over that. Mix soup and water and pour that mixture over the noodles. Bake for 15 minutes at 350 degrees in a preheated oven. Stir it all up and bake it—covered—for another hour.

Grandma's Lemon Meringue Pie

Juice of one lemon
3 egg yolks (save the egg whites for the meringue)
3 T. cornstarch
1 c. water
2 T. butter
1 c. sugar
¼ c. sugar (for the meringue)

Put lemon juice, egg yolks, as well as the cornstarch, water, and butter, in a kettle. Cook until the mixture comes to a boil and thickens. Stir constantly. Remove kettle from the heat. Add the one cup of sugar. Stir some more. Finally, fill an already-baked pie shell.

For the meringue, beat the three egg whites you saved. Beat them until they are stiff. (Cold beaters help.) Add the ¼ cup of sugar. Beat a little more, until the sugar is mixed in. Spread the meringue over the lemon-filled pie crust and, for fun, make curls using the back of a spoon. Bake for about 10 minutes at 350 degrees in a preheated oven. Watch closely. Do not bake too long. The tips of the curls should just turn light brown.

Lime Jell-O Dessert

1 3-oz. package of lime Jell-O
1¾ c. boiling water
¼ c. lemon juice
1 c. evaporated milk, chilled
1 c. sugar
3 c. crushed Graham crackers
Cool Whip

Mix gelatin powder, water, and lemon juice. Let the mixture cool until it begins to set. Then whip it with an electric beater until frothy. Clean beaters and, in a separate bowl, whip the evaporated milk until it stiffens. Add the sugar to the evaporated milk. Mix well. Combine gelatin and milk mixtures. Gently stir before spooning the combined mixture into a 9" x 13" pan lined with crushed graham crackers. Refrigerate until firm. Spoon or cut from pan. And, of course, you can never go wrong by topping it with Cool Whip.

Black Bottom Cupcakes

Sift together the following—

1½ c. flour
1 c. sugar
¼ c. cocoa
½ tsp. salt
1 tsp. soda

Then add the following to that mixture—

1 c. water
1/3 c. vegetable oil
1 T. vinegar
1 tsp. vanilla

Beat the fully combined mixture above with an electric mixer until thick and creamy. Then fill 24 large cupcake papers one-third full.

Next, cream 8 ounces of softened cream cheese with an electric beater. Then, add to it, the following—

1 small egg
1/3 c. sugar
1/8 tsp. salt

Beat this mixture with a mixer before stirring in one **6-oz package of regular chocolate chips.** Place about one soup spoonful of this cream-cheese mixture on top of each unbaked chocolate cupcake. Finally, bake the cupcakes at 325° for 30 to 35 minutes in a preheated oven.

For something extra special, make approximately 60 mini cupcakes by using mini-chocolate chips instead of the regular-sized ones. Then into each mini cupcake paper, spoon 1½ tsp. of the chocolate mixture and ½ tsp. of the cream-cheese mixture. Then bake at 325 degrees, in a preheated oven, for 17 minutes.

ꟾ Pudding Shots ꟾ

White Russian

Whisk together—

1 pkg. vanilla instant pudding mix

¾ c. milk

Add in and beat with an electric beater until smooth and creamy—

¼ c. vodka

½ c. Kahlua

8 oz. Cool Whip

Portion and freeze and top with strawberries before serving.

Banana

Whisk together—

1 pkg. banana instant pudding mix

¾ c. milk

Add in and beat with an electric beater until smooth and creamy—

¼ c. vodka

½ c. Banana Schnapps

8 oz. Cool Whip

Portion and freeze and top with strawberries before serving.

Pumpkin

Whisk together—

1 pkg. pumpkin instant pudding mix

¾ c. milk

Add in and beat with an electric beater until smooth and creamy—

¾ c. Captain Morgan

8 oz. Cool Whip

Portion and freeze and top with Cool Whip before serving.

Chocolate

Whisk together—

1 pkg. chocolate instant pudding mix

¾ c. milk

Add in and beat with an electric beater until smooth and creamy—

¼ c. vodka
½ c. Bailey's Irish Cream
8 oz. Cool Whip

Portion and freeze and top with Cool Whip before serving.

Chicken Dumpling Hot Dish

3-4 c. cooked shredded chicken
½ c. butter
1 c. self-rising flour
1 c. milk
2 c. chicken broth
1 can cream of chicken soup (original style)

Melt the butter and pour it into the bottom of a 9" x 13" pan. Place the cooked shredded chicken on top of the butter. Meanwhile, in a bowl, whisk together the milk and flour and slowly pour it over the chicken, taking care not to move the chicken. Next, whisk the broth and soup together and slowly pour that over the flour and milk mixture. Do not stir! Bake uncovered in a 400°, preheated oven, for 35 to 45 minutes or until the top is a light, golden brown. A can of mixed vegetables could also be added if you want to be really healthy.

Gluten-Free Rhubarb Bars

1¼ c. gluten-free baking mix
½ c. gluten-free oats
½ c. light brown sugar
½ c. cold butter
1 pkg. cream cheese, softened
2/3 c. white sugar
½ tsp. salt
½ tsp. vanilla
¼ tsp. cinnamon
1 egg, slightly beaten
1½ c. diced rhubarb (if frozen, let thaw and drain. Don't squish)

Combine the gluten-free baking mix, oats, and brown sugar in a bowl. Cut in the cold butter until it makes a coarse meal. Set aside one cup of this mixture to use as the topping later. Press the rest of the mixture into a greased, 9"-square, baking dish. Set aside.

In a separate bowl, beat the cream cheese and white sugar with an electric beater until smooth. Add the vanilla, salt, and cinnamon and beat until well mixed. Then add the egg and beat until that's mixed in too. Finally, stir in the rhubarb and pour that mixture into your 9" pan. After that, crumble the remaining oat mixture on top.

Bake for 35 to 40 minutes in a 350°, preheated oven or until the mixture doesn't jiggle like an old lady's upper arm when she's waving. Let the bars cool on the counter for one hour. Then refrigerate them for at least two more hours before serving.

Peaches and Cream Pie

9-in. unbaked pie crust
4 fresh peaches, skinned and sliced
2/3 c. sugar
4 T. flour
¼ tsp. salt
½ tsp. cinnamon
1 c. cream

Place the fruit in an unbaked, 9", pie crust. Mix the remaining ingredients and pour over the fruit. Bake the pie at 400° for 35 to 40 minutes in a preheated oven.

Rhubarb Meringue Pie

3 egg yolks (reserve the whites)
½ c. cream
½ c. milk
1 c. sugar
2 T. flour
2-3 c. chopped rhubarb

Mix all the ingredients. Pour the mixture into a 9", unbaked, pie crust. In a preheated oven, bake the pie for 55 minutes (10 minutes at 425° and 45 minutes at 300°).

For the meringue, beat the three egg whites you reserved until they are stiff. Fold in 3 T. of sugar. Spread over the pie. Bake in a preheated, 350° oven for about 10 minutes or until the meringue tips brown slightly. Watch closely!

I'm Not Kidding Beef Fudge

1 c. ground beef, browned well
¾ c. butter
3 c. sugar
2/3 c. evaporated milk
1 12-oz. pkg. semi-sweet chocolate chips
1 7-oz. jar marshmallow crème
1 tsp. vanilla
½ c. chopped nuts, optional

Brown the ground beef, crumble it fine, and paper-towel it dry to remove the excess grease. Then put it in a blender or food processor to chop it up even more. After that, set it aside in the refrigerator.

Lightly grease a 9" x 13" pan. Mix the butter, sugar, and milk in a heavy saucepan. Bring the mixture to a rolling boil over medium heat, stirring constantly. Boil for approximately five more minutes on medium heat, until mixture reaches 234° on a candy thermometer. Stir all that time to prevent scorching. Remove the pan from the heat. Slowly stir in the chocolate chips until melted. Then stir in the marshmallow crème and vanilla until well blended.

Remove the beef from the fridge and add to mixture above. Finally, pour the final mixture into the greased pan. Don't spread with a spoon or knife if you can avoid it. (It causes the "shine" to disappear.) Instead, simply tilt the pan to allow the fudge to run into the corners.

Fork and Pan Cake

3 c. flour
2 c. sugar
1 tsp. salt
2 tsp. soda
1/3 c. cocoa
¾ c. vegetable oil
1 tsp. vanilla
2 T. white vinegar
2 c. water

In a 9" x 13" greased, cake pan, mixing with only a fork and never beating, mix the five dry ingredients listed first above. Next, make three wells in this dry mixture and pour into each well the oil, vanilla, and vinegar, respectively. Then, over everything, pour the water. After that, mix with your fork until all the lumps are gone, making sure you mix well along the edges and in the corners. Finally, bake for approximately 35 minutes at 350° in a preheated oven. The toothpick test should work. That is, when a toothpick is poked into the cake and comes out clean, the cake is done.

Breakfast Pie

1 lb. pork sausage
1 c. shredded or cubed hash browns
½ large, yellow onion, chopped
1 c. fresh spinach
4 eggs, whisked
¼ c. milk
1 c. shredded cheddar cheese
1 tsp. garlic powder
½ tsp. ground paprika
Salt and pepper to taste
1 T. butter

Press the thawed sausage into a 9" pie plate, including up the sides. Bake it in a 375°, preheated oven, for 18 to 20 minutes. (Place a baking sheet under the pan to catch drips.) The meat doesn't need to be cooked completely through, although it should be close. Remove any excess oil that has formed on the top of it.

While the meat crust is baking, place **2 T. of butter** in a saucepan over medium heat. Add the chopped onion. When the onions are translucent, sprinkle them with salt and pepper. Add the spinach and cover. After a minute or two—once the spinach has wilted from the heat—place the onion-spinach mixture in a bowl. When cool, add in the eggs, milk, cheese, hash browns, garlic powder, ground paprika, and a bit more salt. Mix well. Finally, pour the mixture onto the meat crust.

Bake the filled pie for 25 to 30 minutes in your 375°, pre-heated oven. It's done when the middle bounces back a bit when you poke it.

Orange Jell-O Salad

1 3-oz. box tapioca pudding	1 3-oz. box orange Jell-O
1 large can fruit cocktail	2 bananas
1 can mandarin oranges	¾ c. whipped cream

Drain the juice from the can of fruit cocktail and the can of mandarin oranges into a large measuring cup. Set the fruit aside. Add enough water to the measuring cup of fruit juice to make 1½ cups of liquid. Cook the tapioca pudding powder in this liquid. Let the pudding cool. Make the Jell-O as instructed on the box and allow it to set only partially. Then, when the Jell-O is thick but not set and the pudding has cooled, mix them together. After that, add in the fruit (fruit cocktail, mandarin oranges, and sliced bananas). Finally, whip the cream and fold that in. If you're in a hurry, you can substitute Cool Whip for the whipped cream.

ꕤ Mushroom Wild Rice Hot Dish ꕤ

1 c. wild rice, washed
½ c. butter
2 T. green pepper, chopped
2 T. onion, chopped
1 clove garlic, chopped
½ c. slivered almonds
2 cans sliced mushrooms
3 c. chicken broth
Salt and pepper to taste

Bring chicken broth to a boil. Meanwhile, sauté the rest of the ingredients in a pan until the onions turn yellow. Add the chicken broth. Then, place the entire mixture into a casserole dish and bake it for 1½ hours at 325° in a preheated oven.

ꕤ Pumpkin Roll ꕤ

¾ c. flour
½ tsp. baking soda
1 tsp. cinnamon
½ tsp. ground cloves
½ tsp. baking powder
3 large eggs
1 c. sugar
2/3 c. canned pumpkin

Combine flour, baking powder, baking soda, cinnamon, cloves, and salt in a small bowl. Set aside. In a large mixing bowl, beat the eggs and sugar with an electric beater until thick. Add the pumpkin and beat some more. Finally, fold in the flour mixture.

Meanwhile, line a jelly-roll pan with wax paper. Grease and flour the paper. Then spread the prepared mixture onto the paper and bake in a preheated oven at 375° for 13 to 15 minutes or until the top of the cake springs back when touched. Do not over bake!

As soon as you take the pan out of the oven, turn the cake over onto a cloth towel sprinkled with powdered sugar and gently peel off the wax paper. Immediately roll up the cake—roll the towel up with the cake—starting with the narrow side of the pan. Cool the roll on a wire rack.

Frosting:

1 8-oz. pkg. cream cheese, softened
1 c. powdered sugar
6 T. butter, softened
1 tsp. vanilla

With an electric beater, beat the cream cheese, powdered sugar, butter, and vanilla in a small mixing bowl until the mixture is smooth. Carefully, unroll the cooled cake, remove the towel, and spread the cream cheese mixture over the cake. Reroll the cake—without the towel, of course. Wrap the roll in plastic wrap and refrigerate for at least one hour. Sprinkle with powdered sugar before slicing and serving.

Dog Treats

1 pkg. dry yeast
3 T. warm water
2 c. flour
½ c. whole wheat flour
¼ c. wheat germ
1 tsp. salt
1 c. cooked ground meat (e.g., beef, turkey)
4 T. vegetable oil
1 egg
¾ c. milk

Dissolve the yeast in warm water. Combine the flours, wheat germ, salt, and cooked meat. Stir in the yeast mixture, the vegetable oil, the egg, and the milk. Roll the resulting dough to a ½" thickness. Cut into dog-bone shapes—or simple strips if you prefer—and place them on an ungreased cookie sheet. Bake in a preheated oven at 375° for 20 minutes. Cool. Store in the refrigerator for seven to ten days or freeze for much longer.

Strawberry Pretzel Squares

2 c. pretzel crumbs, finely crushed
½ c. sugar (will be divided)
2/3 c. butter, melted
1½ pkg. (12 oz.) cream cheese, softened
2 T. milk
1 c. Cool Whip, thawed
2 c. boiling water
1 6-oz. pkg. strawberry Jell-O
1½ c. cold water
4 c. fresh strawberries, sliced

Mix the pretzel crumbs, **¼ cup of sugar**, and all the butter. Press the mixture into the bottom of a 13" x 9" pan. Bake for 10 minutes, at 350°, in a preheated oven. Cool.

Meanwhile, with an electric beater, beat the cream cheese, the remaining sugar, and the milk until well blended. Gently stir in the Cool Whip. Spread the mixture over the cooled crust. Refrigerate until firm.

In a large bowl, add the boiling water to the Jell-O powder and stir for two minutes or until the powder is completely dissolved. Stir in the cold water and refrigerate for 90 minutes. At that time, fold in the berries. Spoon the mixture over the cream cheese layer. Refrigerate for at least three hours or until the squares are firm.

Pumpkin Bars

2 c. sugar
4 eggs
¾ c. vegetable oil
1 15-oz. can pumpkin
½ tsp. salt
3 tsp. cinnamon
2 c. flour
2 tsp. baking soda

Cream sugar, eggs, oil, and pumpkin. Add the dry ingredients and mix together. Pour into a greased bar pan (appr. 12 x 15 inches) and bake for 20 minutes at 350° in a preheated oven. (Use the toothpick test to determine when the bars are done for sure.)

Frosting:

1¾ c. powdered sugar
½ c. butter
1 tsp. vanilla
1 3-oz. pkg. of cream cheese

Mix thoroughly and spread over bars after they have cooled.

Lazy Cabbage Roll Hot Dish

2 lbs. hamburger
2 large onions, chopped
2 T. seasoning salt
1 T. black pepper
1½ c. white rice (uncooked)
1 large head cabbage, chopped
2 pints real cream

Brown the hamburger with the onions. Stir in the seasoning salt and pepper, followed by the uncooked rice. Then stir in the chopped cabbage. Place this mixture in a large casserole dish, pouring the cream over the top. Cover the casserole dish and bake for 1½ hours in a 350°, preheated oven. While this dish is baking, occasionally check to see if the rice has soaked up all the cream. That will happen sometimes, depending on the type of rice you use. If the dish seems to be drying out, simply add a bit more cream.

Crouton Hot Dish

1½ lbs. hamburger, browned
7 oz. of croutons
¼ lb. butter
1 c. celery
½ c. chopped onions
1 c. water
1 can cream of celery soup
1 can cream of chicken soup

Layer the croutons over the cooked hamburger, which you have placed in a greased, 9" x 13" pan. In a saucepan, heat the butter, celery, onions, and water until the butter is melted. Pour over the croutons. Mix the soups together, and then spoon that mixture on top of the croutons. Bake the hot dish in a preheated oven for one hour at 350 degrees. Turn off the oven but leave the pan in it for another 15 minutes.

Creamy Chow Mein Hot Dish

2 cans of cream soup, any variety
1 stock of celery, chopped
½ white onion, chopped
1 c. chicken, cooked and cubed
4 T. soy sauce
¼ c. milk
White rice

Mix all of the above ingredients. Place them in a greased casserole dish. Bake at 350 degrees in a preheated oven for 45 minutes or until the celery is slightly soft. Serve over white rice.

Cheesy Chicken & Rice Casserole

1 can cream of chicken soup
1-1/3 c. water
¾ c. regular, long-grain white rice (uncooked)
½ tsp. minced onion
¼ tsp. black pepper
2 c. frozen mixed vegetables
4 skinless, boneless chicken breasts (cut into 1-in. cubes)
½ c. shredded Cheddar cheese

Stir together the soup, water, uncooked rice, onion, pepper, and vegetables. Place in a 2-quart baking dish. Sprinkle the cubed meat on top. Cover the dish and bake at 375° in a preheated oven for 50 minutes, or until chicken is done and rice is tender. Mix chicken in. Stir in cheese. Let stand for 10 minutes. Then serve.

Beef Stroganoff Hot Dish

1 large yellow onion
4 T. butter
4 T. all-purpose flour
1½ lbs. beef sirloin, sliced thin
2 c. beef broth
¼ c. red wine
2 tsp. Worcestershire sauce
Salt and pepper to taste
1 c. sour cream
2 tsp. Kitchen Bouquet browning and seasoning sauce
Egg noodles, cooked

Cook the onions in the butter until soft and lightly brown. Add the flour. Cook for one to two minutes. Scrape this mixture out of the pan and set it aside. In the same pan, cook the beef strips until no longer pink. Don't overcook them. Add the broth, wine, Worcestershire sauce, salt, and pepper. Simmer this mixture for 15 to 20 minutes—longer for *less* tender meat. After that, add the onion and flour mixture prepared earlier, cooking it until the sauce thickens. Finally, add the sour cream and the Kitchen Bouquet. Serve over cooked egg noodles.

To make the hot dish version of this dish, fill a large casserole dish half full of cooked egg noodles. Spoon the final meat and sauce mixture over the noodles. Then, bake the finished dish in a 325°, preheated oven for 30 minutes.

Buttermilk Salad

1 20-oz. can crushed pineapple
1 small can Mandarin oranges, drained
3 T. sugar
1 6-oz. package Jell-O (lime, lemon, or orange)
2 c. buttermilk
8 oz. Cool Whip
1 c. walnuts or pecans

In a saucepan, mix the pineapple, including the juice, along with the sugar. Bring it to a low boil. Immediately add the Jell-O, stirring it until it's dissolved. Set aside until cooled to room temperature. Then, stir in the buttermilk. Fold in the Cool Whip, oranges, and nuts. Pour into a 9" x 13" pan and refrigerate until set. Cut into squares and serve.

Super Rhubarb Bars

1½ c. raw, diced, rhubarb
1 c. dark brown sugar
½ c. white sugar
1 egg
½ c. butter (do not substitute with margarine)
1 c. applesauce
2 tsp. vanilla
½ tsp. salt
1 tsp. soda
2 c. flour

Cream together sugars, egg, butter, applesauce, and vanilla. Add salt, soda, and flour and stir. Fold in rhubarb. Spoon into a 9" x 13" greased, baking pan.

Sprinkle with the following mixed topping:

½ c. white sugar
1 tsp. cinnamon

Bake at 375° in a preheated oven for 30 to 35 minutes or until a toothpick comes out clean.

Blueberry Bars

1¾ c. sugar
1 c. butter
4 eggs
1 tsp. vanilla
3 c. flour
1½ tsp. baking powder
½ tsp. salt
1 reg. can blueberry pie filling
Ground nutmeg

Cream sugar and butter. Add eggs and vanilla. Beat till smooth. Add flour, baking powder, and salt. Stir in gently. Spread half of this mixture in an ungreased jelly-roll pan. Carefully spread pie filling over the mixture in the pan. Sprinkle with a little ground nutmeg. Drop the rest of dough mixture on top of the blueberries, using a teaspoon. Bake at 350° in a preheated oven for approximately 45 minutes.

Pineapple Cheese Hot Dish

2 large cans pineapple chunks (in own juice)
2 c. shredded mozzarella cheese
1 c. sugar
6 T. flour
3 dz. Ritz crackers, crushed
1 stick butter, melted

Drain the pineapple. Mix together the pineapple chunks and the cheese. In a separate bowl, mix the sugar and flour. Then add it to the fruit-cheese mixture. Spread this mixture in an 8" x 11" or 9" x 12" casserole dish. Sprinkle crushed crackers over the top. Pour the melted butter over everything. Bake for 35 to 40 minutes at 350° in a preheated oven. Let cool and serve. Tastes good warm or cold.

Acknowledgments

First and foremost, I must thank my sister Mary Cooney. Once again she was there to share ideas, review drafts, provide encouragement, and make me laugh. Thanks also to Myron Hennen and Gary Bostad for their ongoing lessons about farming in the Red River Valley, as well as David Bergh for teaching me about beet pilers and scale pits. Thanks to the Cooney and Hennen families, both full of funny people who share hilarious anecdotes and spark lots of ideas. Thanks to Mary Keyes and my sister Teresa Cooney, who, along with Mary Cooney, provided critiquing that immensely improved the final manuscript. Overdo thanks to Haley Cooney, who designed the website before the first book came out and continues to manage it, and Elizabeth Young, who oversees the Facebook page. Then, of course, thanks to the booksellers who have taken a chance on me, as well as the readers who have e-mailed wonderful messages, jokes, and recipes. Keep them coming! Finally, thanks to my publisher, North Star Press, where the staff performs editing, layout, cover design, marketing, e-book production, and so much more. Oh, yeah, one final shout-out to the makers of Dove chocolate. I couldn't have done it without you!